Carol Margaret Tetlow

Spoilt For Choice

Éditions
DÉDICACES

First published by Editions Dedicaces in 2016

Copyright © Carol Margaret Tetlow, 2016

First Edition

ISBN: 978-1-77076-636-5

This book was professionally typeset on Reedsy.
Find out more at reedsy.com

Contents

Acknowledgements

To have one book published is amazing but words escape me when I realise that this is the fourth novel in the Teviotdale Series to be published (and there's one more to come).

Thank you as always, Guy Boulianne, who has believed in me and made this all possible.

Thank you to my lovely friend, Helen Norris, who painstakingly proof reads and copy edits for me.

Thank you to my readers, who keep reading and want to know what happens next.

I'd like to dedicate this book to my beautiful god-daughter, Holly and my handsome god-sons, Jason and Max, inspirational young people with their lives ahead of them to be lived to the full. Follow your dreams – they do come true.

1

The rain was driving horizontally into Ed's face as he fought his way up the unmade track towards the house barely visible in the distance. Dismal-looking sheep regarded him with studious curiosity from the other side of the barbed-wire fence, more used to seeing hikers in their standard uniforms of anoraks, red socks and boots than a solitary young man in well-cut trousers, brogues and a sports jacket, carrying a black bag. Wary of bringing his car up, for fear of irreparable damage to the exhaust, or any other component that lurked too near to the ground, he had reluctantly made the decision that it would be less expensive to pay dry cleaners than some car mechanic with a fertile imagination when it came to giving estimates of work required. A quick and frantic search in the boot of his car, the contents of which had been thrown in chaotically, had revealed that his waterproof coat was nowhere to be seen. A sudden mental image then came to him of it hanging on the back of the kitchen door, having been left there since the weekend's climbing when he had again been soaked to the skin.

Only partly able to see where he was going, his eyelids continuously trying to blink away the jagged spikes of water that were lambasting him relentlessly, he cursed out loud as he stepped into a deceptively deep puddle of yellowy-beige mud and felt the water ooze over the top of his shoe and osmose through the flimsy protection of his sock. He now wished fervently that he had accepted the offers of his two partners, Ellie Bonnington and Clare Jennings, to do this particular house call but his sense of fairness had prevailed as both of them already had several of their own visits to do and he had only one.

It had been dry when he set off from the surgery, admittedly not sunny or bright but at least fine. As he had cruised down the country lanes in a relaxed manner, listening to some undemanding music on the car radio, the clouds had thickened and darkened, assumed a menacing air and then the rain had started. Initially, it had been nothing more than an irritating light drizzle, not enough to need the windscreen wipers on continuously but by the time he spotted the signpost for the house, raindrops were ricocheting in all directions and thundering a discordant fanfare on the roof of the car.

More mud splattered up onto the hem of his trousers, instantly obvious as it was far darker than the light fawn of the material and he swore softly under his breath. He was well past the point where he could do anything about it. Rounding a slight bend in the track he saw his destination more clearly and hurried, with relief, to the bottom of a recently paved driveway that led through some large and imposing wrought-iron gates to a meticulous barn conversion of considerable dimensions that was hardly reflective of its diminutive title of Hawthorn Cottage. The main house was to the right, an architectural triumph in some ways, an eyesore in more. Little was recognisable of the original barn now the new build had taken over. A smart new roof, double glazing and red bricks that paid no respect to the far more attractive original stone had created a modern, practical house, rigidly symmetrical with matching turrets at each end and lacking, to Ed's eyes at least, any attractiveness whatsoever.

To the left was a brand-new block of stables. At the sound of someone approaching, three heads appeared over their respective half doors, hoping for treats, longing to be out rather than penned up for the day. Ed knew little about horses but suspected from just one look at them that they were valuable beasts. Ellie would have probably known and Faith, the salaried assistant at the practice, would definitely have been able to tell, never having known a time in her life where horses did not feature strongly.

Joining these two buildings was a garage of substantial size, capable of holding several vehicles. The doors were open and Ed noticed a gleaming, brand-new black 4x4 and a crouching soft-topped sports car, which also boasted the most recent number plate. Further back, he could not help but spot some surf boards – not much call for those in the Yorkshire Dales – mountain bikes and two matching quad bikes, none of which looked as if they had ever been used.

Hanging baskets with flowers spilling out dripped despondently by the front door and curling rivulets from the row of neatly painted tubs, stuffed with colour-coordinated plants, forged their way down towards the gate. Ed stepped carefully over the worst of the water, paused on the doorstep to run his fingers through his sodden hair and rang the bell. Excited high-pitched barking was evident, then a woman's voice remonstrating and finally the indisputable noise of an argument and a small scuffle as the dog was herded back into the kitchen and, after several attempts, the door slammed shut to prevent any escape.

As Ed heard the locks being unbolted, he fixed a friendly smile on his face, hoped that he didn't look so bedraggled as to be unprofessional and picked up his bag.

'Good morning!' he started, holding out his hand. 'Or rather, not such a good morning. Mrs Martin? I'm Dr Diamond from the health centre. I've come to see Kerry-Lee. May I come in?'

Mrs Martin reluctantly shook the very tip of his fingers with a loose touch.

'Of course, you're very wet? Don't you have a car?' Mrs Martin peered over his shoulder to the drive.

'I've left it on the road. I wasn't sure about the track up to your house.'

'It's dreadful. I'm so sorry. We haven't been moved in long. Once we're settled, I'm sure my husband will be pushing for planning permission to have it tarmacked over. I believe it's a public right of way but that won't put him off as it's on our land. I told him it would cause a problem but he wouldn't listen, as usual. He promised me it would be wonderfully private here but droves of walkers seem to come up here every day and most of them stare in quite rudely at our house while they're passing. Some of them even stop and point. I'm sure they're just admiring our lovely home but it does give one the feeling of living in a zoo sometimes.'

Mrs Martin glared worriedly at Ed's feet. 'Perhaps you should slip your shoes off. They're very muddy.'

As he obeyed his orders, Ed could not help but notice the slippers on Mrs Martin's feet. Like two giant tiger paws, complete with claws, they clashed to perfection with her tight leather trousers and over-sized animal print t-shirt which was tied nonchalantly in a knot over her right hip and slipped fashionably off her left shoulder to reveal a bra strap of gold chain and some artificially tanned, freckly skin. She was not unattractive but had gone to too many lengths to stave off the signs of advancing years. Skilfully applied make-up could not hide the signs of previous cosmetic surgery, anti-wrinkle injections and collagen fillers.

'Thank you so much for coming, Dr Diamond. Kerri-Lee's in the snug. This way please.'

Ed could feel his wet feet leaving telltale footprints on the polished wood floor but hoped that they would have dried to invisibility by the time they returned. The snug turned out to be larger than his own lounge, which was the biggest room in his house. A massive flat-screen television somehow miraculously stayed attached to one wall and two generously sized sofas were placed so that viewing was optimal. On one of them was a young girl, almost hidden by a large duvet as she lay spread-eagled and glued to some rather gross cartoon figures that were shrieking at each other on the screen. On the floor by her side were a can of pop, a plate of biscuits and a giant packet of crisps.

Ed advanced towards the sofa. The small girl paid no attention to him whatsoever, other than to twist her body so that she could look past him.

'Hello,' he tried. 'You must be Kerry.'

'It's Kerry-Lee,' Mrs Martin corrected him with firmness. 'Anyway this is Cassandra, my middle daughter. She's not ill.'

'No school today then?' asked Ed.

'Well, there is but Cassie's been quite tired recently, so today she's having a duvet day and catching up.'

Ed raised his eyebrows and Cassie, after a covert glance in his direction, continued to ignore him.

'Where's your sister gone?' Mrs Martin raised her voice to compete with the manic violence that was on the television.

'Don't know. Upstairs maybe. Shh, Mum. I'm watching.'

'I'm sorry, Dr Diamond, she must be in her bedroom. I'm not surprised she doesn't want to watch that rubbish. Follow me.'

The curved staircase wound its way ornately to the first floor. The wood floors gave way to carpets of gleaming white, still smelling new and recently fitted and the thick pile comforted his feet. They paused outside a door covered in notices which included amongst them a badly drawn skull and crossbones and a warning to keep out or face the consequences. Mrs Martin knocked timidly.

'Kerry-Lee?' she called softly, waiting a moment before turning the handle and opening the door slowly.

Expecting to find an ailing child in bed, Ed was taken aback to find a young girl, no more than eight years old, dressed from top to toe in pink, busy playing on her computer. The room was also mostly pink, from the bedspread to the curtains, the carpet and the clothes that were visible through the half-open wardrobe door. There were pink fairy lights weaving their way around the bed head and yet more decorating the mirror on the dressing table. Even the toys that were visible were pink.

'It's the doctor, darling.'

Kerry-Lee looked up.

'Hello!'

Ed smiled and returned the greeting. Kerry-Lee was a pretty girl with a huge grin.

'Stop doing that for a moment and come and tell him what's wrong.' Mrs Martin was beginning to sound a little weary.

'Hang on a mo, I've just got to save what I've done so far. I'm playing that new game Daddy bought me yesterday – it's cool.'

'Daddy buys you far too many things,' muttered Mrs Martin, under her breath but loud enough for Ed to hear.

Sitting down on a chair, after moving a ridiculously large floppy pink dog to one side, Ed opened up his bag and extracted his stethoscope, ready to begin his consultation. As he hoped, Kerry-Lee left her computer and came to sit on her bed, facing him. His first impressions were that she looked far from ill.

'How can I help?' Ed offered, his gaze moving from mother to child.

Kerry-Lee looked at her mother for approval and, on the receipt of a nod, picked up her right foot.

'It's my toes,' she complained.

'What's wrong with them?' asked Ed.

'They're horrid and they hurt.'

'Let me see. Have you injured them?'

'No.'

Gently, Ed took the petite foot onto his knee and examined it carefully, finding nothing wrong until he looked between the toes and spotted a mild fungal infection.

'Is that what you're worried about?'

Kerry-Lee cringed hysterically.

'It's gross. I can't bear to look at it.'

'It's nothing to be concerned about,' Ed promised.

'What have you found?' Mrs Martin sounded alarmed.

'A very slight infection. Athlete's foot.'

'Oh my goodness. What's that?'

'It's caused by a fungus. It's very common and easily treatable with some cream you can buy from the chemist. I'll give you the name.'

'But why on earth would she have a fungus? Our hygiene is perfect.'

'I'm sure it is. But this is easy to pick up. Does Kerry, I mean Kerry-Lee, go swimming?'

'Yes, she does.'

'Well, she probably picked it up there then. In the changing room.'

He scribbled quickly on a scrap of paper from his bag.

'Apply this twice a day and be careful to dry properly after you've been in the bath or shower. A good way of doing that is to use a hairdryer. Sounds silly, I know, but it works.'

Kerry-Lee skipped back over to the computer and was quickly immersed back into the game she had been playing. Ed closed up his bag, trying to formulate how to say his next words.

'Thank you so much for coming, doctor. Such a relief to know it's nothing serious,' gushed Mrs Martin, leading him back to the front door and waiting while he persuaded his feet to go back into his damp, unwelcoming shoes, which seemed to have shrunk. She cast a disapproving glance in the direction of frantic scratching noises that were coming from the back of the house.

'Mrs Martin, I have to say that it was hardly a problem that necessitated a house call. You could easily have brought Kerry into surgery to see us. We're very busy with house calls to patients who are genuinely unable to leave their homes.'

'It's Kerry-Lee,' insisted Mrs Martin. 'I didn't like to bring her to the surgery in case she was infectious. You can't be too careful these days. There are all sorts of horrible bugs around. Alternatively she could have caught something from someone else. Plus it's raining and my car's just been washed.'

'Well, if you're ever unsure in the future, you can always ring and speak to one of us, or one of the practice nurses and we'll be able to advise you and make you an appointment. Don't forget, apply the cream twice a day. Good morning!'

'Doctor!' Mrs Martin called after him.

Ed turned to look at her.

'Yes?'

'You've forgotten to leave a prescription.'

'You can get the cream at the pharmacist's in Lambdale. It's not expensive.'

'But if you leave a prescription it won't cost anything...'

Ed looked round at the sumptuous surroundings, estimated roughly how much all of the work must have cost and then studied Mrs Martin, her perfectly manicured hands, expensive jewellery and glamorously coiffured hair. Shaking his head sadly, he turned on his heel and began to splash his way angrily back to the car.

In the staff room at Teviotdale Medical Centre, Ed was recounting the details of his frustrating house call to a captive audience of John Britton, senior partner, Ellie and Clare. Ellie had made tea, found the biscuit tin which Joan the receptionist had hidden and a towel for him to dry his hair on.

'Then to rub salt into the wound, as I was plodding back down that horrible track, she bounced past me in her infernal 4x4, made no attempt to stop and I'd put money on the fact that she chose the biggest puddle to drive through for maximum drenching impact. I don't think she'll be in a hurry to see me again.'

'Who are they?' asked Ellie, dunking a biscuit and just catching the sodden result in her mouth before it dropped onto her blouse. 'I'm sure I've never heard of them.'

'New folk,' replied John, who had a remarkable ability to know something about all his patients. 'The husband works in Leeds – high up in some investment banking group and disgustingly wealthy. I met him last week when he came in with a knee problem, probably a torn cartilage. They've three children, all girls, who go to that outrageously expensive private school outside Harrogate. They bought that place and did it up so his wife could live in the countryside. Her mother lives with them. More money than sense if you ask me. There's nothing wrong with the local secondary school. It did extremely well in the latest Ofsted visit.'

'Of course not,' agreed Ellie, aware that John was one of its governors. 'That's where my girls will be going,' she added for good measure, referring to her twins, Lydia and Virginia.

John smiled magnanimously and smoothed his cord trousers, brushing off crumbs onto the floor before pulling the biscuit tin towards him and rummaging in the contents until he found two fig rolls, his favourite and fortunately despised by everyone else. He popped one into his mouth and rested the second on the arm of his chair before picking up some letters and starting to read. Slightly overweight but avuncular and sympathetic, he still adored the patient contact aspect of general practice, even after over thirty years in the job. The administrative side, the constant derision from the government and the institution of more and more guidelines drove him to distraction however and every Sunday evening while he pretended to watch television with his wife Faye and a glass of whisky in his hand, he was mentally calculating just how long it was until he could retire but not sacrifice any of his pension.

Ellie, mid thirties, was still young and flexible enough not to be fazed by change. She was blessed with the ability to balance her home and professional lives, seemingly effortlessly. At work, she was efficient, well organised and excellent at her job. At home, she adored family life with her husband Ian and of course the twins, to say nothing of the selection of animals, which seemed to grow on a regular basis. Ian, whose only brush with the medical fraternity had been when he had had appendicitis at the age of fourteen, instinctively knew how to be a tower of support to his wife when she needed it and the twins were still young enough to be natural levellers without realising it.

Clare was the opposite – a worrier and a perfectionist, constantly self-critical and striving to do better. Her patients always came first, regardless of what else was going on in her life. Repeated gentle persuasions to leave her work behind her when she left the building fell on deaf ears and David, consultant psychiatrist and husband, knew that it was unlikely that she would ever change. Recently returned from long- term sick leave, she was still, to an extent, trying to integrate herself back into ful-l time work and sat quietly, checking and double checking that she had written up her notes from her surgery and had completed the work that had been generated, such as referral letters and research. She was only half listening to what the others were discussing, hoping that they had not noticed that they did not have her full attention, worried lest they think she was not behaving normally, not coping with her workload and showing the first hints that her mental health problem was starting to rear its ugly head again.

The door opened and in came Faith Faber, late morning surgery having just finished. She had joined the practice to cover for Clare while she was off sick, proved herself to be a hard worker and had been asked to stay on. She loved working there and dreamed of being offered a partnership. In awe of John and his consummate skills, she envied Ellie's glamorous good looks, appreciated Ed's sense of humour and his ability to make the job look easy, but still felt wary of Clare, with whom she had not really had much of a chance to become acquainted.

Following closely in her wake was the new registrar, Abigail Watson, who had been sitting in with her. Faith looked fraught, weary no doubt from Abigail's endless stream of questions and criticisms, which had already exhausted the partners in the brief time she had been with them, to such an extent that the remaining eleven and a half months of her training that she would spend with them seemed a very long time indeed. Serious and, as yet, having revealed not even a glimmer of a sense of humour, she wore harshly rimmed spectacles and always dressed in what appeared to be the same navy blue suit and green checked blouse, a look which would not have been out of place behind the counter of the local building society branch but that was too severe for her new place of work. Academically, they could not fault her. Her knowledge was jaw-droppingly awesome. From the esoteric to the rare, she knew the symptoms that were characteristic of rare syndromes most of them had forgotten about once they left medical school to enter the real world and she could quote facts and figures from the latest research projects from memory. Sadly, she was finding it very difficult to make the transition from hospital medicine to general practice and her communication skills lagged far behind her encyclopaedic mind.

She had a way of talking to patients as though she was barking, uttering a quick fire of closed questions which invited only the briefest of replies. Her sole objective was to make a clear-cut diagnosis, send off a barrage of investigations, prescribe at great cost and ignore the social aspect of her patients' lives. Unsympathetic to those she felt were the victims of their own indiscretions, she ordered smokers to cease, had no time for alcoholics and was convinced that weight loss was simply a matter of putting your mind to it and anyone could do it. Her ability to sit and listen had yet to be conceived.

Ed, bestowed with the dubious honour of being her trainer, had spent some considerable time trying to help her, which had proved awkward in the extreme as she had no perception that there was a problem in the first place. She had sat in with him for a whole week and failed to see how he related to his patients. She had even become irritated by his inability to run to time. So, in an attempt to acquaint her with the subtler nuances of consultation techniques, it had been suggested that she sit in with each of the other doctors in turn, to see how their styles compared and contrasted. Ed, initially optimistic, now felt this project was, so far, not proving to be the success he had hoped it would be. Rather than emerging from each session with a burning desire to read the classic works on doctor-patient interaction, all she brought back to Ed was a list of clinical omissions that she thought the other doctors had made, failing to consider the bizarre and nigh impossible in their differential diagnoses. The novelty of explaining about general practice was wearing off rapidly and Ed was glad of the support and help of his colleagues.

'But why didn't you do some blood tests on that last lady but one?' Abigail was demanding of Faith.

'Because she had food poisoning. All she needed was a stool sample.' Faith justified her actions.

'How can you say that? It could have been ulcerative colitis, Crohn's disease or even a tropical disease. You never asked her if she'd been abroad recently.'

'Abigail,' Faith turned from the sink where she was filling the kettle, 'didn't you listen to what she told us? She admitted that she had had seafood last night and her symptoms started during the night, which admittedly were horrible for her but she's already starting to feel a bit better. You've got to remember that common things are common. The only reason she came to surgery was for a sick note because she works in a kitchen.'

Faith raised her eyebrows at Ed, who smiled with his eyes to reassure her.

'Come on, Abigail,' he called, heaving his lithe but rather etiolated body out of the chair, 'let's go and have a chat for twenty minutes before lunch.'

She was proving to be such hard work that it was increasingly difficult to keep up an air of enthusiasm. His last registrar, Rob, had been so straightforward. Unassuming but competent, he had grown in confidence on a daily basis and by the end of his attachment with them had not only been working as efficiently as a partner but he had also started going out with Faith, who had escaped, in the nick of time, from an engagement that was hurtling towards disaster faster than she could see. He was now working some ten miles away at the local district general hospital but was still in contact with Ed, who had proved not just to be a trainer but a good friend and drinking partner on alternate Thursday evenings. Somehow, Ed could not envisage sitting in the pub with Abigail, laughing at ridiculous jokes and putting the world to rights.

2

Clare, Ellie and Ed had escaped from the surgery for lunch and were sitting across the road in Delicious, the small but appropriately named delicatessen that boasted a small café towards the back of the premises. Abigail was on call for visits, a task she had already grown to hate and Ed, aware of her increasing tendency to try to fob off requests for house calls with an insufficient telephone call, had made her promise that she would contact him about everything and not make any decisions without first running them past him. Despite this safety net in position, he was still looking worried as he sat down.

Unusually, there were a lot of free tables, possibly explained by the persistent pouring rain which had started mid morning and showed no sign of letting up. They were waiting for their order of coffees and sandwiches, which they knew would be in the freshest of bread rolls, made on the premises, crammed almost to the point of obscenity with filling and served with crisps and an assortment of salads.

'How did it go with Abigail?' asked Ellie, gazing hungrily across to the counter where there was a spectacular display of irresistible cakes, biscuits and gateaux – all homemade.

'Still no signs of progress, I'm afraid,' he admitted. 'I can't stay long, much as I'd like to, as I'm afraid of leaving her too long on her own. Who knows what she might do?'

'She's got to learn to be independent,' argued Ellie.

'Yes, that's fine and I agree. But she's also got to make sensible clinical decisions and act on them. Just at the moment, I'm frightened of what her next move might be. Last week she tried to get a bed-bound patient to call a taxi to bring them in for an appointment, rather than go and visit herself. I've even asked the receptionists to let me know what she's up to.'

'It's a hard one,' agreed Ellie. 'On the one hand you don't want to be breathing down her neck all the time as that will make her feel you don't trust her...'

'I don't.'

Clare laughed.

'....but at the same time, you can't let her off the lead as it were. Our first priority has to be our patients.'

'Exactly. Clare, you used to be a trainer. What would you do with her?'

Clare pulled a sympathetic face. 'I feel really sorry for you. All of my registrars were very good by and large. I certainly never had a challenge like Abigail. I don't know how I'd have coped. So far, I think you're doing a remarkable job. You're being caring and attentive, you're trying to emphasise her positive qualities and yet doing your utmost to turn her into a GP. What more could she ask of a trainer? She's only been here three weeks or so. For all we know, she might be terrified and all this bluster is a front to impress us.'

Their food arrived and they sat back to allow the waitress, the teenage daughter of the owner, place large plates in front of them.

'Clare's got a good point there.' Ellie nibbled on a crisp, lifting up the top half of her roll and inspecting the contents. 'It's easy for us to think that we're friendly and approachable. Some people might think we're quite the opposite.'

'I'm sure she'll change soon.' Clare tried to be optimistic.

'What, out of that suit?'

Ellie spluttered into her lunch and Clare tried not to laugh.

'Ed! That's the sort of thing I'd say,' Ellie snorted, pretending to be aghast. 'Seriously though, Ed, you know we'll all help you with her training. If it does prove to be really difficult, then we'll all do extra with her, share it out between us. And if it comes to it, John will sort her out.'

'Thanks,' Ed mumbled, half way through a mouthful of tuna mayonnaise. 'But,' he swallowed, 'I'm determined not to let this defeat me. Even if at the end of her time with us, she doesn't want to be a GP, she'll still have had a shedload of invaluable experience.'

'Quite right,' nodded Ellie emphatically. 'She should know when she's well off.'

The enjoyment of their lunch took over and they said little more apart from murmurs of appreciation until Ed wiped his mouth clean at almost the identical time that Ellie did the same.

'As good as ever!' he announced.

Ellie scooped up the last remaining blob of coronation chicken with half a crisp and popped it into her mouth.

'Clare, are you okay? You've hardly eaten anything.'

'I'm fine. I thought I was really hungry but then as soon as I took the first mouthful, I didn't want any more. Sorry.'

'Oh, I hope you're not coming down with anything. There's apparently a ward closed at the hospital because of diarrhoea and vomiting. I tried to admit a patient this morning and was given a really hard time as they have so few empty beds. What about David, has he been all right?'

'He's fine. I'm sure it's nothing. Please don't worry.'

'You'll not want pudding then, I suppose.'

Clare shook her head.

'Ed, what about you?'

'No, I'm going to get back to the surgery. The suspense of not having heard from Abigail is proving too much.'

'No news is good news...' suggested Ellie and Ed looked unconvinced.

'Tell you what, get me a slice of the apple and almond cake and bring it back for me. I'll have it mid-afternoon.'

'I'll have another coffee, if you'd like a dessert, Ellie,' suggested Clare.

'Excellent!' Ellie went over to scrutinise the choices from closer quarters while Ed, throwing some money on the table to cover his share, waved to his two colleagues and left, turning to wave to Clare as he turned his collar up against the elements and set off at a brisk run.

Ellie returned balancing a plate of cake on top of a coffee cup, her other hand clutching Ed's takeaway.

'Mmmm, caramel and chocolate. Hideously fattening but who cares? I've worked really hard this morning and there's another surgery to get through this afternoon. I've already checked who's booked in and there are some names that strike terror into my heart, so I need some energy. That's my excuse. Want to try a bite?'

Clare declined and watched her good friend tucking in. Aware that she was being observed, Ellie turned her head and put down her fork, temporarily. She cleared her throat.

'So how are you really? Is it going okay, work I mean? Sometimes you look very pale.'

Unable to conceal a slight sigh, Clare studied the cruet on the table.

'It's hard, Ellie. I feel that I'm on a tightrope and everyone's underneath, watching me, holding their breath, just waiting for me to fall off. I'm so glad to be back though and my patients seem genuinely glad to see me.'

'I'm sure they are. They were always asking how you were getting on.'

'I was worried that they'd forget about me,' Clare confessed.

'No fear of that. Yours are ferociously loyal, you know that.'

'I wondered if they might all want to go on seeing Faith.'

'Faith's good enough, but she's not you.'

'She seems very competent.'

'Well she is. We wouldn't employ someone who wasn't, would we?'

Clare tried to smile, while wishing that she had even half of Ellie's down to earth common sense.

'And we're not all watching you like you think we are. We're all so glad that you're better and back at work. We've missed you. We're all your friends too, not just work partners. Try to relax and look forward, rather than over your shoulder all the time.'

This time Clare managed a more genuine smile.

'That's what David's always saying. Thanks, Ellie, I'll try.'

Clare took a sip of coffee but Ellie had not finished.

'There's something else though, isn't there? We've been friends long enough for me to spot that.'

Ellie pushed her plate to one side and rested her elbows on the table, allowing her chin to rest in her hands. Her thick auburn hair fell forwards off her shoulders.

'No, there's nothing,' Clare assured her, over-nonchalantly, too quickly.

She was aware of Ellie's interrogative gaze still upon her as the two sat in silence, Ellie waiting patiently, knowing that more was to come. The use of silence, she thought. It always worked with patients. If you kept quiet for long enough then they would inevitably speak and reveal some secret they had previously kept hidden that was often the clue to why they had come to see you. Now she was going to see if it worked with Clare. Tempting though it was to prompt her, Ellie said nothing but at the same time made no effort to avert her gaze. Eventually, after looking over her shoulder to make sure that no one could hear her, Clare leant forward, closer to Ellie and whispered.

'I'm pregnant.'

'That's fantastic!' Ellie shouted, genuinely thrilled.

'Shhhh,' Clare hissed at her. 'It's a secret.'

'You've wanted this for so long. Congratulations. How many weeks are you?'

'I don't want anyone else to know yet,' Clare warned her. 'I'm only about eleven weeks.'

'But it's still wonderful news,' Ellie dropped her voice.

She wondered why Clare was not looking ecstatic. David and she had been desperate for a family for years and at one point had been considering IVF. As if able to read her mind, Clare continued.

'I've conceived naturally. Goodness knows how after all this time. Maybe because I've been so busy worrying about work I stopped thinking about getting pregnant. But I'm still on medication, so that worries me. Even though David says it's nothing to cause concern, I can't forget about it. I wanted my baby to get off to a perfect start.'

'Well it has done because he or she has the two of you for parents. Think about it, lots of our patients have conceived while taking antidepressants and have had perfectly healthy, bouncing babies. So will you.'

Clare did not look any happier. 'But there's an even bigger problem.'

'What?'

'I feel I'm letting everyone at work down. I've only just come back from long- term sick leave. I'm so lucky that you've all supported me through that as you have done. What on earth are they all going to think when they find out I'm going to need maternity leave now?'

'They won't think anything, Clare, other than be overjoyed for you. Don't forget we've got Faith helping out. She's got a year's contract with us and I'm sure would be happy to stay on longer if need be.'

'I suppose. But what about the patients?'

'No sooner will they have found out than you'll be inundated with more knitted garments of every colour under the sun than you know what to do with. Clare, let yourself be happy about this. Don't worry about anyone else. It's not worth it. This is your life, it's what you've always wanted, at least as long as I've known you, so enjoy.'

'I am happy about it, really.'

'Good. Physically, how are you feeling?'

'The first few weeks were fine, apart from feeling that I'm walking on eggshells all the time in case something goes wrong and I start to bleed. I've had some period-like pains but that's normal, I think. It's so different when it's happening to you. I don't seem to be able to think logically. Now, I feel sick all the time. Sometimes not just feel sick but actually vomit as well. This morning I had to be sick in the basin in my room between patients. I'd probably have been okay if one of them hadn't brought in an old jam jar half full of the stuff they'd been coughing up off their chest for me to see.'

'Ugh! I think I'd probably have been sick too,' Ellie sympathised. 'And, what's more, while they were still in the room.'

Clare's face relaxed. 'Thanks, Ellie. You're a good friend. You always make me feel better.'

'Seriously though, it's a good sign. You must have lots of hormones hurtling through your body. Think of it from that angle.'

'That's what David keeps saying too. He's been amazing. Cooking the tea every night – well his own tea at least, doing the housework, making me put my feet up each evening and generally spoiling me rotten. He brings home flowers, chocolates, lotions to soften my skin and potions to ward off stretch marks. No husband could be more attentive. I just pray that nothing goes wrong. He'd be so devastated.'

'It won't,' Ellie replied emphatically. 'Everything will be fine. You deserve some good times after what you've been through. Hey, look at the time, we'd better get back. Feel okay?'

Clare nodded and quickly drank the dregs of her coffee, one of the few things that still tasted normal to her hypersensitive taste buds.

'You won't say anything just yet, will you?' implored Clare, as they rose to leave.

Ellie linked her arm into Clare's and squeezed it. 'Your secret's safe with me, I promise. Though I feel so excited for you, I want to tell everyone. But that, of course, is for you to do.'

Side by side, drawn even closer to each other by the news that Clare had shared, they half jogged back to work and arrived laughing, out of breath and shaking the rain from their hair. Aware that her coffee had re-awoken feelings of unrest in her stomach, Clare made a bee line for the toilet but was relieved when a series of loud belches seemed to settle things down. Relieved, she sat down for her umpteenth wee of the day.

The upheaval of her illness, then returning to work and David's concern for her welfare had meant that trying for a family had been the furthest thing from their minds. For the first time in years, they had stopped planning when she might be ovulating and she had stopped fretting about whether David's underpants might be too tight for healthy sperm to develop. Also, her periods had become chaotic, a fact that she attributed to her medication. So irregular in fact that her fertile days, if there were any, could have been at any time. If it hadn't been for the exquisitely tender breasts that she had developed, which also seemed to have doubled in size overnight, she might not have had any suspicions at all and as these symptoms first started, she had kept them to herself. They hadn't gone away, in fact they had got worse. She had waited until David had left for the hospital, willing him to stop agonising over whether he had all the papers he might need that day and go, wanting to do the test when she was on her own, in case it was negative. Lighting the blue touch paper to his hopes, only have them dashed was the last thing he deserved.

But this time, the test was positive, not just a maybe but a definite blue line that appeared within seconds. It had been minutes before she felt steady enough to get to the telephone and even then had been shaking to such an extent that she had barely been able to dial his number correctly and had to try several times before she was successful in getting through to his secretary. The receiver had rattled against her earring while she had waited for him to answer. At first his voice had sounded anxious and afraid, worried that she was ringing to say she was ill. When she had told him, he had gone so quiet she had thought they had been cut off. After his initial disbelief and then his incredulity, he had burst into tears of euphoria and so had she which led to a totally incomprehensible conversation with them both sobbing at each other. He had sent flowers later that day, blues and pinks – the florist must have thought that he was colour blind and then had arrived home with a bottle of champagne, which admittedly he had drunk most of. Clare doubted that he had ever been so happy.

She made her way to the washbasin to rinse her hands. Examining her reflection closely in the mirror, she was not overly impressed with the black rings around her eyes, the pallor of her complexion and the new crops of unsightly spots which were erupting with frightening velocity around her chin and nose. It seemed so unfair that she should look so awful when David was walking around with an unmistakable handsome rosy glow that simply screamed at people, 'I'm going to be a father.'

Clare half smiled and stroked her lower abdomen, wondering if the tiny person in there had any idea of what was going on in the outside world. Acid refluxed up into her mouth and she suddenly vomited. The bitter-tasting bile in her mouth made her gag repeatedly.

Only eleven weeks gone which meant twenty-nine to go or two hundred and three days.

Her pregnancy was merely in its infancy. Still, it was all worth it, wasn't it? The end of the infamous first trimester was in sight and surely after that she would feel so much better.

3

Hannah was curled up on the settee, her head resting in Ed's lap, the two of them watching a DVD which she had picked up at the local shop on her way over. It did not live up to the rave reviews on the box, which had promised 'you won't be able to sleep after watching this' and 'blood curdling thrills' but was passable enough to entertain them on a Friday evening after their hard weeks at work. Ed had ordered in pizza and while Hannah had pronounced herself full some time ago, he was still methodically chomping his way through both his and the remains of hers. A snoring tabby cat was draped over the back of the armchair, like a striped antimacassar, tail swishing gently, paws twitching at times, lost in a dream that was probably far more exciting than the film her owner was watching.

Unlike Mrs Martin's snug, Ed's lounge was a cosy room that emanated warmth and an invitation to relax as soon as you walked into it. Ed had decorated soon after moving in. The name of the paint he had chosen was banana, which sounded very off putting, but the walls, when painted and dry, had turned out to be more of a light primrose, which created the cottage-y feel that he was hoping for, lightened up the room considerably, thus making it feel considerably bigger and provided the ideal backdrop for the framed photographs he wanted to hang up. These were all his own work, mostly landscapes, taken on days when he was out climbing or walking. Among them were views of desolate scenery with wild skies, sunrises taken from the top of mountains and shots involving water, cascading, turbulent and tumbling over rocks or eerily calm and still as a mill pond.

There had been an open fireplace, which had thrilled him until he discovered how much work it was to prepare and light the fire, to say nothing of the cleaning up the following day, so reluctantly, after deciding the cons outweighed the pros, he had replaced it with an electric one, which admittedly would never convey the same look of homeliness and was useless when it came to toasting crumpets and melting marshmallows. On either side there were bookcases, jammed full randomly; books lying on their sides, others upright, some upside down. Their content was equally unpredictable, from medical books to novels, photography books and tomes on outdoor sports, even a pile of annuals, saved from his childhood – to any outsider a mess, but to Ed, who could immediately go to whichever book he was after, just perfect.

Flaked out on the thick sheepskin rug was his second cat, Toby. Barely more than a kitten, he was fast asleep, absorbing the heat to recharge his batteries before the next game with a tiny fluffy toy mouse or a chase round the house after an invisible prey. Hannah had bought Toby for him. She thought that the other cat, Hebe, needed a friend but their relationship to date looked as though it would never advance past mere tolerance.

On the television screen, there was so much blood that it was hard to make out where it had come from. Accompanied by a variety of gargling noises and screams, plus the unmistakable sound of a chain saw in the background, there was clearly something very unpleasant taking place. Ed shifted in his chair, gently moving Hannah's head. Sleepily she sat up, yawning as she did so.

'Sorry,' he apologised. 'I was just going to make a coffee. I can't stand much more of this rubbish, can you? I thought you said it was a murder story, not a murder massacre. Can I get you a drink?'

'Don't leave it on for me. I've been dozing for the last I don't know how long, so I haven't a clue what's happening. And yes, I'd love a hot drink, though I'd prefer a green tea if it's no trouble.'

Ed levered his long limbs out of the soft, squashy sofa, gathered together the pizza box and the last remaining two arcs of crust and, switching off the DVD, flicked onto the news, which was nearing the end, so that he could watch from the kitchen doorway while he was waiting for the kettle to boil. He was eager to see the weather forecast for the weekend, not that the promise of rain and cold would stop the two of them from spending tomorrow in the Dales, walking. The plan was to be up early, just after dawn and then tramp the Three, aiming to beat their previous time of eight hours, which both of them secretly thought a bit pathetic. Hannah had put the blame on Ed, chastising him for stopping to take so many photos and holding them up. He had laughed and retorted that if only her legs were longer then they'd have covered the ground more quickly.

He was lucky to have found someone who was as big a devotee of outdoor pursuits as he was. Mountain biking, climbing, abseiling and white water rafting –Hannah was up for all of them and more. Her enthusiasm was directly proportional to the amount of adrenaline that her body would release.

Ed's previous relationships had fallen by the wayside because girls had found it difficult to cope with his favourite pastimes. Some simply refused point blank to join in, not owning any flat shoes. Others, more adventurous, would agree to go walking but rarely finished the course, Ed's idea of a proper walk being ten or fifteen miles longer than theirs. One even arrived, ready to set off, in full and obviously brand-new walking gear, set to impress but had begun to whine after a few miles, when her socks were wet through and her feet, unaccustomed to the boots, had developed an ugly crop of throbbing blisters.

Ed was not impervious to feminine charms such as beauty or a desirable body but could not tolerate being made to feel like a pariah when he chose the great outdoors over a lie-in (which admittedly might involve some good sex) and then a shopping trip in some bustling city or town centre where it was impossible even to walk side by side. He loathed loitering outside the changing rooms, along with other sheepish-looking blokes, waiting for their girlfriends to appear from behind the curtains, to twirl and preen, waiting for adulation, exclamations of perfection and preferably an offer to pay the bill.

He had grown up in the Lake District, his father a disillusioned accountant but a keen climber, his mother a teacher at the local primary school. Every day, he had felt the freedom of the rolling, glorious scenery and loved the fact that the indigenous sheep population far outnumbered that of the humans. His was a childhood of running wild, outdoors from dawn until dusk, exploring, cycling, straying miles from home with his two best friends, brown as berries in the summer, ruddy cheeked and no less energetic in the winter. Not for them the lure of the television and video games. There was far more excitement to be found in the hills and valleys surrounding them.

True, it was bleak at times. In the winter, the rain and snow made any visitors wonder why on earth they chose to stay there but even in these extreme moments, to Ed, there was still a magical feel to this part of the world he was so attached to. His plan had always been to return after qualifying, having half promised to get involved with the mountain rescue but he had been offered the partnership in Lambdale, where he had done the last part of his training and the prospect of working in the Yorkshire Dales, part of the country with its own unique beauty and challenges, had proved irresistible. Instantly, he had known that it was perfect for him. After joining the practice, he had, after some searching, found his house, an end terrace cottage, ideally situated for everything outdoors, big enough for all his possessions and yet small enough not to require a great deal of cleaning or looking after. There was even a small outhouse, imaginatively called a garage in the estate agents' details, which was ideal for his climbing gear and bikes. It hadn't taken long for Gary, one of the receptionists, to volunteer his mother, Barbara, a reliable cleaner and cat lover, as someone who was more than happy to come in and tidy up twice a week and look after the animals when Ed wanted to go away, in exchange for a reasonable wage which helped towards the upkeep of her little car. Toby and Hebe had quickly ingratiated themselves with Barbara, smarmily weaving their way in and out of her legs, purring their best purrs, which of course had helped seal an arrangement which had gone on to stand the test of time.

Hannah had come into his life only a few months earlier. Introduced to each other by a mutual friend when they had all just stopped to get their breath half way up a rock face near Malham, Ed had been impressed not just by her athleticism but also by her joie de vivre in general. With very short, curly hair, a tiny but muscular body composed of androgynous hips and no breasts to speak of whatsoever, she was a world apart from the usual girl he fell for with long hair and generous curves demanding exploration. There was something different about her, which he had found indefinable but tantalising and before they left that day, he had asked her out and she had accepted.

On their first proper date, he drove over to Harrogate, where she lived, and took her out for dinner, Hannah having chosen the restaurant. Ed, looking forward to a thick steak or, failing that, a rib-sticking slowly cooked lamb shank, found himself reading through the vegetarian menu with horror, blinded by the choices and desperately trying to find something to order. In the end, he chose lentil lasagne, hoping against hope that it might have some resemblance to its meaty relation and baulked slightly as Hannah nonchalantly ordered butter bean and cider casserole with potato and turnip purée. Trying to sound as if he knew what he was talking about, he asked for a glass of the same drink that she had requested, elderflower and pomegranate pressé, correctly assuming that his preferred request for a glass of lager would not be well received.

Whilst he was pretending to enjoy the aubergine fritters with tomato sauce that were placed before them as a starter, he paid more attention to conversing with Hannah. Initially there was awkwardness between them, stiff and uncomfortable in their good clothes and reserved in unfamiliar surroundings. She was hesitant to chat other than superficially, so Ed had to persist gently and help her relax before she gave anything about herself away. By the time the waitress came to clear the plates after their main courses, he noticed that she had barely eaten anything either. Attributing this to her nervousness, he sipped on his pressé, which admittedly, when you got used to it, did not taste too bad at all.

'How long have you been vegetarian?' he asked.

Hannah looked down at the table, moving the remaining cutlery to one side and resting her elbows on the table. Ed's heart flipped over as she looked at him, dark eyes sparkling with mischief.

'I've a confession to make,' she began. 'I'm not a vegetarian at all. I just thought it would be interesting to come here.'

'So that's why you've hardly touched your food,' surmised Ed.

'Yes, I'm beginning to thing that it was something of a mistake.'

Ed laughed and took her hand. 'How about I pay the bill and we go somewhere for a proper drink?'

'That'd be great. Sorry about this! I feel awful.'

Twenty minutes later they were in the corner of a small wine bar, sipping glasses of wine and chatting naturally. The new ambience, perhaps the alcohol and the sharing of a bowl overflowing with hot, golden potato wedges, sprinkled with sea salt, acted as a catalyst to help the real Hannah emerge. Opening up, she became willing to talk about herself and Ed quickly learned that Hannah was a solicitor, working in a small firm that specialised in divorce and family law. Originally from the South coast, she had studied at Manchester and then worked for a short time in Leeds. She was taken aback to hear that Ed was a GP, expressing the view that he did not look like one. When asked to expand on this, she became very embarrassed and muttered something about all the doctors she had ever met being elderly, overweight and cynical – a far cry from the good-looking, fit, amusing young man who was sitting with her now. Her discomfort had been palpable and Ed had tactfully regaled her with as many funny stories about his work as he could think of, gratified to see her initial polite laughter turn to genuine amusement.

By the end of that first evening, they had become closer and the kiss that they shared when saying a lingering goodbye left neither of them in any doubt that this was the beginning of something very promising. Ed had driven back home with his heart singing and mind a-whirl with exciting thoughts. With both of them having a vocation rather than a job, work inevitably took first place but they quickly established a routine where, on Friday evenings Hannah would motor up to Lambdale and stay until late Sunday afternoon. She refused to stay until Monday morning, emphasising that she had to get back, take stock and prepare for work. They seldom saw each other during the week, relying on telephone calls in the evenings, Hannah claiming to be far too busy, but they made up for lost time at weekends, indulging in their favourite hobbies and enjoying each other's company.

Their sex life was unremarkable. Hannah's libido was easily satiable and Ed, though left frustrated at times as he found her so erotically attractive, did not push her, happy to have a multi-faceted relationship, rather than one that was largely based on carnal desire. What he loved about her was her personality, her ambitious streak, her dedication to the enjoyment of life and her unique outlook on the world. He also understood her work ethic. She had made it clear from the outset that her career was vitally important to her. It was one that required commitment and resolve and she had set her sights on doing extremely well. Without being told as much, Ed realised very quickly that trying to dissuade her from the path she had mapped out for herself would probably be the beginning of the end of their liaison.

On a couple of occasions he had come very close to asking her to move in with him. Their relationship was going really well, superficially relaxed and easy-going but with a tacit undercurrent of trust and loyalty. Something, though, at the last minute made him backtrack, sensing that perhaps she was not ready to put things on a different footing just yet. Ed was happy to leave things be, not wanting to make a suggestion that might unsettle what had grown between them. Time enough for more formal arrangements.

Eager to show her off, he had taken Hannah one evening to Ellie's where the partners were all having a get together, enjoying each other's company away from the confinements of work. He had so been looking forward to but it had turned out to be a disaster. She had been totally overawed by the laughter, the chat, the stress of being the newcomer and had reacted by withdrawing into herself, looking gauche and close to tears and having a miserable time. With hindsight, he realised that perhaps it had been tantamount to trial by fire, meeting everyone all at once, being the only stranger amid a group of very good friends and had sought to rectify his mistake by arranging smaller, less raucous supper parties where Hannah had felt more comfortable and had let her natural charm show through.

Ed turned towards the boiling kettle and made the drinks, unable to stop his head from shaking imperceptibly at the green tea bag which looked as if it might contain dried lawn trimmings. Cutting a piece of fruit cake – left by Barbara who decided every so often that he needed feeding up – he heard the first dulcet tones of the current favoured weather lady and hurried back to catch what she had to say. He leant on the back of the settee and handed Hannah her drink.

His heart sank when he saw the British Isles covered by a swarm of angry-looking black clouds with big dark raindrops descending from them and heard the confirmation that the whole country was going to be wet for the weekend. Flood warnings followed and the local weather forecast was no more optimistic and accompanied by, as if to labour the point, clips of distraught-looking people standing in their kitchens, ankle deep in water, ineffective sandbags by their doors.

'Oh shit,' he swore. 'Just look at that.'

'It's been quite a nice week,' complained Hannah. 'I thought it would hold up for us tomorrow but it doesn't look like it, does it?'

'I'm afraid not. What do you think? Shall we still go?'

Hannah thought for a moment.

'We'll never beat eight hours if it's pelting with rain. The ground will be really slippy, which will make climbing and running really difficult.'

'Let's give it a miss. If it turns out better than we think, we can always go on a bike ride somewhere closer to home.'

'Okay. I'd far rather do the Three on a good day. It's a shame, but never mind. There'll be other opportunities.'

Ed walked round to sit next to her, stroking Hebe as he passed her and smiling at the indignant look on her face. Hannah snuggled up next to him and flicked through a number of channels before switching off in disgust. They sat silently, watching the hypnotic artificial flame of the fire. Ed slipped his hand under her jumper and tentatively started to stroke her firm little body.

'Ed,' began Hannah, extracting herself from his embrace.

'Yup?'

'I've a bit of news.'

'What's that?'

'I've been offered a job.'

'What? A partnership? That's fantastic.'

He made a move to give her a congratulatory kiss but she backed off.

'No, not exactly. Well, yes, I suppose you're right. It could well lead to a partnership, if I work really hard, but it's not where I'm working at the moment.'

'Oh, you've been head-hunted, have you? Which firm recognises talent when it sees it?'

'McGregor Moran. I saw the advertisement and sent in my application.'

'Never heard of them.'

'It's unlikely that you will have heard of them.'

'Why, are they a new firm?'

'No, quite the contrary. Long established, very well thought of.

Experts in divorce. It really is a golden opportunity for me.'

'Then that's great. Well done. Come here and have a hug. If I had champagne, we could celebrate but you'll just have to settle for another green tea.'

Hannah laughed quietly, then became serious.

'I don't think you realise what I'm saying, Ed. This firm isn't in Harrogate. It's in Edinburgh.'

Ed felt his heart starting to race.

'What! I thought you were happy where you are at the moment.'

'Well, I am, I suppose. But this would be such a chance to progress. Jobs like this don't come along every day, you know.'

'You're not going to take it are you?'

'Yes, I am. In fact, I've already said yes.'

She watched him as he struggled to make sense of all that she was saying.

'But you never told me you were looking for another job... Did you never think to discuss it with me...?'

Hannah sighed. 'I know. I wasn't really looking seriously for a new job but I always keep an eye open, just in case something crops up which will be a step up for me. I saw this one and knew that I just had to go for it. I never really expected to get it. But you know how important my career is.'

Ed nodded. 'Yes I do. I just can't get over the fact that you've never said a word about this before. Presumably you've been for an interview and not thought of telling me about that either.'

'Sorry,' Hannah apologised.

'I don't know what to say. How could you do that?'

By now Ed had moved down onto the hearthrug, seeking solace by stroking Toby's soft fur. Hannah shuffled down to be beside him. He scooped up the little cat into his lap, possessively.

'When do you start?'

'Next month.'

'Very soon then. Well, I hope it lives up to your expectations.'

'I'm confident it will.'

She took his hand. 'Don't be cross Ed, you know how much work means to me.'

He looked directly into her eyes. 'I thought that I meant a lot to you. I thought we were a couple that shared everything. Hannah, I love you.'

'And I love you, Ed. That's why I want you to move there with me.'

They sat up talking long, long into the night. Now that the arrangements for the next day had been postponed and the proposed early start no longer necessary, the need for sleep had become less important. The cats woke up, became playful and full of the joys of life but had to be content with amusing themselves, Ed and Hannah being too wrapped up in their own dilemma to notice them. Ed kept himself going with regular cups of coffee, laced with slugs of whisky, each one rather more generous than the last, refusing to let matters lie unresolved overnight. Upset with Hannah for even thinking of such a change to her life without consulting him, he was trying hard to control his temper. The last thing that either of them needed was a quarrel, with raised voices, comments getting out of hand and mud slinging which would be later regretted. But he could not comprehend how she was able to remain so detached. Surely this only meant that what feelings she had for him were of secondary importance or maybe he had been demoted even further down her list of priorities without his noticing.

Never one to wear her heart on her sleeve, Hannah tended to respond to topics of emotion by hoisting her professional façade to act as a barrier behind which she could conveniently hide. So much so that Ed had felt that he had achieved a major breakthrough when Hannah confessed that she loved him and though since that moment she had only repeated these words on a handful of occasions, he had not needed to hear them, trusting her, secure in her actions and knowing that there was a new closeness between them. He had taken it for granted, foolishly, it now appeared, that they were planning a future together but that there was plenty of time to discuss more formal footings such as engagements or marriage.

He told her this, in a sad soliloquy, broken into short bursts while he fumbled through his brain for the words that would best describe the way he was feeling. In doing so, he alternately held her hands loosely, gripped them tightly and once let them go as if scalded by a hot coal that was exacerbating his pain. She sat cross legged and listened silently, head bowed. At a loss for anything further to say, he sighed and looked at her, questioningly, intimating that it was now her turn to do the talking. To his amazement there were tears rolling down her cheeks.

Clearing her throat, Hannah voiced out loud the way she felt about Ed and that she could no more contemplate a life without him than envisage her not having a career. Ed was flattered and surprised. Her apologies were profuse – she accepted that she had allowed the situation to run away with her and in the excitement of concentrating on her career, had not given due consideration to Ed. She went on to paint a tempting picture of life in Edinburgh, a city he had never been to. Her research had gone so far as to canvas local estate agents and acquire details of likely looking properties. She was looking near the city centre, near to where her office would be. Work would be ferociously hard and long hours but the money exceptional, making a larger mortgage attainable. The less she had to travel the better. A local Harrogate agent had valued her house generously and it would be on the market within a week. Expectations were high that it would sell in no time.

Having completed her sales pitch for the city, during which she waxed lyrical about its modern vibrancy and historical connections, Hannah went on to point out the potential of not just the surrounding countryside but the rest of Scotland, facts that Ed could not dispute. It was bound to be easy for him to find a job, she had decided, with his skill and reputation plus his partners would surely give him good references.

Ed, at this point, held up both his hands as if to stop her mid-flow.

'Hold on a mo, Hannah. You're like a runaway train that's left me on the platform of the station before last. Don't I get a say in this? You seem to have it all organised.'

'Well, now you know all about it, we can make plans together. We could even go up there tomorrow as the weather's going to be so foul and start to have a look round, stay in a top notch hotel and spoil ourselves. What do you think?'

Ed shrugged.

'My treat?' she cajoled him.

'Thanks, but no thanks. Not this weekend. My head's reeling with what you've told me. I'm not ready to make such a commitment just now. I don't think you realise what you're asking me to do. This may be a great career move for you, but remember that I'm already in a partnership that I'm very happy in. I'm lucky to have good colleagues and I love my work. I can't just up and leave. I don't know if I'd want to.'

'Ed, it'd be great, I promise.'

Yawning, Ed reached out to turn off the fire.

'It's no use, Hannah. There's no way I'm making any decisions just now. I'm really pleased for you but I'm still uncomfortable with the way you went about it. Let's go to bed now, enjoy tomorrow and what we have of Sunday and I promise I'll think about it over the next few weeks.'

'Please think more quickly than that,' Hannah pleaded.

'We'll see. Even if I did leave, I'd have to give considerably more notice than you, it's in the practice agreement. But you'll still come down some weekends, won't you?'

'Of course, we can alternate – me here one weekend, you up in Edinburgh the other. It won't be easy for us, which is a good reason for you to make your mind up as soon as possible.'

Ed yawned, stretching his arms above his head before rubbing his face. 'I'm bushed, Hannah. Come on, let's get some sleep.'

Lying in bed between the cool, fresh linen that smelled of Barbara's fabric conditioner, Hannah was asleep almost before Ed joined her, having lingered over his teeth brushing on purpose. She murmured indecipherably as he got in beside her and put out the bedside light. While she slept, her face serene in rest with a small smile on her mouth, Ed lay awake for most of what was left of the night before finally dozing just before dawn.

4

Clare was thumbing through the obstetric text book she had used both as a student and when she was doing her training in maternity. When written in black and white, pregnancy looked so straightforward, that was of course if she ignored the chapters on what could go wrong, complete with gruesome diagrams of potentially disastrous situations. Cord prolapse, undiagnosed breech presentations and shoulder dystocia did not bear thinking about. It was one thing to deal with them as a doctor but quite another to think that it might happen to you. She snapped the book shut and instead turned to the rather twee booklet called 'And Baby Makes Three', given to her by the midwife. This was more what she needed – a pictorial diary of a group of women, each basking in a halo of happiness as they travelled from conception to birth. Not for them the vulgarity of stretch marks and humiliation of piles – they lived in a world where maternity clothes were always flattering and never included the anonymity of shapeless leggings and husbands' shirts. They smiled their way through morning sickness, laughed with their husbands as they inflated like beach balls, barely broke into a sweat as they gave birth and were back in bed, with a clean nightie and not a hair out of place cuddling the new arrival in less than twenty pages. Clare sighed as she made comparisons. Now just out of the first trimester, she had foolishly dared to hope that the goddess of pregnant women would wave her magic wand and overnight she would start to feel better.

Not so. Disconcertingly, the vomiting, if anything, was worse. Last night and the one before, she had even woken in the night, knowing that she had to dash to the bathroom yet again. And if that wasn't bad enough, in between times, she was visited by persistent nausea, melancholic burps and acid refluxing into her gullet. Her appetite was virtually non-existent. All food had assumed the same taste, approximating to a mixture of damp cardboard and half-wrung-out dishcloths, yet she had, conversely, become hypersensitive to aromas and the merest whiff of cooking could make her heave. She tried hard, repeating the old adage 'eating for two', over and over in her mind, desperate for her baby to have the nutrients it needed to grow and develop. Nibbling dry biscuits was useless, ginger revolting and indigestion remedies a waste of money. Nor did she have the least desire to eat coal, pilchards with marmite or ice cream drizzled with tomato ketchup. She wished that she did. David tried repeatedly to coax her to eat with a variety of surprises – new textures, unexpected tastes, sweet, acid, bland or spice. All had the same effect.

With huge reluctance, she even tried prescribed anti-emetics as eventually the awfulness of her symptoms led to desperation and a desire to try anything, if it would only help. The very first one seemed to be a success and her heart leapt with joy, only to descend with a crash as it turned out to be a coincidence of the cruellest kind and as for subsequent doses – well, she might just as well have been swallowing sweets for all the difference they made. She drew the line at suppositories and spent one undignified and awkward weekend on the gynaecology ward, being rehydrated intravenously before taking her own discharge on the Sunday evening so that she could be back at work the following day thus not arousing the suspicions of her partners.

Her midwife, Marjorie, was a large-bosomed woman with a frighteningly booming voice but a kind heart. The epitome of optimism, she had reassured Clare that there was no need to worry – she had seen more cases like this than Clare had had hot dinners, perhaps not the wisest analogy to use in the circumstances. The baby would be fine, safe in the little incubator of Clare's womb. Her own body would see to that and it would be no time at all before she was able to enjoy her food and make up for lost time. Besides, she was probably going to be one of those women who just pile on lots of weight at the end of the pregnancy. Clare, now over a stone lighter than her normal fighting weight, found little consolation in her words and said nothing, merely smiling gratefully, all the while hoping that she was right.

The sickness was not the only hardship she had to cope with. Dermatologically, her face now resembled the lunar surface. Literally spotted around her forehead, chin and nose were pustules and inflamed cysts, oily patches and blackheads, all alien to her as she had, to date, been fortunate with her complexion, even as a teenager. Her fine hair hung in lank and lifeless clumps, no matter how often she washed it. She felt that she was living proof of the fact that exfoliating scrubs, anti-bacterial washes and revitalising shampoos did not live up to their promises.

Fatigue of the most unimaginable ferocity set in but she was determined not to take any time off. She resorted to her bed within minutes of arriving home, slept as though drugged for the best part of twelve hours and got up hoping that she would have enough energy to get her through the forthcoming day at work. If she was really fortunate then she found time for a half hour nap in her room at lunchtime, which went some way to revitalising her for the afternoon surgery. Her examination couch left a lot to be desired when it came to providing comfort.

Patients were beginning to notice, despite the carefully applied make-up, which was supposed to cover up acne and the bags below her eyes. Whilst they had said nothing directly to her, one or two had passed comment to the receptionists, who had also not been oblivious to the changes taking place and had started to compile a list of their own concerns, which they were prevaricating about whether to pass on to Dr Britton. Joan had actually asked Clare if she was all right. Blushing furiously, Clare had muttered something about having had a terrible sickness bug which had completely knocked her for six but was now confident that she was on the mend. Attempting to add gravitas to her excuse, she had even blamed David for bringing the illness back from hospital. She hoped that she had got away with it. But that encounter had made Clare realise, if nothing else, that it was time to tell the partners, or rather, confirm out loud what she suspected they had already guessed.

She chose her moment wisely, waiting impatiently and nervously until the end of a practice meeting. They talked long and late about some of the more serious aspects of management and finance, potential effects that this might have on Teviotdale, knocking ideas back and forth ad nauseam without reaching any concrete solutions, a state of affairs that left everyone weary and slightly dissatisfied. Never a partnership to bicker or fall out, they finished up rather despondently and were very quiet when Elliot Douglas, the practice manager, moved on to any other business.

Spontaneously, Ellie suggested supper at her house that weekend, as an antidote to the heated debate of the evening, promising good food, plentiful wine and a chance to relax as friends and forget about work. Ellie's prowess as hostess and cook being famous, the mood lifted instantly and Clare, gulping down her fear, seized the opportunity to make her announcement before anyone could get up and put on their coat.

Quite why she had tortured herself with worry, she would never know, for their reactions were unanimously those of joy, sincere congratulation and a barrage of concerned questions as to her current state of health. John had had his suspicions that something was going on for some weeks, not that he told Clare this and had shared these with his wife Faye who had instantly proposed the diagnosis with the benefit of woman's intuition rather than medical acumen. Ellie felt very relieved that Clare's secret was out in the open as the burden of not telling anyone had proved heavy, particularly on the days when it was quite clear that Clare was not fit for work. Elliott, in his usual customary manner of efficient organiser, asked when the baby was due, wrote down a reminder to start looking for maternity cover and asked Clare if she would spend a few minutes with him the next day to talk about her plans.

Only Ed was completely taken aback. Pleased for Clare, of course, but he could honestly say that he had not had the slightest idea. He had been so pleased when she was deemed well enough to return to work as he had missed her common sense and her experience as a trainer that he liked to call upon, to say nothing of the contribution she gave on a daily basis to the practice. Her virtues far outweighed her drawbacks but Ed often wished that he could do something to ease her daily battle with her perfectionism and devotion to her patients. But for the last fortnight, Clare could have sprouted horns and grown a beard for all that he would have noticed, his mind having been totally preoccupied with Hannah's invitation to move to Edinburgh.

Again, he had suspected nothing, but then why should he have done? Hannah, playing her cards close to her chest as usual, had let no clues slip and he still bristled at the thought that she had been so clandestine about her plans. Weren't couples supposed to discuss such matters? The rest of their weekend had been tense, to say the least. After a Saturday morning sitting indoors, going round and round in circles with their discussions, he had gone out, not exactly in a huff but he had certainly made it clear that he wanted to be alone and had accidentally slammed the front door on his way out. Despite the promised teeming rain, he had cycled for miles, oblivious of his soaking condition, just glad to be in the fresh air, wind blowing through his mind, trying to make some sense of the jumbled thoughts that were in there. Drenched, he had enjoyed two greasy egg and bacon sandwiches, bought from a mobile takeaway van he happened upon in a lay-by at the summit of a hill, doing a roaring trade as sight-seers, who had stopped hoping to take in the views, usually a panoramic photographic opportunity, were disappointed that day by the appalling visibility. He found a certain catharsis eating the hot meat while thinking angrily of Hannah and treated himself to a home made flap jack and a squidgy chocolate brownie to eat on the way home. Checking his watch, he set off on the return run, cranking up his speed a couple of notches, putting his adrenaline to good use, forcing his legs to pump faster and faster.

Once back at his house, he had acknowledged Hannah with a curt nod – she was lying on the settee reading some heavy legal tome – trying to look stern, an effect rather ruined by his dripping all over the carpet and gone up to soak in the bath for as long as he could. Finally warm and dry, in clean jeans and soft cotton shirt, he had felt able to face her. She had made dinner. There was wine – clearly a peace offering along with the meal which consisted of Ed's favourites – a casserole full of hefty chunks of local beef, carrots and onions, served with jacket potatoes and broccoli. A bought apple pie was produced for dessert, plus vanilla ice cream and by the time he was eating this and Hannah was gnawing at a banana, at least they were talking civilly, albeit in a rather stilted way. That night they had slept back to back, Hannah having retired while Ed stayed up to watch the football.

Ed had been almost glad, when, on the Sunday morning after breakfast, Hannah announced that she was off back to Harrogate. Due in court first thing on Monday, there was no way that she was not going to allow plenty of time for preparation. Since then, there had been telephone calls, some brief, some protracted, none leaving Ed feeling that he was any nearer to making a decision.

One of the things Ed found so hard to understand was why Hannah could not see what a huge deal it was for him, leaving a practice where he had worked for over five years and even trained at. Regularly, he took stock and appreciated his good fortune in having acquired partners who were friends away from work as well, who did not sulk or take umbrage, who were supportive, equally hard working and good fun. He was the envy of many of his friends, who had not had such good experiences themselves, ending up in groups where the dynamics were unbalanced and unpleasant, tainted by rifts and disharmony. To be blunt about it, he loved going to work. Meeting new people socially, he would almost brag that he had the best job in the world. It wasn't just his partners but the practice staff – all of them from the cleaners to Elliot, the nurses, health visitors and counsellor. Each one contributed in some small but vital way, like pieces of a jigsaw. Last but not least were the patients. He knew lots of them and they knew him. He was looking forward to acquiring the same encyclopaedic knowledge that John had, with the passage of time. He had already been privileged to be part of their lives for some years and wanted to stay with them, to help them stay healthy, celebrate births and commiserate over illnesses and death. What other job offered such an opportunity? For sure, there were the heart-sink patients, the ones whose very name conjured up visions of impossible demands and circuitous conversations but the majority were good folk, grateful for the excellent service they received. And while Ed was able to retain enough objectivity to be sure that there would be parallels of all these people in Edinburgh, that wasn't the point and why did Hannah persist in thinking that it was all so easy?

He wished it was his day for going out for a pint with Rob. As the others donned their coats and made their way to the car park, anxious to get home to their respective families, Ed dawdled behind, took his bike out from the small room at the back of the building and gently cycled away.

The telephone was ringing as he unlocked the door and he threw his rucksack onto the stairs, narrowly missing Hebe who was descending graciously to greet him. Grabbing the receiver he heard Hannah's voice and sat down to talk to her. Hebe leapt noiselessly onto his knee and curled up, digging her front paws rhythmically into his thighs. Hannah was excited, chattier than usual. A client had asked especially for her and she was thrilled, thinking that this was a sign that her reputation was spreading around the town. She was sickened to have to turn it down but there was no way that she would finish the

42

job in the time left to her. Still, it had given her a good feeling to start her day and then there had been a phone call from her new boss, who was already looking out for cases that she could be involved in and would be emailing her papers to start working on. It was going to be hectically busy, almost akin to working in two places at once, but she was so looking forward to it. Ed tried to listen patiently to her selfish ramblings but found his attention was more on tickling Hebe's ears and the sound of her ecstatic purring. Not once did Hannah ask after his work, not once did she ask him how he was. A fleeting thought of telling her about Clare's news came and went. Her departing words of 'I love you', sounding obligatory rather than heart felt, did nothing to appease his loneliness and although he dutifully repeated them back to her, he felt deflated once she had rung off.

After fixing some supper of sausages and macaroni cheese – the latter left by Barbara, who believed that stinting on the cheese was a cardinal sin – Ed sat with a beer and rang his parents. His mother answered and the sound of her voice instantly made him feel better. They chatted for a while, just about everyday things, she interested in his work, he wanting to know about his father, news from the area, anything that he could take comfort from. Wisely, for she appreciated as soon as she heard his voice that there was something amiss, she answered his questions and made him laugh with some ridiculous sally about the neighbours' dog and a bed of rhubarb before asking him what he was worried about. His knee-jerk reaction was to deny that there was anything wrong, insisting that he had just rung for a chat as he frequently did, but his mother, able to detect the slightest nuance in his voice that varied from his normal cheerful tone, repeated her question.

He told her all about Hannah and her proposition, feeling a weight lift from him as his words came tumbling out. Diplomatically, rather than giving her own opinions, she stayed quiet on the other end of the line. Not expecting to be told what he should do, Ed thanked her for listening, feeling in some way that she had helped him and felt her warm, familiar laugh wrap around him protectively.

'You've always said that you love it in Lambdale,' she finished as he was about to ring off.

'I do, Mum,' he corroborated her words.

'I know you do and I know how happy you are there.' He could hear her smile. 'What about Hannah? Do you love her that much more?'

'That's the problem. I just don't know.'

'Be patient. I know you'll make the right decision. Just don't do anything in a hurry.'

5

'I came to see Dr Watson last week,' confessed Kevin Ackroyd, corpu-
lent, apple cheeked and balding. 'She told me – hang on a moment –
I had to write it down as I hadn't the first clue what she was talking
about, ah here it is, hypertensive disease, hyperchol-something and
impaired glucose something or other. She'd completely lost me by
then. Out of the blue she asked if I'd any trouble getting an erection. I
was speechless. She gave me five different lots of tablets. Something
has given me the squits. I guess it must be one of them and so I've
stopped taking them and brought them all back. I felt quite well when
I went into the surgery. I came out feeling bloody awful.'

Ed sighed inwardly and turned slightly so that he could see the
copious notes that Abigail had made.

'Okay, let's have a look. You'd been for a medical for work, had
you?'

Kevin nodded, mopping at his forehead where some beads of
perspiration were forming.

'I have one regularly. There's never been any problem before.'

He waited patiently for Dr Diamond to absorb all the details, making
a mental note not to come back to see Dr Watson again.

'It's quite simple really,' began Ed. 'At your medical, your blood
pressure was a little raised. Then your blood tests showed your
cholesterol could be lower and your blood sugar was a little high.
Had you eaten that day?'

'Yes, breakfast. Orange juice, cereal, toast, bacon and eggs. The
usual. What anyone has.'

Ed's eyebrows rose a little, casting his mind back to the bowl of branflakes he had hurriedly consumed that morning.

'Fine. Then let's start at the beginning and try to sort this out. Firstly, I need to check your blood pressure today. Then, we need to arrange a blood sugar test for first thing one morning when you've had nothing to eat or drink since the night before. And we'll give you an information sheet about cholesterol, what it is, what is does and how you might be able to lower it a little by altering your diet.'

Ed moved towards his patient, who dutifully tugged up his right sleeve and pulled faces while the cuff inflated around his arm, squeezing it uncomfortably.

'That's a bit better than in your medical but not perfect. You were probably nervous on the day. To be on the safe side, I'd suggest that you book a couple of appointments with the practice nurses, a week or so apart, just so that we've got a few readings to see how you're doing.'

'What about all these tablets, doc? They cost me a small fortune. Have you any idea how much a prescription charge is these days?'

Ed looked at the array of boxes that Kevin had produced from his jacket pockets. Three to control blood pressure, one for diabetes, one to lower cholesterol.

'Mmm,' he pretended to consider them professionally, hoping that Kevin was oblivious to his real desire to jettison them all into the nearest bin. Talk about inappropriate prescribing – another difficult discussion with Abigail loomed.

'Do you know what? Let's leave all these for now until we've got the other blood pressure readings and the blood sugar result. Come back and see me in say, three weeks – I'll ring you if there's any need for me to see you sooner – and we'll just go through everything again.'

Kevin relaxed visibly. 'But why did she ask me about erections? I was mortified. I'd not tell a young girl a thing like that.'

Ed nodded, sympathetically. 'Dr Watson has only just started in general practice. She's highly qualified in hospital medicine, very keen and has a huge amount of knowledge. We're very lucky to have her with us for a few months. High blood pressure is usually caused by hardening of the arteries – have you heard of that? Good. This can progress to cause heart disease. I'm sure you know people with angina? Maybe even someone who has had a heart attack? Exactly. Sometimes, an early warning that this is happening in a male patient is that they start to have problems with getting an erection.'

'Bloody hell.' Kevin looked horrified, his hand automatically going down to cover his groin.

'I shall tell her that you've been back to see me and what we've spoken about. I'm sure that it will all help her become a better GP with time.'

'I hope she's got plenty of it,' Kevin murmured. 'She's going to need it.'

Following a few more placatory pleasantries, Ed escorted Kevin to the door and shook his hand. Before he could call in the next patient, he saw Abigail gesticulating wildly at him from the other side of the waiting area, beckoning for him to come over. She was having a tussle diagnosing a rash in a happy-looking toddler who, having explored every nook and cranny in the surgery, was now trying to empty the bins. With him, looking bewildered, was his mother, young, chicly dressed, ostentatious diamond engagement and eternity rings hanging loosely on the fourth finger of her left hand and impractically long designer nails.

'Ah, Ed. Thanks for coming over. I thought you'd like to see this very interesting case. I'm not sure if it's Stevens-Johnson syndrome or possibly Henoch Schonlein.'

'Hello, there,' Ed held his hand out. 'It's Mrs Robeson isn't it? And this is Jacob? He's having a whale of a time, isn't he?'

'Hi, Dr Diamond. Yes he's full of beans, as usual. No, Jacob! Put that back. Sorry! He's just got a bit of a rash on the front of his elbows and behind his knees. I thought it was probably eczema – I remember having it when I was little and came along to get some cream. I almost didn't come but I'm glad I did now as it seems to be something much more serious. Dr Watson was talking about him having to see a consultant urgently.'

'Let's have a look. Jacob, can you come over here?'

After some kicking and a fair amount of screaming, a disgruntled Jacob permitted a brief but sufficient examination.

'Dr Watson,' Ed turned to Abigail. 'What made you come up with your ideas?'

Abigail commenced with what sounded like a verbatim recitation from a text book and kept up the flow for a full three minutes at which point Ed decided it was time to butt in, fearing that she might be capable of going on for a good while longer. Mrs Robeson was looking very afraid. As gently as he could, he pointed out the reasons why Jacob's rash was indeed classical of mild atopic eczema and did not exhibit any features to suggest an alternative condition. Promising to go into more details with Abigail at their post-surgery de-brief, he instructed her to prescribe some emollients and a weak steroid cream and took his leave, aware that his own surgery was now running late.

His next patient was well known to him, an elderly lady, Kathleen Clarke, small in stature, now almost bent double by the ravages of osteoporosis and sentenced to a life where she was destined to study the floor rather than what was in front of her. If that wasn't enough to contend with she fought a daily battle against chronic backache, continual grumblings from her abdominal organs which due to her concertina-ed physique were vying with one another for space and osteoarthritis in the small joints of her hands and feet. Yet somehow, she refused to let her disabilities get her down, blessed with the ability to be optimistic and see the best in life at all times. Living alone in a ground-floor council flat she somehow managed to maintain an independent, if precarious, existence, even though this required some imaginative adaptations on her part. Ed vividly recalled their first meeting, when she was housebound with a hacking cough. As he stood at the door waiting for her to answer the bell, his eyes were diverted to the letter box, protruding from which was a stiff cardboard tube. Thinking that perhaps this was some elaborate but probably not very safe mechanism for hiding the front door key, he suddenly realised that it was moving, panning the horizon, very much in the manner of a telescope, which indeed was just what it was being used for. No longer tall enough to view her visitors through the conventional spyhole in the door, Mrs Clarke had concocted her own alternative and was thus able to screen, to the best of her ability, all callers before allowing entry.

Today she was accompanied by a youngish woman, perhaps in her early thirties, dressed hurriedly in a plain fashion that comprised a long tweed coat of non-descript brown and some flat slip-on shoes that had obviously seen better days. A stark contrast to Mrs Clarke whose silvery grey hair had been recently forced into stiff curls, the woman's hair was scraped back from her unmade up face. She looked tired and concerned, dark rings under her eyes implying little recent sleep. She ushered Mrs Clarke in with care, helping her negotiate the doorway and find her way to the chair by Ed's desk.

'Mrs Clarke,' Ed greeted her, 'have a seat. How lovely to see you. Who's this who's come with you today?'

Taking a moment or two to settle herself and balance her handbag on her knees, Mrs Clarke cleared her throat.

'This is my great niece, Tina.'

'How do you do?' Ed held out his hand. 'Lovely to meet you.'

'Tina Baxter. I'm sorry I look such a mess.' Tina returned his handshake and smiled a pleasant smile that did wonders for her otherwise pale features.

'No need for apologies,' Ed assured her.

'Nice to meet you, Dr...?'

'Diamond,' answered Ed, pulling up a chair for her before sitting down.

Mrs Clarke fumbled for a handkerchief to wipe her nose.

'I've come to see you today, doctor, because I've decided to move into a home. I've given the matter a lot of thought but it really is getting too difficult for me to manage on my own in the flat. We'd like your advice about these places please. It's a big step for me to take – that's why Tina's come along with me, so that I remember all you tell me.' Mrs Clarke did her best to extend her neck and look at Ed. Her face contorted with the discomfort that resulted from doing this.

'Aunty had a fall as well, last week,' Tina added.

Mrs Clarke tutted. 'I told you not to mention that, Tina. Anyway, since you have, I think that's probably what made me make my decision. There were a lot of bruises but mercifully nothing broken. I can't afford to be doing things like that, not with my bones.'

'You're absolutely right,' agreed Ed, admiring of his patient's good sense.

'So, what do you think?' Mrs Clarke demanded.

'I think you're a remarkable lady,' Ed began, glancing quickly at Tina who returned his smile and nodded. 'Too many people try to carry on at home when it's not safe for them and end up having to be admitted to hospital when there's a crisis. You're very insightful to think of making this change while you're well enough to do so.'

'Aunty's very level-headed about her life,' commented Tina. 'She's given considerable thought to the matter. At first, we'd thought of asking for some carers to visit her at home...'

'And I said that I didn't want that, Tina. All those people traipsing in and out, a different one every time, looking in all my personal things. No, that's not for me. Doreen, that's one of my chums from the Day Club, she's gone into a home and she loves it. They have proper puddings every day and a glass of sherry before lunch and dinner. Oh and there's a huge bath that you're lifted into and allowed to soak in for as long as you like. She says it's like being in a hotel but you don't have to go back home after a fortnight.'

Ed laughed softly. 'I can see your mind's made up. I'll help however I can.'

'I knew you would. You've always been good to me.'

Tina leant forward towards Ed. 'So where do you recommend, Dr Diamond?'

Ed rummaged in one of his desk drawers and produced a small leaflet. 'It's not really for me to recommend anywhere in particular. But I can give you this list of homes, some residential, some nursing, some both, in the area and a bit further afield. I've been to quite a few of the nearer ones and they all seem very pleasant – you know, clean and friendly. Why don't you both pick two or three and go and have a look at them for yourselves. It's the best way of doing it. You'll get a feel for the place as soon as you walk in the front door. Where's your friend Doreen moved to?'

'Cherry Tree House,' replied Mrs Clarke. 'She's going to ask for me if there are any spare rooms.'

'That sounds like an excellent plan.'

'We could go this afternoon, if you like, Aunty Kath,' suggested Tina, eager to please.

'That'd be lovely. There's one very important question left for me to ask though.'

'Yes?' Ed smiled expectantly.

'Will you still be able to be my doctor? I'd not want to change to any one else. Not at my time of life.'

Gracious in his response, Ed patted her hand. 'So long as you stay in the practice area, of course I'll be your GP. When you look at the list I've given you, you'll see we've marked the ones that we visit.'

'I'm so pleased, Dr Diamond. Isn't that good, Tina.' Mrs Clarke's neck could be heard to creak as she attempted to turn her head towards her great-niece.

'I can see why you want to keep the same doctor, Aunty. He seems very nice and caring.'

'Tina's just moved into Lambdale. She's been working away in London but she's fed up with the noise and all the people, so she's come to live up here.'

'Just for a few months,' qualified Tina.

'So you can be her doctor too!' Mrs Clarke experienced a eureka moment.

'If that's what she wants,' agreed Ed, looking at Tina who was staring quite intently at him, studying his face. 'Just register at the receptionists' desk any time.'

'You make it sound so easy,' Tina commented.

'It is,' Ed found it hard not to sound bewildered.

'It certainly isn't, in London. I'm due for a check up soon and a smear.'

'We've several female doctors here as well. When you register, there'll be a practice booklet for you to take away with all our details in.'

'You've been very kind, as always, Dr Diamond.' Mrs Clarke shuffled forward in her seat and descended precariously on to her feet. 'Come along, Tina, we've taken up enough of this good doctor's time already. Next time you see me, Doc, I'll have a new address, God willing. Keep your fingers crossed for Cherry Tree House, won't you?'

She grasped Ed's hands in her own as best she could, her bony, misshapen fingers and dry skin rubbing awkwardly against his joints, chafing and squeezing gently. Tina rose to her feet and pushed some stray tendrils of hair behind her ears.

'Thank you so much, Dr Diamond. It's been a pleasure to meet you at last. I'd heard so much about you. And thank you so much for all the help you've given Aunty Kath.'

Ed walked with them to the door of his room and watched as they left before viewing with satisfaction that his waiting area was empty, a sign that his surgery was over. His contentment was short-lived however as he remembered that he needed to see Abigail.

She was waiting for him upstairs, putting the time to good use, doing a search on a medical website. Having expressed a desire to do some worthwhile research during her time in general practice, an issue with which Ed had no problem at all and was happy to encourage, she was trying to decide on a topic to look into. Her first few ideas had been gently kicked into touch by Ed, who had explained that they were not really relevant to general practice and that perhaps she should be looking for something simpler and more patient centred. His comments had not been met with gratitude and as a result she was banging the keyboard with some anger and doubtless would have been much less reserved had it not been for the fact that John and Ellie were in the room also.

'Ah, there you are, Abigail,' began Ed, traversing the floor towards the kettle, badly in need of some caffeine.

'I've been waiting for some time, Ed,' she remonstrated. 'Our tutorial's supposed to start at 11.30.'

'Sorry, but you know how it is. You can never guess what the next patient's coming in with and I got a little held up, talking.'

Abigail looked at him crossly, as if this was not an option, and logged out.

'Let's go and talk downstairs,' he suggested. 'It'll be quieter there.'

She stood up and pulled down her dark blue jacket, thrusting out her chest in the manner of an indignant chicken. Holding the door open for Ed, who had coffee in one hand and a sheaf of letters in the other, she then followed him down to his surgery, the usual place for their meetings.

'Right,' Ed began, matter of factly, leaning back in his chair and crossing his stretched-out legs in front of him. 'How was surgery this morning? Any problems?'

He could have predicted her response.

'No. All very straightforward. I think you could be wrong about that child though, so after you'd gone, I sent him up to the paediatric ward to be checked out properly.' She placed a heavy emphasis on the final word.

Ed was appalled. It was one thing dealing with an uncertain registrar but quite another to have to cope with one who ignored advice. The former, while wearing, was infinitely preferable. Confidence came with time and experience and he was more than happy to nurture

53

this skill and enjoy watching it grow. Always better to ask and learn, however stupid the question may seem – he was always telling his registrars this. What the patients appreciate is honesty. Respect is born for doctors who are prepared to admit that there are things that they don't know but are prepared to go away and find out about. A good rule of thumb for the rest of their lives. Ed and his partners were always swapping ideas, asking each other for advice, comparing management of different conditions. It was what made the job unique, kept them up to date and cemented the bond between them all. Registrars that had come to Teviotdale in the past had absorbed this atmosphere and become like minded as they enjoyed the camaraderie and mutual support.

Abigail, however, was proving to be different. She was arrogant and unwilling to listen. Her lack of respect for him and his colleagues was a big worry. There was little prospect of him ever forming any sort of worthwhile working relationship with her while she continued in this vein. And he didn't know how to help her change. Ed kept reminding himself that she had only been working with him for a few weeks and that her previous jobs had all been in hospital, where the environment was very different. Clare's words kept coming to him. Perhaps this was all a front.

Looking at her, she was putting on a pretty miraculous façade for someone who was really petrified. Rather more than an award-winning performance in fact. Her face was a picture of pugnacity, daring him to challenge her decision. That was the last thing he wanted to do. Friction between the two of them was the last thing he needed to have to cope with.

'That's interesting,' he opted for. 'Why don't you ring up later and find out what they thought? It's always a good idea to follow up interesting cases.'

Abigail, momentarily taken aback, agreed. 'Okay, I'll do it later.'

'Good. Let me know the outcome. I'm keen to know.'

Ed viewed Abigail's surgery list and decided that he couldn't face an hour of confrontation, so decided to veer off at an unexpected tangent. Abigail was expecting him to talk through each patient that she had seen and she had braced herself to stick up for the decisions she had made with regard to diagnosis and management. But today she was caught on the back foot. Frustratingly, Ed seemed to have no further interest in her surgery, instead preferring to chat in a casual way about why he had chosen general practice as a career.

'I've always been interested in people, not just their illnesses, but how they live, who they live with and where they live. The more you know about someone, the more fascinating they become. It helps you understand how they tick, why they react to certain circumstances as they do. This is the only branch of medicine where you get to share a person's life, where you're privy to so much that goes on, the good, the bad, everything from life to death.

'In hospital, all you see are snapshots of a patient's life. For us, it's the whole feature film and what's more, we're part of it. It's a great honour and not one to be taken lightly. People are so surprising, you know, Abigail. Some are resilient and never come to see us, others are here almost daily, using us not just as doctors but as priests, counsellors and advisors for all aspects of their lives.'

Abigail assumed a look of disbelief.

'I can assure you they do. They know that what they share with us is confidential. They don't want or need blood tests or prescriptions. They know that we listen and don't judge. Of course sometimes they do have a physical illness that needs to be addressed but often they just want to talk. I'm sure that you've experienced that yourself. You know the sort of thing. Something's worrying you, you talk about it to someone else and feel better for having got it off your chest. The more you know your patients, the more you can understand how events in their lives, be it illness or other sorts of things, will affect them. It's a unique service to supply and it's hugely gratifying when you realise that a patient trusts you so much.'

Abigail was starting to look uncomfortable. They had strayed across the boundaries of her comfort zone. She liked to live in a monochrome world, preferably one with a strong scientific basis so that she could apply her vast repertoire of medical knowledge. Not for her the softer side which involved empathy, sympathy and patience. Briefly, Ed spotted a look in her eyes that conveyed the way she was feeling at that moment. Only for a second, but he felt in some ways he had made a breakthrough and hoped that he had given her food for thought.

'I've an idea for your morning surgery tomorrow. I'm going to give you twenty minutes for each appointment and I want you to find out three interesting facts about each patient during the course of your consultation. Jot down what you've found out and tell me about it afterwards. I'll do the same and then we can compare notes. Okay?'

Abigail emitted a huge sigh. 'Okay, I'll try.'

'Good. I'll look forward to it. Now, let's go out on some visits, then when we get back you can ring about Jacob.'

6

'That is so good.' Ed drank gratefully from a pint of locally brewed beer, dark and strong, leaving a white froth moustache on his upper lip.

Hannah laughed, leaned towards him and wiped it off.

'Careful, you look ridiculous,' she commented, but not unkindly.

He took her hand and kissed it gently. 'We did it!'

'Six hours and thirty-three minutes. I'm really pleased.'

Their heads were buzzing and their limbs aching in an enjoyable way, tingling, glowing from the recent exertion, a good example of the fine dividing line between pleasure and pain.

As it was warm enough to sit outside, he and Hannah had eschewed the dingy interior of the pub, which smelled of beer-soaked bar towels, and ventured out into the garden, where they were fortunate in finding a table out of the wind. Enjoying what little warmth the sun had to offer that day, they surveyed their surroundings, basking in the satisfaction that comes with achievement. Some very late daffodils were still flowering in a selection of tubs near the door and the dead- looking strands of forsythia were speckled with fresh buds. A few other like-minded but well-wrapped-up customers huddled together in small groups, chatting and laughing over their drinks, crackling crisp packets, preferring to enjoy the fresh air as well. The lawn had been mowed, perhaps a little too enthusiastically for so early in the year, but it looked neat and well tended alongside the recently turned- over flowerbeds which, given another couple of months or so, would become chaotic with colour and beauty.

It was Hannah's last weekend. Her house was all but sold, an offer of the asking price had been put on the table almost immediately, fulfilling the estate agent's prediction. She had just about packed up all her possessions, some of which had already left in a large removal van and the remainder would be stashed into her car on Tuesday, three days from now. She had persuaded Ed to have one last try at the Three walk before she went and so they had left Lambdale at a time when sensible people would have been fast asleep to drive to the starting point at Horton in Ribblesdale. Hannah had chosen her moment to perfection. This time the ground favoured speed and as they laced their boots before setting off it was agreed that they were both determined to concentrate on the job in hand and break their previous record. This having been decided they alternated between jogging and brisk walking, time for sight seeing, photography or idle chat having been vetoed from the word go and so few words passed between them as they pushed upwards, scuttled down hill and forged onwards only briefly pausing to check their watches and pass comment about keeping up the same pace or even cranking up a gear. This approach had suited Ed. Having to channel all his energies into physical activity helped to keep his mind focussed on their challenge when all the time it wanted to concentrate on matters of far greater sensitivity.

Over the past month, they had grown close again, possibly even closer, aware that time was running out and that to waste what was left arguing would be counterproductive. Ever conscious that Hannah was leaving the area, Ed's mind was awash with things he wanted and needed to say to her, but had never got round to because he had no idea how or where to begin. No clearer in his own mind as to what he wanted to do, he thought that by voicing it out loud then it might assume some sense. He had lost count of the number of times he thought that he had constructed a suitably worded opening. Each time he rehearsed though, the words sounded trite and laughable.

So for six hours and thirty-three minutes he had been granted a stay of execution but now there was no excuse for prevaricating any longer.

He was about to open his mouth when fate intervened, albeit temporarily. Their lunch arrived. Huge oval plates heaped with sausages, eggs and chips were placed before them by a young waitress wearing low-cut black trousers and a short- sleeved shirt that had once been white.

'Fantastic,' he thanked her and delved under the chips to find the sachets of brown sauce and vinegar.

Hannah bent over to rummage in her rucksack and produced a light jacket which she put on and zipped up to her chin, shivering slightly.

'Want to go back inside?' he inquired tenderly.

'No, it's far better out here,' Hannah replied, shaking her head.

She looked wonderful, her face happy and alive with delight. She had no need of make-up to assume a look of beauty. Her complexion was clear, her eyes danced with joy and her taut thighs, encased in dark blue Lycra shorts, were decidedly erotic. Ed was unable to resist stroking one of them. Hannah leant against his shoulder and turned her face towards him, waiting for a kiss then pretending to be repelled by his beery breath. He put down his knife and fork, enveloped her in a huge hug and clung to her. He would miss her dreadfully.

They ate in silence to begin with, both ravenous after their exertions. Hannah went to the bar for more drinks, bringing another pint for Ed and promising to drive home.

'So,' she began when she was starting to feel comfortably full and had begun to nibble rather than eat, 'how's your week been?'

'Good, by and large,' Ed replied through a mouthful of chips, glad to be on home territory with the topic of conversation.

'How's Clare?'

Ed paused. 'She says she's fine.'

'And you think?'

'That she's not.'

'Why?'

'In a nutshell, she looks awful, she's still being sick all the time and she's exhausted.'

'Oh, that's sad. Couldn't she take some time off?'

Ed rolled his eyes. 'Of course she could, but you know Clare. She'd be mortified if she had to admit she wasn't managing. You're right though, she probably shouldn't be at work. The others have all noticed too. If she doesn't improve soon, we'll have to have a word with her.'

'If it were me, I'd want to do what was best for the baby,' Hannah considered.

'Exactly,' Ed turned his attention to his food again.

'Seen any interesting patients?' asked Hannah, chopping up what was left of her chips and scattering them around for the birds that were hopping around hopefully.

'Of course. A lot of familiar faces and a few new ones. Oh, I'll tell you something curious that happened...'

He swallowed in preparation for his tale, in a hurry to get started, keen to keep the topic of conversation to one with which he felt secure and unthreatened. Briefly he filled in the details about Kathleen Clarke.

'She came with her niece, great-niece perhaps. I didn't think much of it at the time. Tina, she was called, if I remember correctly. Very ordinary looking, almost drab. But obviously very caring when it came to her aunt. She was pleasant enough and said she was going to register with the practice while she stayed up here.'

'So what's curious about that?' Hannah pulled her knees up to her chest and hugged them.

'I'm getting to that bit,' Ed answered, a little exasperated. 'She came back to see me last week. Bearing gifts would you believe? A big box of chocolates as a thank you for helping her aunt.'

'That's great. I bet you've eaten them all.'

'Yes, I have actually.' He looked sheepish.

Hannah glared at him, pretending to be cross.

'Typical! Anyway, go on.'

'But the thing was, I hardly recognised her. She looked amazing, really attractive, she'd had her hair cut, put on some make-up and her clothes really suited her. You know the sort of thing, high heels, tight skirt, girly little blouse and jacket.'

Hannah guffawed at his description.

'Do you always notice your patient's clothes?'

Ed nodded. 'I do as a matter of fact. You can learn a lot from how a patient dresses. Baggy black and grey clothes often hint at depression for example. But she looked great.'

'Careful, Ed, or I'll think that you fancied her.'

'Of course I didn't. She's a patient. No, I was just amazed at the transformation.'

'Come off it, Ed. She'd been helping an elderly relative. She'd maybe been awake all night after sleeping on an uncomfy camp bed or something and had just thrown on the first thing she'd found. I know men think that women should look perpetually wonderful but sometimes, you know, it simply isn't possible. What was wrong with her?'

'Nothing, she'd just come to say thank you. Told me that her aunt had got her name on the waiting list for the residential home she wanted and had started packing in anticipation.'

'What a waste of an appointment. Next time, save some of the chocolates for me. Let's talk about something else. How's the terrible Abigail?'

Ed puffed his cheeks. 'I think I might just have made the tiniest of breakthroughs this week. With any luck, she's actually starting to see patients as people.'

He started to expand on this announcement but realised from the look on Hannah's face that she was not really listening. 'What's up? I thought you wanted to know about Abigail.'

'I was just thinking, that's all. Taking all this in. You know – me, you, this lovely

countryside. This time next week, what will I be doing?'

'Settling into your new house?' Ed suggested.

'Yes! And do you know what? I can't wait.'

There was something in her voice that bothered him. She sounded too excited and too eager, as though she was counting the hours. Not even a tinge of regret or sorrow. Perhaps she suddenly realised this as her next words seemed to be chosen to placate. 'And I can't wait for you to come and see it. I love it so much more than I did that shoe box that I had in Harrogate. It's double fronted, has a kitchen to die for, four bedrooms and two bathrooms. The mortgage is terrifyingly huge, so it's a good job I'm getting a pay rise.'

'I think you've mentioned this just once or twice before. You were lucky to find somewhere so quickly,' agreed Ed, not wanting to sound miserable.

'So when are you coming up?' Hannah turned to him.

'Soon.'

'The weekend after next?'

'What's wrong with this weekend coming?'

'I'll be too busy unpacking. Nowhere looks good when it's full of half unpacked boxes. I want it to look really good when you come for the first time, Ed. Then you'll want to come and live there too... Have you given that any more thought?'

Ed put his arm around her shoulders. 'I've thought about little else. Hannah –you know I want to be with you but there's so much going on here at the moment.'

'Such as?' Hannah interrogated him, pulling away.

'I've a lot of responsibilities. I can't and won't let down my partners. If Clare goes off sick then we're going to be short staffed and if I left as well the others would simply not be able to cope. It would be a disaster – even with really good locums. Then it would be completely unfair to leave them with Abigail. I'm her trainer and, as I was trying to tell you, I think I'm just starting to make some progress. Then there are the patients...'

Hannah sighed. 'Ed, will there ever be a good time? You sound as if you don't really want to come at all. Sometimes in life you've just got to make a leap into the unknown.'

'Give me a chance, Hannah. I've told you umpteen times that it's a really hard decision for me. It might have been easier if we'd planned this as a couple from the beginning. Sorry, that was a cheap jibe.'

'Then come up and stay,' retorted Hannah, ignoring him. 'Have a look round. It's a fantastic city. We'll do all the touristy bits, see the sights and have some fun. We can eat haggis and stovies followed by Edinburgh rock and oddfellows.'

'Maybe, I'll let you know.'

'Ed, we're just going round and round in circles and we're running out of time. I know you can't make long-term promises, at least not yet, but at least agree to come up soon and visit?'

He kissed her emphatically on the lips.

'Put me down for the weekend after next then. But be sure and have that house looking spick and span!'

'I'll do my best. I want you to be so impressed that you don't want to leave. Oh, and don't forget the house-warming present.'

Ed smiled wanly and Hannah assumed a more serious tone.

'Ed, this is as hard for me as it is for you. But I'm trying to be positive. We're strong, you and I. We're not just some passing fling that means nothing. Okay so we're only going to be able to see each other every weekend but that's what we do now and I'm sure we can withstand that pressure. Don't you believe that?'

'Of course I want to. It's just that everyone I've ever known with a long-distance relationship has had problems, usually ending up with them breaking up and going their separate ways.'

'Hey, Ed, we're not just anybody, are we?'

'I guess not. But I guess that's what they thought too.'

'Then we'll buck the trend. Don't be so bloody miserable about it. If it's going to work then we've got to believe that it is. So start doing that right now. That is, of course, if you want it to.'

'Of course I do. I'm sorry, I'm just being silly. Ignore me.'

'I love you, Ed. We can do this, I know we can.'

'You're right, as usual. So, what shall we do with the rest of the day?'

'Whatever you want. If it's okay with you, I'm staying until Monday morning. My packing is all but finished so we've got all tomorrow as well.'

'That's great,' rejoiced Ed. 'Let's eat out tonight and then perhaps climb tomorrow?'

'Perfect. Shall we make a move now? My body's crying out for a long hot bath. But we did it! Beat our record into the ground. You see, Ed, we're a formidable team. It's going to take more than a few miles to break us up.'

Contrary to his expectations, the rest of the weekend, at least up until the Sunday evening passed like a dream. Led by Hannah's indefatigable cheerfulness, the subject of Edinburgh was put to one side and replaced by a determination to make the most of their time together. Once the muscular aches had been bathed away, Hannah changed into a short, vermillion-coloured dress which did credit to the few curves that she had and made Ed go weak at the knees when he saw her.

'I hope I look as good as that patient of yours!'

'You look out of this world,' Ed whistled.

'It's one of the few items of clothing I've got that isn't either in a suitcase or creased,' she explained, twirling round so that he could be equally admiring of the back.

Happily tired, he took her, on a whim, to the Golden Dog, a popular pub on the outskirts of Lambdale, within walking distance, and noted for its restaurant which specialised in French cuisine. Perhaps not the best choice on a busy Saturday evening but they were fortunate in having to wait only a short while before being seated and were delighted to find Ellie, together with her husband Ian, sitting at the adjacent table.

'Hi,' cried Ellie, 'I bet you didn't recognise us without Virginia and

Lydia! They've gone to a sleepover at some friends. It all sounded fairly fraught when we rang earlier. I could hear them bickering in the background. Love the dress, Hannah.'

'Thanks. I used to love going for sleepovers,' admitted Hannah, taking a menu from an attentive waiter who was also wanting to know what she would like to drink.

'I think it's maybe simpler when their friends come to ours. That way I can keep an eye on them. They spend most of the time at home fighting each other but when they go out, they join forces and can become quite a handful. That's why I'm ashamed to have my mobile phone on the table, normally something I would abhor but, this evening, I daren't take any chances and miss hearing it ring.'

'They really aren't that bad,' apologised Ian in his usual laid-back way. 'They're just high spirited and discovering their own personalities.'

Ellie spluttered into her wine before roaring with laughter.

'Of course, darling. If that's how you like to think of it.'

'What are you eating?' asked Hannah, unable to make her mind up.

'We started with the pâté. It's home made on the premises and really, really good.

Now, Ian's waiting for sea bass and I'm having the chicken. But choose anything and I'm sure you'll not be disappointed.'

Hannah looked at Ed who winked at her. Ellie, never one to miss a non-verbal cue pounced.

'What's this then? Is this some sort of special occasion? You're both looking uncommonly smart.'

Ed teased her. 'Sort of...'

'Could you be... celebrating?'

'We might be.'

'Oh, that's wonderful,' began Ellie, before being interrupted by Hannah, who was keen that no one should jump to the wrong conclusion.

'We broke our record today for walking the Three.'

Ellie's face fell visibly then politely brightened up. 'Well done. For a moment I thought you were going to say something a little more scintillating.'

Ed joined in. 'And it's our last meal out for a while. Hannah starts her new job next week.'

'Oh, how exciting. Ed was talking about it at work the other day. Edinburgh did you say?'

Hannah nodded and was about to add how very much she was looking forward to it but tactfully changed her mind when she saw Ed raise his eyebrows to attract her attention.

'Right, let's make our minds up. I'm starving,' he prompted her. 'They're anxious to take our order.'

A splendidly enjoyable evening was had by all. True to form, the food was delectable. Not the gargantuan portions of lunchtime but exquisitely presented and each mouthful perfection to the taste buds. Ellie and Ian were forced to leave first, before they had time for dessert, summoned by a garbled message on the telephone which they correctly interpreted to mean that there was trouble at the sleepover, bad enough to warrant their intervention. Ed was pleased when they left. Not that he had been the slightest bit dismayed to find them there as he had huge affection for them both but he had wanted the evening to be particularly special, not just for Hannah but for them as a couple.

They wandered home, arms wound around each other, taking their time, gazing up at what stars were visible between the clouds, stopping to kiss and whisper endearments. Inside, they snuggled down together to watch some late television, drink cups of tea and play with the cats. This is how it should be all the time, thought Ed. I'm really happy. I've got everything I need. A stunning girlfriend, a great house which I've made my own, Hebe and Toby and the best job in the world. Why can't it stay like this? Why do things have to change, just when I've got it right?

The next morning the weather had changed for the worse. Rain had returned and looked set in for the day. Bitter winds howled around the cottage making the window frames rattle and the cats refused point blank to go out into the tiny garden. They lay in, uncharacteristically, before rising, eating bacon sandwiches whilst reading the Sunday papers and drinking coffee. By midday they were agitating to be active, never good at being consigned indoors for any length of time and so they fetched their walking boots and waterproofs from the car before setting out on a local walk, devised by Ed, which took them on a circuitous but pretty route through the countryside around Lambdale. They managed to keep up the bonhomie until their return when it all began to feel a bit strange as though some silent clock had started a countdown. Hannah would usually at this point be leaving for Harrogate, had she not already done so, and her very presence created an atmosphere that suggested all was not right. Their conversation became more stilted, concentrating on the trivial. Their laughter sounded forced. Her enthusing over the supper that Ed threw together was over the top and she noticed that he was drinking far more than he was accustomed to. They searched in vain for something to watch, something that would take their attention and remove the need for talking. Little choice was available, just the repeat of a period drama, a blood and guts police series or a new comedy programme that proved to be completely devoid of humour to all but the well- primed studio audience. Both professing to be tired from the previous day's walk, they settled for an early night and lay spooned together, listening to each other's breathing, Ed willing time to slow down and the morning not to come.

Daybreak brought hurried goodbyes and promises to phone later in the day as Ed rushed round trying to get ready for early morning surgery and Hannah packed her bag. This was good, Ed decided. He hated protracted partings where melancholy conducted the proceedings and the world seemed cold and heartless. But this felt like any other morning, the two of them busy, him off to work knowing that within seconds of arriving he would be swept into the tide of other people's problems which would keep his mind occupied for the whole day.

They kissed quickly and hugged before leaving the house and again before Hannah got into her car. Waving her off, promising to see her the weekend after next, he immediately felt a shiver of desolation run down his spine and longed to call her back. He stood on the road, still waving though her car was out of sight – holding on to a last lingering hope that she might turn around and come back – before climbing into his own vehicle, taking a large breath and setting off for the surgery.

7

A month later, he had barely closed the door after seeing his first patient, wanting a moment to write up his notes before the next, when an email popped up on the screen to inform everyone that Clare was not going to be in for a few days. Her patients would be contacted and reappointed where possible but if their need was urgent then the others would be required to see them. It was hoped that she would be back by the end of the week. Sighing slightly and hoping that it was nothing serious, he flicked through his surgery, already full with two extras fitted in at the end. Oh well, at least this would keep his mind off Hannah. Ed felt tired and uninspired. Wanting to stay in Edinburgh until the last possible moment, he had risen at a ridiculously early hour and driven back that morning. What little sleep he had managed had been restless, broken by clock watching, not the least bit restorative. He rang through to reception and asked one of them to bring him a cup of strong coffee, swallowed two aspirin and mentally girded his loins for the onslaught of the day.

For once, he would have gladly swapped places with Clare, who was sitting in the armchair that David usually liked to relax in when he came home from the hospital, her feet curled up under her, still in her nightdress and dressing gown, watching a flurry of birds attacking the niger seeds that she had put in a couple of feeders and hung in the garden. Half past ten in the morning and she felt frustrated and worried. An insipid sun was continuing to shine despite a shower of rain and the resultant rainbow almost definitely had its end in one of their neighbours' gardens. She was half tempted to go and look – a crock of gold might be quite useful. But this was not allowed. Nor as far as she could work out, was anything else. She was on enforced rest and digging would definitely not fall within the definition of that word.

She had been feeling so much better and now this.

About a fortnight previously, Clare's appetite had returned, as if a switch had been flicked and now she was able to both taste and enjoy foods again, with no fear of their return shortly after ingestion. As a result, she was starting to look better, her cheeks were filling out, her skin was clearing and the bags under her eyes, which she had begun to assume were with her for life, had shrunk considerably. If anything, now she had to be careful that she did not overeat, for at times her desire for food seemed insatiable, perhaps because it was such a relief to feel more normal after weeks approximating to hell. And she did, she kept reminding herself, have to make up for lost time. With this came energy, more than she remembered ever having, and suddenly days at the surgery became enjoyable again rather than feeling as if she was wading through week-old porridge. Best of all there was life enough left in her to cook when she got home, to talk with David and enjoy her spare time at weekends.

A few days earlier, she and David had been out for the day, wandering round shops in Harrogate looking at cots, prams and pushchairs, trying to decide exactly what they would need. It had been a wonderful day in many ways. Just having the exclusivity of her husband for so long at once was both a novelty and a joy. Latterly he had been working even harder than usual, writing up a paper which was soon to be published. This had necessitated a weekend conference in London with the result that Clare had been left feeling rather lonely and unsupported. However, his excitement about the pending arrival knew no bounds and in the manner of controlling a new puppy that is not yet used to his lead, she had to steer him in the right direction as his attention was diverted by the softest of teddy bears, cutest of mobiles and tiniest of Baby-gros. Before they had even found the cots, he had already amassed a handful of carrier bags, stuffed with items that he had been unable to resist and Clare had to laugh as he hopped from one side of the shop to the other, holding things up for her approval, boyishly incredulous at the choice available.

To begin with, she was more cautious with her spending, an admonitory inner voice telling her not to tempt fate by buying too much so early on the pregnancy, just in case something went wrong. But David's infectious glee was irresistible and she found herself agreeing to have new trousers, some tops and even two dresses, one for work and one that would do nicely for a smarter occasion, should the need arise. All of them looked deflated when she tried them on, as though something was missing, but David's reassurance that she would fill them out in no time at all was all she needed to hear to convince her that their purchase was necessary. Currently in an awkward in-between phase where most of her usual clothes no longer fitted, at least certainly not anything that possessed a waistband, she was in fact desperately in need of more appropriate clothing, but up to that moment had been afraid to buy, preferring to make do with what she could find that looked passable. By now this had boiled down to a tent-like pinafore dress that she had always regretted buying and a pair of linen trousers with a drawstring waist which were inevitably creased and looked as though she had rolled around on the floor in them. Paying for her new things seemed to exorcise what prudence she had exhibited earlier and before they left the shop, it had taken David little of his persuasive skills to convince her to think along the same lines as him and they had bought a Moses basket and a rather expensive pushchair in a dark blue material covered with tiny stars, which he felt sure would be relaxing for his progeny. A de luxe cot was on order.

They lunched at their, but also sadly everyone else's, favourite restaurant and were forced to stand and queue for a table for a considerable while. As always though, it was worth the wait and they were seated next to a couple with a toddler in a high chair, giving

David every excuse to share the details of Clare's pregnancy to date, much to her embarrassment.

Carrot and coriander soup with warm bread rolls, followed by a choice of amazingly intricate cakes from a trolley that was wheeled to their table, recharged their batteries and they walked up through the gardens to listen to the brass band that was playing and people watch before heading for home.

It was while they were in the car, waiting at some temporary traffic lights, that Clare became aware of dampness between her legs, followed by a discomfort reminiscent of a period pain. Trying to ignore it by reminding herself that increased vaginal discharge was completely normal during pregnancy, she shifted her position and said nothing to David, who had tuned the radio to the football and was listening avidly to the half-time results. The journey back seemed to take forever, punctuated by the dreary accounts of various matches and each jolt as they drove over an unevenness in the road accentuated her ache and created a sickening feeling in the pit of her stomach, instinctively knowing that something was not right.

She was out of the car and into the bathroom within seconds and cried out loud when she saw the blood, feeling more trickling out when she sat down on the toilet. David, leaping into action with an authoritative air, passed her pads, implored her not to worry and had her back in the car before she knew it. He drove as fast as he dared, breaking all the rules by telephoning ahead on his mobile phone, thanking God that at least the traffic was light, there were no hold-ups and no patrolling police cars.

They spent a horribly anxious hour in the obstetric unit, sitting on a hard bed around which some blue and green curtains had been drawn, segregating them from the rest of the world. Clare was unable to speak for her mouth was so dry; David so anxious that he shouted angrily, intent on chivvying up the midwives, demanding that something be done and asking to see their consultant, Professor Corbett. No sooner than the words were out, he was apologising, explaining that he was so frightened lest anything should be wrong with the baby or his wife in any sort of danger. Clare persuaded him to go and find them both a cup of tea, more to give him a purpose than because she wanted one. She felt confused and bewildered. Part of her wanted some time on her own, the rest of her wanted him near her constantly, to help her through this ordeal.

A junior doctor came and examined her, rather roughly, before informing her that the bleeding seemed to have stopped but a scan was mandatory and should be available later that day. Turning to leave, Clare begged him to try to find the baby's heartbeat with the Sonicaid, knowing that he had refrained from doing so because he was afraid that he might not be able to find one. He relented and went away, but sent back a friendly, smiley midwife, having delegated this meaningful task to one whom he felt more able to deal with the possible repercussions than he was. Fortunately she was experienced and empathic.

'This happened to me with my first,' she sympathised. 'Let's see if we can find this little one's heart.'

The cold jelly on her lower abdomen made Clare flinch but she laughed a little with the midwife who asked for forgiveness.

Time stood still while they waited. The ward went quiet as though everyone was on tenterhooks, listening. Her heart leapt into her throat as she tried desperately to discern the rhythmic beat of a heart against the background noise. Nothing, just indeterminate whooshing and bleeping – more like extraterrestrial signals than signs of human life. Clare's own heart was pounding. She felt barely able to breathe. Then suddenly, just when she felt that there was no hope, there it was, unmistakable, regular and best of all, strong.

'There you are, my dear,' announced the midwife, doing a noble job of concealing her own relief. 'That sounds good to me. Feel better now?'

'Oh yes. Thank you so much. I can't tell you how much. Oh, here's my husband, could he possibly hear it too?'

David wiped the tears from his eyes as he listened, clutching Clare's hand as if he would never let it go.

'Thank goodness. Clare, do you hear that? The baby's fine. How wonderful is that?'

The midwife departed discretely, promising to arrange the scan for as soon as possible. The cup of tea, bought from a machine in the corridor, was stewed, too strong and had remnants of milk powder floating menacingly on the surface but it still, to Clare and David, tasted like vintage champagne. They shared a chocolate biscuit and hugged each other, alternately laughing and weeping.

'How hopeless are we?' gulped Clare, screwing the silver paper up into a little ball and throwing it at her husband.

'Past hope, I think,' David concurred, catching the missile deftly and depositing it in the bin.

'I love you so much, David. Thank you for being here.'

'Don't be daft!' David stroked her cheek. 'Hey, guess who I met when I was getting this disgusting tea?'

Clare shrugged.

'Do you remember Zoë Ferguson from medical school?'

Clare looked bemused.

'Yes, you do,' David insisted. 'She was in my year. Big girl, a formidable lacrosse and tennis player. Big brown eyes and lots of wavy dark brown hair that was always all over the place.'

'Oh, yes. Of course I do. I was always a bit frightened of her. What's she doing here?'

'She just started as a new gynaecology consultant.'

'Oh that's lovely. Good for her. Has she still got mad hair?'

'Nope, she looked really good though. It was very nice to see her.'

'We'll have to have her round for supper. It'd be nice to catch up.'

'Fine, but only when we're sure that you're okay. Hey, great – they've come to get you for your scan.'

The scan was unremarkable. Nothing accountable for the bleeding was obvious but the baby looked unconcerned, had grown appropriately from the twelve-week scan and was performing some daredevil loop-the-loops which amused everyone in the room. Just before they left to go back to the ward, Zoë popped in to see them. David had been right, thought Clare. She'd lost a lot of weight and tamed her hair, resulting in a look that was young, fresh and decidedly less scary than it had been. Trendy glasses together with casual trousers and a blouse made her look most un-consultant-like.

'I can't stop but I just wanted to look in and say how I'm so pleased for you that everything's fine,' she told them. 'You must have been so worried.'

'Thank you,' replied Clare. 'I can't begin to tell you how awful it was. But fingers crossed, things are looking good. Give David your phone number, Zoë, and we'll be in touch.'

Despite advice to stay in overnight, Clare pleaded with Professor Corbett, her obstetrician, to let her go home, arguing her case with the facts that she would be able to relax so much better there, that David was capable of coping with any form of problem and that surely the hospital bed would be better occupied by someone whose need was far greater than hers. The professor looked moderately unconvinced and agreed, but only after securing a promise from Clare that she would rest, ring him at home day or night if she had any worries whatsoever and on no account go to work before he reviewed her in the antenatal clinic the following week. She agreed without hesitation.

It was a wobbly Clare who made her way back to the car, suddenly feeling vulnerable once out of the hospital surroundings. Her heart fluttered slightly at the sight of the pushchair in the back of the car, still waiting to be unpacked. Perhaps she shouldn't have thrown caution to the winds – just look what the result had been.

Uncharacteristically, she allowed David to make her a nest in the lounge, put her feet up on a stool and bring down a duvet for her to curl up in. To her surprise she fell asleep, no doubt exhausted by the emotional energy expended that day and woke to find David watching the football with the volume turned off and the subtitles on, so as not to disturb her. He made her cocoa and toast before helping her up to bed. Terrified, she went to the bathroom, dreading to find evidence of more bleeding, but there was none and their relief was palpable.

That had been three days ago and there was still no sign of any more fresh blood, just some old dark brown discharge, so her confidence was just starting to return. It no longer felt as though she was perpetually living on the edge of a precipice and her average speed of walking was no longer that of an aged tortoise. Her emotions oscillated from impatience to be back at work to fear that something else might go wrong. Desperate for something to do, having finished the novel that she was reading and given up on the jigsaw puzzle which seemed to be composed of identically shaped pieces of either sky or sea, and unimpressed by what the television had to offer, she got up and wandered into the kitchen. David had left it spotless apart from his cereal bowl and mug which were sitting in the washing-up bowl and took only seconds to clean and dry. Clare peeped into the fridge and managed to resist the temptation of the remains of last night's dessert. The combination of rest and a gargantuan appetite would, if it continued for any length of time, doubtless result in her assuming the appearance of a basking elephant – not a good idea.

She went upstairs, straightened the duvet and looked in the dirty linen basket but, yet again, David had beaten her to it and there was only a pair of socks and a shirt, hardly enough to justify using the washing machine. Unnecessarily, she rearranged her perfumes and jewellery on the dressing table before deciding to put some proper clothes on. Half naked she pulled a face at her reflection in the mirror and turned to contemplate her profile which was now convincingly looking pregnant. Something flickered, as if on cue, and her hand automatically went to protect her lower belly. That was definitely not wind. Again, more pronounced, then a pause.

Clare beamed at herself, overjoyed to realise that this was her baby moving. Savouring the moment, she threw on a baggy jumper and some leggings, stroking her bump and talking to the tiny person inside. She wanted to ring David but knew he was in a meeting all morning so had to make do with sending a text message instead, aware that his phone would be on, just in case. Predictably he replied immediately, thrilled and Clare was unable to stop smiling as she went back downstairs, loving him all the more for his transparent excitement.

Having exhausted any ideas of how to occupy herself in the house, she decided to go for a short walk, sure that she would come to no harm. Damp still hung in the atmosphere, the sun had disappeared but it was mild. The air was intoxicatingly refreshing. Clare strolled carefully, suddenly feeling vulnerable in the great outdoors, in the manner of one convalescing after a protracted illness. At the end of the road, she felt steadier and decided she would walk a little further before turning back. It felt really good to be outside, almost human again after her days of incarceration. She freely admitted that she was not a good patient. It was verging on hypocritical how she found it so easy to advise others but invariably failed to transpose the same advice into her own life. Quite why she should have been blessed with some additional protection against morbidity and mortality, she never actually stopped to consider.

A car slowed down beside her and the window rolled down.

'Hi, Clare,' shouted Ed. 'How are you?'

She was overjoyed to see him.

'Fine, well, I think I am. I felt the baby kick for the first time just now. Have you time for a cup of tea or coffee? I'd love some company for a bit.'

'And I'd love a drink. That's great news about the baby. Hop in, I'll give you a lift home. You're quite wet. Are you supposed to be out?'

'Not really,' she admitted, before filling him in with regard to her antenatal complications in the short trip back. Letting him into the house, she led him into the kitchen and switched on the kettle.

'How's work?' she was unable to keep from asking.

'Busy, but fine. Don't you worry. I'm just out on my visits.'

'Are there many?' she asked, anxious in case they were run off their feet and cursing her absence.

'No! What did I tell you? Don't worry!' Ed ordered her. 'We're coping. It's fine. Just put yourself first for once.'

Clare laughed and fetched milk.

'You know me too well. Let's go in the lounge, it's more comfy. I've biscuits somewhere. David hides them, because he knows that I'll eat them all if he leaves them somewhere easily visible. I seem to have turned into a human dustbin. Oh, here they are! His hiding places are very predictable, I'm glad to say. Oh good, chocolate.'

Ed insisted on carrying the tray through and waited until Clare was resettled in the armchair before passing her mug and sitting down.

'Any news?' Clare interrogated him.

'John's got a new car,' Ed volunteered.

'About time. His old one was about to fall apart there was so much rust on it. What about my patients?'

'They're fine too. They've all been sorted. Stop worrying. They understand and so do we. You just concentrate on looking after your baby and do not take any chances.'

'I'm in clinic the day after tomorrow. Hopefully Professor Corbett will let me come back to work. The bleeding's all settled so I can't see why he won't.'

'Don't be in a rush, Clare. Just wait and take his advice. He knows best after all. Think what advice you'd give to a patient.'

'I suppose so.' Clare looked fed up.

Ed took a sip of his drink. 'I've been up in Edinburgh this weekend,' he started, making a conscious effort to change the subject away from work.

'Oh! How was it? How's Hannah?'

'Great. I'm shattered though. Only drove back this morning. Not a good idea.'

'Is that the first time you've been up?'

'No, the third. I'm trying to go most weekends. I had hoped that she'd come down here for alternate ones but as yet, she's been too busy. You know what it's like when you start a new job.'

'But she's enjoying it?'

'She loves it. If there's one thing Hannah thrives on it's hard work. She's so ecstatic that she's got this job – it's apparently a very prestigious law firm – and nothing's going to stop her proving to them that they made the right decision taking her on. She's working all hours. She looks worn out and frazzled.'

'I bet she was glad to see you and have a bit of time out.'

'A bit is the appropriate word. The first weekend I went up we had a fantastic time, walking up Princes Street, visiting the castle, Greyfriars Bobby – it's a wonderful city and I couldn't wait to go back. Next time, she worked quite a lot but there still seemed to be time to do things together. This last visit, if I'm honest, was a bit of a disaster. The only time she had off was on the Saturday evening when we went out to eat but she'd arranged for us to meet up with some of her new friends from work, so even then I didn't get her to myself at all. Plus they were all talking about some important court case they've got coming up. Then on Sunday, she was back up to her ears in paperwork. I felt a bit like a spare part.'

'So what did you do?'

'Some housework, some shopping – stocking up her cupboards with food, a bit of sightseeing but it's not a lot of fun when you're on your own.'

'No, I don't expect it is. Still,' Clare paused optimistically, 'it's probably only while she gets started, isn't it? Things should settle with time, I'd imagine.'

'I hope so,' agreed Ed, with feeling. 'I hate to say it, but there were times, when I was alone, when I wished I hadn't bothered going up. I could've been climbing – the club were off to the Lakes and I felt bad about not going with them. I could have popped in to see my parents. Plus the driving is completely knackering.'

Clare muttered some sympathetic noises.

Ed continued. 'It's great when we're together but there's not enough of that,' he added, sadly.

'It'll get better,' Clare assured him. 'Just be patient. Are you going up this weekend coming?'

'I don't think so. I've stuff I must do at home. It'd be great if Hannah came down but I doubt she will. She promised to think about it though.' He sounded unconvinced.

Absent-mindedly, Clare reached out for the last biscuit, unaware that she had in fact eaten them all while Ed had been talking. He glanced at his watch.

'I'd better get a move on, Clare. Sorry to leave you but I'll pop in again if you're not back at work.'

'Where are you off to?'

'Cherry Tree House. Kathleen Clark's gone to live there. She needs a prescription review.'

'I quite like it there. It always smells nice when you walk in the door. Clean and fresh, not at all like some of the fusty homes we go to. Real flowers as well, not plastic plants covered in dust.'

'I think she'll be very happy there. See you soon. Give me a ring any time if you want a chat.'

Clare waved him off and returned to her chair, picked up a new novel and with a sigh, after a cursory glance at the back cover, opened it up at page one.

8

'Your go, Doreen. And hurry up about it.'

Kathleen Clarke glared at her friend sitting on the opposite side of the Scrabble board and started drumming her fingers irritatingly on the table.

'Stop doing that! Just give me a moment. I need to think.'

Doreen, peering myopically through her magnifying glass at the letters in front of her, wondered how she could make the best of the appalling selection that faced her. Much as she was delighted that Kath had come to live at Cherry Tree House, she did not enjoy the Scrabble game, which had somehow become a daily humiliation, taking place between elevenses and lunch, except on Thursdays when the hairdresser came and it was postponed until mid afternoon. Invariably, she lost by a large margin and then had to suffer the advice on offer of how to improve her performance. She had never been much of a wordsmith and now her eyesight was so poor, she found it even harder. The final straw was the aggravating fact that Kath always insisted on having the board facing her, which meant that she had to wrestle with everything being upside down as well. Once she suggested, in what she hoped was a tactful way, that maybe it would be fairer if they were to turn the board round each go but Kath would have nothing of it, refusing to let anything spoil the concentration she was putting into her next move.

In contrast to Kathleen, Doreen was slim and upright. Salt and pepper hair was scraped back into a stern bun and her thickly lensed glasses made her grey eyes look huge and verging on the macabre. Good quality pearls hung around her neck over the pale pink twinset and a bracelet, laden with charms, the end result of many years' Christmas and birthday presents weighed down her left wrist. Oedematous ankles, resistant to any medication that her doctor advised, hung over the edges of her specially made shoes. Beside her was her delta walking frame, complete with string bag attached to the handlebars, necessary to provide a safe place for her handbag and the mobile phone her relatives had thoughtfully given her when she had moved into Cherry Tree House but that she had no idea how to use.

'It must be nearly lunchtime,' she suggested hopefully. 'We ought to be going down for our sherry. It's fish pie today. You really enjoyed that last week.'

'Plenty of time to finish the game. And I've got the doctor coming too, so get a move on. Here, let me look at what you've got and I'll give you a hand.'

Kathleen reached out across the board but Doreen was too quick for her and snatched up the rack of letters, grasping them to her bosom in order to keep them secret. In doing so, she also inadvertently took hold of the tablecloth with the result that tiny tiles spewed onto the floor bringing an abrupt and premature end to the game.

'That's done it,' cried Kathleen, exasperated.

'Sorry, Kath,' was the none too sheepish reply. 'We'll have to call that game a draw. It's too late to start another one.'

'I don't think so. We were nearly done anyway and you'd never have caught up with my score, so that's another victory for me. I'm looking forward to tomorrow's game already. Now your problem is that you never remember that you can make more than one word, if you arrange your letters carefully. Let me show you how I scored twenty-five with just two letters...'

There was a knock on the door saving Doreen from the imminent lecture and Mrs Barnabas, owner of Cherry Tree House and an expansive smile, entered with Ed following close in her wake. She was a strikingly tall woman with large bones and a generous amount of flesh covering them. Over her pale beige checked trousers and short-sleeved white top with crocheted collar, she wore a large butcher's apron, which was splattered with evidence of her recent activity in the kitchen.

'Here she is, Dr Diamond. Happy as a sandboy and beautifully settled in to her new home!'

Ed looked around him with approval. It was, without doubt, a majestic room, spacious with a bay window, which let in a flood of sunshine and an en suite bathroom discretely fashioned in one corner. The walls were neutrally coloured, the carpet dark green and the curtains a green floral mix, enough to add interest but avoid being intrusive. Basic furniture consisted of a bed, wardrobe, chest of drawers and a couple of comfy chairs, leaving plenty of scope for Kathleen to add her own possessions and put her individual stamp on the room. There were some signs this process had already started. A display cabinet had been positioned near the window. Inside, carefully arranged on each of the three shelves, were the remains of a tea set together with a selection of cut glass, some cherubic figurines cavorting in unlikely poses and a collection of china cats. A few dog-eared but much-loved paperbacks were stacked neatly in a small bookcase, the top of which had been livened up with some grainy photos in a variety of mismatched frames, both old and new and then there was the small bridge table and chairs that were currently in use. Kathleen watched Ed as he took everything in.

'So, Dr Diamond, marks out of ten?'

'Ten, definitely. This is a wonderful room. I think it's perfect for you. How do you like it?'

'I love it. That old flat of mine was dank and dreary. This is warm, there's lots of folk to help me and the cooking is just fine.'

Ed laughed. 'It's good to see you settled in so quickly.'

'I've some more things to come from the flat. Tina's bringing them over bit by bit. She's only got a small car so she can't do too much at once.'

'That's probably the best way. It gives you time to unpack and decide where to put things without creating too much upheaval.'

'This is my friend Doreen. Remember I told you she was here?'

'Of course,' nodded Ed, shaking Doreen's outstretched hand warmly. 'Nice to meet you. You must be very pleased to have Kathleen here.'

A rather forced smile appeared on Doreen's face. She was still smarting from yet another loss at Scrabble. Stretching out for her frame, she accepted Ed's offer of help and wobbled to her feet.

'I'll leave you to it, Kath. See you at lunch. I'll make sure they save yours if you're late.'

Mrs Barnabas steered Doreen to the door, in the manner of a duck rounding up her errant ducklings, and they left together leaving Ed studying his patient. Confident that the door had been closed firmly, he started to speak.

'Is it really as good as you say?'

Kathleen chuckled a little and shifted in her chair, stiff from the board game, her back aching uncomfortably.

'You're very astute, Dr Diamond. Of course not. I miss my home and all my possessions more than I can say. I could weep when I think of all the things I've thrown out and that I'll never see again. It's like my life being dumped in a dustbin. But I'm trying to be positive. I know I've done the right thing and I'm sure I'll get used to it. Mrs Barnabas is very kind but gushes a lot. I wish she wouldn't hug me quite so much. She means well so I shouldn't be critical. The food is good and there's plenty of it. This is a nice room – you get a lovely view of the gardens from the window. Have a look. It feels a bit queer that someone had to die for me to have all this and then it'll just pass on to someone else when I go. I have to try not to think about that side of things or else it'd get me down. Still, it'll be better when I've a few more knick knacks about.'

She sighed and looked about her.

Ed searched for something encouraging to say. 'You're a very wise woman. Give it time. I'm sure you'll settle here and make the most of it.'

She reached out to pat his hand. 'I'll do my best, but it won't ever be home. Thanks, Dr Diamond. I'm so glad you can still be my GP.'

'It's a pleasure. Right, let's check your blood pressure then and make sure you've enough tablets.'

'Mrs Barnabas has taken all of those. They arrive at certain moments of the day in little plastic cups. Then they stand over me until I've taken them. It's as though they'd don't trust me.'

'Most homes do that. It just makes life easier for the staff and it's safer all round. It's not a criticism of you in the slightest. Think of it as something less to worry about.'

Kathleen waited until he had taken her blood pressure and indicated that it was satisfactory.

'I'm not very keen on it, whatever you say. They might make a mistake. They might try to give me sleeping tablets to keep me quiet.'

'They are not going to give you any tablets that I haven't prescribed. I think you've been reading too many murder stories. Believe me, Mrs Barnabas is an excellent manager. Now, may I listen to your chest, please?'

It was while Ed was leaning over his patient, paying careful attention to some crepitations at her lung bases, that Tina came in. He had no idea of her arrival until he straightened up and took his stethoscope out of his ears.

She looked as delightful as she had done the last time he had seen her but in a different way. Today she was wearing tight, skinny jeans, high-heeled boots with pointed toes and a chunky knit jumper in russet which came down to mid-thigh level.

'Hi there,' she started, setting down the two bulky carriers that she had lugged up from her car. 'Oops, sorry to interrupt. Do you want me to wait outside?'

'Tina, dear, come in,' Kathleen was effusive with her welcome.

'How lovely to see you. You remember the doctor don't you?'

'Of course. Hello, how are you?'

'Fine, thank you.'

Ed shook her hand, wondering momentarily whether it was in his imagination that she had squeezed it a little more than one would with a passing acquaintance but then dismissed the thought from his mind as absurd.

'How's Aunty settling in?'

'Quite nicely, thank you,' Kathleen butted in. 'I can speak for myself.'

'I've brought some more clothes and those books you asked for. In the car, there's a box of paintings and more photos. I'll get them for you now, while you're with the doctor.'

'Thanks,' Ed replied. 'We've very nearly finished.'

'I'll be back in a mo then.'

Ed tried hard not to notice how her figure flattered the jeans as she walked away from him. Kathleen coughed theatrically, dragging Ed's concentration back to the matter of her wellbeing and he carefully explained how he felt that it would help if she increased the dose of water pills that she took each day, a suggestion that filled her with despondency, anticipating yet more trips to the toilet than she was already making. The frequency was one problem, the ferocity of the urgency that accompanied each trip was far worse and for someone like her, whose mobility knew only two speeds, either very slow or not quite so slow, more water pills were undoubtedly bad news. Like many patients, she kept quiet, wanting to keep her dignity intact, unwilling to discuss such a personal problem as incontinence with the doctor. She would just have to send Tina out to buy more of those cumbersome pads, which, although they served a useful purpose, she loathed vehemently. So far, she had managed to keep this problem to herself but it was only a matter of time before Mrs Barnabas did some snooping and found out and she would really rather deal with it on her own. So busy was she formulating her plans that she missed

86

hearing most of Ed's explanation, including the opportunity to ask any questions and the next words that sunk in were clearly those of someone who was on the verge of leaving.

'...so all in all, I'm very happy with how you're doing. I'm sure that living here is going to be beneficial for your health generally. Give me a call in about a month and I'll pop out and see you – obviously call sooner if you've any worries.'

He reached for Kathleen's hand and she clutched it.

'Thank you,' she whispered, then more loudly, 'ah here's Tina back. That looks heavy, dear. Are you sure you can manage?'

Puffing and rather red in the cheeks from the effort required, Tina put down the cardboard box inelegantly and arched her back to stretch out.

'There's one more box to bring in. I'll get it in a minute.'

'Perhaps Dr Diamond would give you a hand,' Kathleen suggested.

Ed put down his bag. 'Of course. Which one is your car?'

'The blue hatchback. You can't miss it as I had to leave the door wide open. Thanks so much, that'd be great. I'll come down with you then I can lock up.'

Regretting his offer somewhat and hoping that the reward for his good deed was not an inguinal hernia, Ed heaved out another cardboard box, overflowing with papers, which tried to escape in the breeze, balls of wool, knitting needles and nondescript memorabilia. A tea caddy rolled off the top and onto the drive, neatly fielded by Tina who walked behind him, picking up anything that fell off as he staggered erratically up the stairs.

'Goodness,' he remarked, breathlessly. 'What has she got in here?'

Tina sympathised. 'I'm so sorry. It's good of you to help. I'd really have struggled with that box. One of her old neighbours had to help me get it into the car, so I'd been wondering how on earth I was going to manage at this end.'

'Is there much more to come yet?'

'No, that's it. It's sad to think that this is what over eighty years of life amounts to.'

'Maybe that's made it easier for her to make the decision to move here.'

Ed paused at the top of the stairs, resting the box, which by now was in grave danger of falling apart, on the banister rail.

Tina looked into his eyes. 'I hope you're right.'

He was touched by the hint of tears that he saw, not having quite appreciated just how close she was to her great aunt.

'Try not to worry. I'm sure she'll be okay. We've several patients who live here and they're all well cared for.'

He only just made it into the room before the bottom of the box finally gave up the strain. The contents landed in an untidy heap, luckily on a chair.

Kathleen, just emerging from her bathroom, having successfully completed yet another trip there, was now keen to go and join Doreen for sherry and lunch.

'You go down, Aunty,' suggested Tina. 'I'll stay here and make a start, then when you come back, you can tell me what you want where. There's plenty here to keep me occupied.'

'You're a good girl. I'll ask Mrs Barnabas to bring you up a cup of tea. With any luck my kettle will be amongst that lot and then I'll be more self-sufficient. Come on, Dr Diamond, you can escort me down the stairs.'

Her bony hand nestled into the crook of his elbow and slowly the couple made their way across the landing before negotiating the stairs with great care, one step at a time and reaching the dining room without mishap.

'There is a lift, you know,' she chatted conversationally, 'but I want to use the stairs for as long as I can. I think it's good for me. I'm not going to go and give up all my independence.'

Ed contained his mirth and commended her for her resolve before saying his goodbyes, hesitating a moment to watch her shuffle into the dining room, ease her way into a chair at the table where Doreen was waiting and then take a decidedly un-ladylike slug from the schooner of sherry that stood on the dinner mat before her.

Visits completed for the day, Ed checked his mobile phone, hoping for a message from Hannah but predictably there was nothing. She rarely contacted him during the day. Once at work, it was as though she was blinkered and the outside world ceased to exist. While on one hand he admired her resolve and dedication, there was a part of him – quite a large part if he were honest – that wished she would behave like a more normal girlfriend who was separated from her lover and send affectionate, perhaps slightly risqué texts and leave breathy messages on his voice mail that would make him tingle with anticipation of their next meeting. He knew, though, that Hannah would never be like that. He tried to imagine her at work, hobnobbing with her new friends, the ones he had met two nights ago. They had seemed pleasant enough folk but he had felt ostracised from their legal world with its own jargon and in-jokes.

'Stop feeling sorry for yourself,' he remonstrated out loud, starting the engine and backing into a space before heading for the gate. 'It's no different from a group of medics getting together and talking about work. Speaking of which, I should get on with mine. I've a tutorial to give. God, I'm tired.'

Abigail was waiting for him to arrive back at the surgery, in the staff room, occasionally glancing up at the clock on the wall. She was a firm believer in structured timetables and protected teaching time. Ed's inevitable lateness grated on her nerves although she had to admit that it did so slightly less of late than when she had first arrived at Teviotdale. She was, as the partners suspected, finding the transition from hospital medicine to general practice far harder than she could ever have predicted, but it was against all her principles to go so far as to admit this. She had loathed the first few weeks, feeling that she was in an alien environment over which she had no control and had sat at home each evening convinced that she had made a terrible mistake. Gone was that reassuring feeling of being on a ward or in an out-patient clinic, with nurses around to delegate tasks to and senior doctors to nurture and appreciate her excellence. Gone was the ritual of the ward round, parading in order of seniority to the foot of each bed and striving to impress the consultant. In hospital, patients were ill, state-of-the-art investigations were at hand and consultants were easily impressed by academic knowledge – at least the ones she had worked for had been. Her last job had been on a cardiology ward, the professorial unit in a teaching hospital where rare and difficult cases were the rule of the day, each one a challenge in its own right. There she felt safe, confident in her own skills, her unique intelligence and the back-up that protected her. She also felt powerful, as though elevated above her patients on some small pedestal and expected to be treated with respect and held in awe. Part of her wanted to be back there, studying for a consultant's post but she had always wondered about general practice and thought that a spell in that speciality would at best help her decide between the two and at worst do her career no harm whichever path she chose.

Whilst she would never tell anyone, least of all Ed, to begin with she had lain awake at night, dreading the next surgery and the patients that might sit before her. Here in the community, medicine was like being on another planet and being surrounded by creatures who spoke an entirely different language, for which no dictionary existed to help her translate. Though the days were busy, everyone seemed more relaxed and no hierarchical structure existed. The practice staff called her by her first name, worse still, so did some of the patients, men and women she had never met before. They sat almost beside her as she consulted. There was no desk between them to act as a barrier, as she was used to. Then she had to make decisions on her own. She had to cope with requests for raised toilet seats and tablets to postpone periods so as not to disrupt a much anticipated holiday, to say nothing of babies who screamed for seemingly no reason, toddlers who wriggled and female patients who wept inconsolably and wanted someone to listen to their woes.

For sure, Ed was there if she wanted advice, but to ask for it was admitting defeat and weakness, which had never been part of her repertoire.

Try as she might to amaze, it wasn't quite working the way she had anticipated. Ed and the others were clearly stunned by her vast array of medical facts but not in the way she'd hoped. Nor did they seem impressed by her choice of clothing, carefully chosen to look official, smart, commanding. They dressed casually. The female partners often wore trousers, Ed rarely wore a tie and as for the ridiculous jacket with leather elbow patches that John Britton seemed to be sewn into, that looked as if it had been snatched from a wartime museum – well, the less said about that the better. Ellie, on the other hand, possessed some fantastic clothes. Low-cut tops, figure-hugging skirts, boots with precipitously high heels and as the weather was warming up, she had started to appear in sleeveless dresses and impractical sandals. All chic and beautiful but none that came under the umbrella of power dressing. The difference was that somehow Ellie and the other partners looked relaxed and efficient, while Abigail, sweating slightly under the auspices of her rather tight suit, felt overdressed and out of place.

Which was why, that morning, she had dared to dress down, well slightly, as she thought of it, in a pair of well-tailored, wide-legged trousers and a blouse covered with spots and a demure bow at the neck. She felt as if she stood out like a sore thumb but no one had said anything, apart from Faith, who had admired the trousers and asked where she had bought them. Despite feeling awkward and uncomfortable, Abigail had survived surgery without mishap. One patient had even complemented her on the way she looked. Encouraged she had thought of trying to put into place one or two strategies that Ed had taught her but fell at the first hurdle when faced with an elderly and very deaf gentleman who misheard everything she said and so gave up. Unbeknown to Ed, Abigail had now turned her attention to, and read, some books on consultation skills, but still felt too unsure to apply these, cynical about the results they might bring. Asking an open-ended question ran the risk of a time-expending trip down memory lane, screeds of irrelevant information and unnecessary gabbling. She remained convinced that it was better to ask direct questions, which surely saved time and much waffling from the patients and kept her firmly in control of the consultation.

To be fair, she found that she had so much time with each patient, as Ed was continuing to allow her twenty minutes for each one, that she did venture to inquire about their home circumstances and social lives, more to use up the time than because she was interested. The revelations had left her reeling at times, the honesty and trust placed in her was humbling and she felt the beginnings of a distinct desire to try to find out more.

Talking was all very well but no substitute for the cut and thrust of acute medicine, the suddenly breathless patients, the cardiac arrests and other emergency scenarios, for these were now few and far between, having been replaced by a gentler world but one in which each patient presented with a far more diverse range of problems that stretched her problem-solving skills to the limit.

Slowly, she felt she was making some headway but knew she had a long way to go. Ed was admirable, so unflappable and patient. She could appreciate why he was such a popular trainer. Like a huge sponge, he always seemed to have time for more questions, more discussion, more reflection. When she was at her wits' end with a patient, he was there, willing to listen, to go through the history from the start and help her decide where to go and what to do rather than simply tell her the answers. It had been a tough start but things were definitely getting that little bit easier.

Gary put his head round the door.

'Dr Diamond's just phoned. He's on his way. He suggested you pop out and get some sandwiches while you're waiting and then you can both have lunch while you do your tutorial.'

Abigail sighed. 'Couldn't you go?'

'No way, I'm busy on reception. Joan's on her lunch break, so I'm on my own.'

'Okay. What does he want?'

'He'd like ham salad in brown, with mayo and some crisps – plain or cheese and onion. Oh, and a can of something to drink and a banana.'

'Okay,' she repeated, looking at her watch. 'Just how long is he going to be?'

'He's just left his last visit which was in Upper Slattersby – that's about five miles from here but the road isn't good, so I'd say probably fifteen minutes. Oh and if you want to get into his good books, he really likes those flapjacks that they do.'

Abigail stretched and got to her feet. There was a queue at the bakers and Ed was back, typing in his visits when she returned, arms laden with his order, including flapjack and a smaller bag containing her own plain salad roll and an apple.

'Hi, sorry I'm late. Thanks for getting lunch. I hope you don't mind eating and talking but that way, we'll have a good hour.'

'No that's fine.'

'Right, so what was it we were going to talk about today?'

'Sexually transmitted disease.'

'Ah, yes. Perhaps not the most delightful subject to discuss while we're eating but still a very important one. We might not get through all I wanted to in the time we've got but let's give it a go. Did you do the reading I suggested?'

Abigail nodded, starting to feel on firmer territory, mentally rehearsing the signs and symptoms of conditions such as gonorrhoea, syphilis and non-specific urethritis. She reached into her bag and took out a wad of notes, ready to start, only to be totally thrown when all that Ed said was, 'How do you think a patient feels when they're told they've got an STD?'

9

Ed was stomping up and down Princes' Street, angrily. It was frantically busy, mostly, as far as he could see, with tourists milling this way and that and he had lost his good temper hours ago. He felt hot, sticky and slightly dirty having been out on his own since after breakfast, when he left Hannah at the door to the imperious- looking building that housed her office.

Hannah's persuasive cajoling had resulted in him driving up the night before for the weekend. He had a certain amount of misgiving about the trip. There was plenty for him to be doing at home, plus he was conscious of having neglected the climbing club of late. The original plan had been for Hannah to come to Lambdale and perhaps take off the Friday or Monday (even better, both) and make a long weekend of it. Good weather was promised and it was sacrilegious not to make the most of the opportunities the long days of late June offered. Ed had believed the arrangements were signed and sealed and had been looking forward to them with an almost childlike enthusiasm, confident that Hannah was also. He had bought in food and drink that he knew were Hannah's favourites, including the first of locally grown strawberries and booked a table for Saturday evening at the local pub. He had started to plan both a cycle ride and a climb, desperate to maximise their time together. He also was nurturing a tiny, embryonic hope that Hannah, when she saw the Yorkshire Dales in all their summer glory, Lambdale's Saturday market in the square and got some good fresh air into her lungs, would see how preferable this lifestyle was to the one she was currently so devoted to, stuffy central city life which consisted of little other than work.

The last thing he had planned was the long drive up to Edinburgh after Friday afternoon's surgery but he had known, by some psychic force, as soon as the telephone rang on the Thursday evening, just as he was getting ready for bed, what was going to happen. Something had come up, Hannah had said. Impossible for her to get out of without risking the wrath of her boss, which was just unthinkable. She was so sorry but knew he'd understand. In a way it was thrilling, wasn't it, because she'd been entrusted with important work which normally wouldn't happen with such a new member of staff, so she needed to prove she was up to it. She'd have to work on the Saturday, but only for a couple of hours, then she'd be free and they would get out of the city and into the countryside, escape and explore, she'd vowed. So please, please, please would he come up and stay with her? Next time, she'd come to him, really she would. She'd already started looking at the feasibility of flying to Leeds to save time.

It had been useless to argue but Ed had been unable to keep the disappointment out of his voice and Hannah had picked up on it. Their conversation had become overformal and monosyllabic at times, culminating in Ed capitulating and agreeing to subject himself to the journey yet again and making a mental note to tell Barbara to take as much of the fresh food from the fridge as she wanted, so that it didn't go to waste. The strawberries he could take with him.

His last patient of the day was a last-minute extra. A woman in her late thirties, brought along by a distraught-looking husband who had begged the receptionists for an urgent appointment. He described in detail to Ed how his wife, Eve, had started to behave increasingly erratically over the last few weeks, spending recklessly, way more than they could afford, staying out all night, being definitely over-familiar with the neighbours and lying in only her underwear on the front lawn, saying that she was sunbathing, regardless of the weather. Ed had listened carefully, all the while watching his patient who was pacing round his room, picking things up to examine them, throwing open the window and leaning out, shouting at people outside. She had been dressed bizarrely, a slipper on one foot and a sandal on the other. Impressively endowed, her loose breasts swayed dangerously under her close-fitting pink t-shirt. Her skirt was flamboyant orange, a cerise scarf wafted from her neck and her head was crowned with a garland of plastic flowers and a pair of sunglasses.

Ed had turned his attentions to her, asking her to sit down while he did so, which she did, but he had found it impossible to steer her in the direction he wanted to go as she chattered incessantly, barely pausing for breath, describing to him in detail how she had a fantastic plan that would make their fortunes and change the world for ever. When he had finally grabbed a moment to ask what this was, she had set about elaborating on her idea for a seven-sided cube, with such conviction that Ed found himself almost believing her and wondering if perhaps it would work. She had been thrilled that Ed has been so intrigued and had been flattered by his suggestion that she go to talk to one of his colleagues at the hospital about it, though she hotly denied that she was in any way ill.

The diagnosis of hypomania was in no doubt, but the consultation had taken up far longer than he would have liked and then yet more time had been spent discussing the case with the psychiatrist on call – sadly not David Jennings, which would have made it all so much easier and arranging a time for her to be assessed. Ed was just grateful that she had agreed to this, removing the need for a possible section under the Mental Health Act, which would have taken even more time.

So he had started out on his journey drained and wound up. Had fate bestowed good fortune upon him then the drive would have been long but straightforward but no, it had been even worse than usual, tediously slow, just stopping and starting. All his least favourite tracks on the radio station. His favourite CD of the moment lent to Rob. Large lorries and scores of caravans. Odd that, he had mused, stuck in a jam, north of Newcastle. When your mind-set was negative, things started to go wrong, which just made you feel more gloomy than when you started out. He had drunk two cans of oversweet pop which just made him feel thirstier and finished off the strawberries which then led to another delay as he had to stop at a filling station to use the toilet.

It was dusk when he had arrived. Hannah was in but working, her table covered with papers, lap top humming, mobile phone to hand. There had been no sign of supper and close inspection of the kitchen revealed bare cupboards and nothing more than some semi-skimmed milk and a large bar of chocolate, half eaten, in the fridge.

'I didn't know what time you'd be arriving,' Hannah had explained, hugging him briskly, which had initiated a slow thawing process in Ed's grumpiness. 'Here, phone for a takeaway. Your choice, my treat.' She had flung a handful of leaflets at him.

His protestation that he was tired and suggestion that they just snuggle up on the sofa with a beer or glass of wine had caused Hannah to shrug her shoulders, intimating that there was nothing she would like better but... Ed had kissed her gently on the forehead and gone upstairs to bed, alone. Surprisingly, he had slept well, perhaps eased into unconsciousness by the feeling he was still moving in the car. He had no idea what time Hannah joined him or indeed left him, for when he woke her side of the bed was crumpled but empty. Blearily, in only his pyjama bottoms, he had made his way downstairs to make coffee and toast, only remembering halfway down that there was no bread. Hannah was dressed, working. It was almost as though she hadn't moved from the night before.

'Morning.'

She had angled her cheek to be kissed, without taking her eyes off her papers.

'How's it going? What time did you get up?'

'About an hour ago, maybe a bit more. It's going really well. Do you mind making your own coffee? Sorry about breakfast but I'll show you a good place to get some if you walk me to work.'

'Okay,' agreed Ed, not wishing to start the day acrimoniously. He sat down on the sofa and flicked on the television.

'Er, Ed,' began Hannah.

'Yes,' he looked up.

'I need to leave in a couple of minutes and it's vital that I concentrate on this last little bit. Sorry – again.'

He had dutifully exited, showered and dressed, returning with still wet hair to find Hannah at the front door, key in the lock, anxious to be off.

'How long will you be?' he'd asked as she'd kissed him goodbye, rather hurriedly, after looking all round, which had made him feel she didn't want anyone to see.

'Two hours, certainly no more than three. I'll ring you, promise.'

And with that, he watched her be sucked into the cold, austere-looking hallows of McGregor Moran.

It would not have taken a genius, looking at Ed, to realise that Hannah's promise of three hours at the most had not been fulfilled. His feet were weary with trudging, his stomach protesting because it wanted lunch but Ed had chosen to wait, feeling sure that Hannah's call was imminent and the clock reminded him that it was four-thirty in the afternoon. He wandered back to her house and perched on the little wall outside. The key she was having cut for him had failed to materialise, which had not seemed a problem until now. Exasperasted, he punched out her number on his phone, but, as usual, was passed on to voicemail after one ring. He looked at his car and thought about getting in and driving home. There was nothing left inside that was vital and an action like this might just make Hannah realise how left out he felt. It was one thing to be tolerant and supportive but this was something else. She had all week to work, just as he had. They should make the most of their time together, goodness knows there was precious little of it at the moment and not much prospect of change in the near future. Ed contemplated moving up to Edinburgh, for the umpteenth time, looking around him, up and down the road, trying to envisage whether he would be happy living here, whether having Hannah every day would compensate for the open fields that he could see from his bedroom window, country lanes and the rural life that he adored.

His phone trilled and he answered immediately. Hannah sounded breathless. 'I've finished, Ed. Where are you?'

'Outside your house. I've been waiting ages.' The none too subtle jibe was out of his mouth before he had time to think and stop it.

'Sorry,' she replied airily and then laughed. 'Oops, all I seem to have done today is apologise. Anyway, I'm on my way. Wait for me there or walk down to meet me.'

She rang off leaving him no time to agree or otherwise.

There were dark shadows under her eyes when they met. The previous evening's late night followed by the early start was taking its toll. He suspected that she would not be wanting to rush off out on some adventure and was proved right when, as they made their way into the house, she flung herself onto the settee and sighed.

'I'm done for, Ed. My head's buzzing with all the thinking I've had to do. Still, it went well and Sebastian seemed really pleased with what I'd done.'

'Sebastian?' asked Ed.

'Yes, he's the partner who's overseeing my work on this case. I've told you about him before.' There was a trace of annoyance in her tone, suggesting that Ed did not listen to her.

'Of course. That's good. But, more importantly, you're finished. What shall we do? Go out for dinner, or for a drink? There's still time to get out into the country if you want?'

Theatrically, Hannah threw her arms behind her neck.

'I can't think beyond a shower and hair wash right now. Tell you what, if I go and do that, would you be an angel and go to the supermarket for me, if I write a list? I'm ashamed how I haven't even got the basics in.'

'Okay. But tell me, what on earth do you live on during the week? I'm always going shopping for you.'

'Well, I don't have time to cook, so I don't shop. I grab a coffee and a pastry on the way to work – did you go to that little café for your breakfast? It's great, isn't it? Then someone comes in selling sandwiches at lunchtime and in the evening, we often have working suppers at work, otherwise I'll grab something at the wine bar when I go with the others or a takeaway – hence the vast number of leaflets in my possession.'

'That doesn't sound very healthy,' Ed commented. 'And what about exercise? When was the last time you had any?'

'Don't get all doctor-like with me, Ed. I'm tired out. I calculated that I've worked over sixty hours this week and now I'd like to unwind if it's all right with you.'

'Sure. I didn't mean to nag. I just want to know that you're looking after yourself. You've always taken that sort of thing so seriously.'

Hannah relented and reached out for him.

'Sorr–' she started and they both giggled. 'I'm going for my shower. I'll feel better afterwards.'

'Perhaps you'd like some company, I'm very good at soapy massages.'

She laughed softly, gently pushing him away.

'Ed, I need a little time on my own. My head's still buzzing. You know how it is. By the time you get back with the shopping, I'll be fine. Promise.'

Ed was tempted to comment on her choice of words but resisted the temptation and left, feeling more than a little rejected, list in one hand, bags in the other.

The supermarket was busy; there seemed to be a preponderance of solitary men looking miserable but maybe Ed was biased in what he saw. He loaded up a trolley with all Hannah's requests and then added his own ideas. She never used to be one for microwave-ready meals, chocolate and biscuits. What she needed and would appreciate, he decided, was more fresh fruit, cereals and packets of healthy snacks such as nuts and dried fruits, food that was energy packed, easy and nutritious. At the last minute he added a couple of bottles of red wine, looking forward to a drink at home before they went out and then maybe carrying on later when they got back. They both needed to chill out and relax. The evening would be fine.

Opening the front door, Ed found the house was quiet. No sound of the television or music playing and nothing to suggest that Hannah was preparing herself upstairs. Quickly he put the shopping away, nodding with satisfaction at the much improved sight in the fridge and cupboards. He uncorked the first bottle of wine and left it to breathe. A mix of nuts and raisins he decanted into a little glazed pottery bowl that he found at the back of one cupboard and placing this on a chopping board, as there was no sign of a tray, along with two glasses and the bottle, he went into the lounge to wait for her. As soon as she came down, he would have his shower and then the evening could begin. He was starving and hoped that she had picked a good restaurant for them to go to. Italian perhaps, a plateful of pasta with a rich garlicky sauce would be good, just for starters and then who knows. He licked his lips in anticipation. A steak? Chicken? Fish? Tiramisu for dessert? He hadn't had what his mother would call a proper meal since Thursday evening.

Scooping up a handful of nuts, he strolled upstairs, tossing them into his mouth as he went. The bathroom door was wide open, so he took advantage of this, showered briskly and then went into the bedroom, towelling his hair, to find clean, fresh – if creased – clothes. Hannah was on the bed, curled up into a foetal position, snoring unfemininely, dead to the world. Ed carefully sat on the edge of the bed beside her but needn't have worried. It was clearly going to take considerably more than that to wake her. Stroking her short hair he nudged her only to receive an incomprehensible grunt before she rolled over, pulled the covers on top of her and retreated back into her dreams. He tried again, a little more forcefully and she woke, looking disgruntled and bemused.

'I'm so tired. I've got to sleep. Leave me alone, Ed.'

Disappointed, he threw on some clothes, old comfy jeans rather than the smart trousers he had brought and a polo shirt, thrust his feet into some flipflops and left her to it. He turned on the television, picked up his glass of wine, opened up the photography magazine he had bought earlier and prepared for a lonely night in on his own. After sitting through one ghastly variety type show there was still no sign of Hannah. He made an omelette which turned into scrambled eggs, laced liberally with cheese and tomato and toasted a pile of bread to go with it. Two films later – one excellent thriller and one so-so comedy, he called it a day and snuggled down beside his still deeply asleep girlfriend.

Remorseful, Hannah brought him breakfast in bed.

'I feel so much better for a good night's sleep,' she confided in him, watching him eat.

'Good.' Ed was encouraged by the cheeriness in her voice. 'So, what shall we do today?'

'I'd wondered about a good walk. What do you think? Along the beach perhaps.'

'Fine by me. Anything, as long as I can have you to myself for a bit. Come here. You're mine for the day.'

He placed his plate and mug on the bedside table and pulled her towards him, starting to caress her neck and lick her earlobe. His hand moved to probe inside her dressing gown, longing to refresh his intimate knowledge of her body. Acquiescing, Hannah kissed him on the lips with feeling before pulling back and wrapping her clothes around her, protectively.

'There's no time for that,' she tried to make light of the situation. 'Come on, I thought you were in a rush to get off.'

'Hey, Hannah, come back to bed. It's early and I need a cuddle.'

'I can't, Ed, I'm on my period.'

'Hannah… We can still…'

He implored her to return to his arms but by then she already had her clothes on and was bouncing off to the bathroom. He flung the bedclothes back, frustrated, and sat briefly, on the bed edge, scratching his head with both hands, unable to understand exactly what was happening. The weekend was turning out to be a complete let down.

Nothing ventured, nothing gained. He willed his rising bad temper to lie down and rooted around for his clothes. They could still have a good day. One glance out of the window showed that it was fine and sunny, a good omen. Ever the optimist, thought Ed, that's me.

Ed drove. Not exactly what he wanted to do, with a long drive home pending but Hannah took charge of the map and leapt into the passenger seat before he could suggest otherwise. She wanted to see the beach at East Lothian and had earmarked somewhere for lunch once they had walked. But barely had they got to the end of the road and argued briefly about whether it would be better to turn right or left when her phone rang. She cursed softly, Ed swore out loud and asked her why she had bothered to bring it with her.

'Just in case,' she answered before squinting to see who was calling and taking the call. 'Hi, Sebastian, how are you?'

Ed kept on driving as she was talking, trying not to listen to the one side of the conversation that he could hear and knowing which direction it was going in.

'Of course I can come in and help,' she was saying, pulling rueful faces at Ed as she did so. 'When? Half an hour? Okay. Yes of course. No, no problem. I hadn't planned anything for today. See you soon then. Bye.'

Without waiting to hear what she had to say, Ed swung the car round and set off back for her house.

'Don't even begin to say you're sorry,' he snapped.

'But I am. You know what work's like. I can't refuse.'

He snorted, revving the engine needlessly waiting for some traffic lights to change.

'The very least you could have done would have been to explain that you had a visitor and that, yes, actually, you did have some plans for the day.'

'He's my boss, Ed. I must do what he asks. I think I'm making a really good impression so far so there's no way I'm going to risk jeopardising my track record. It'll only be for a while. We can go out this afternoon.'

'Ha!'

Ed's normally placid nature had been tried to the limit.

'Hannah, I think I'll just get my things and go home. At least that way, I'll arrive back in good time and not feel shattered tomorrow.'

Hannah looked aghast. 'No, Ed, please don't. Look, I'll ring Sebastian and tell him I've got to be back for lunch. How about that? You could read the Sunday papers without me disturbing you for once.'

Ed was pensive as he skilfully negotiated his way into a tiny parking space outside Hannah's house.

'I don't think so. I spent all day yesterday waiting for you and that was a waste of time. We've barely said two words to each other since I arrived and you don't even want me to hug you. I'll get my bag and get off.'

He strode into the house, Hannah busying along behind him, torn between the demands of Sebastian and Ed's ultimatum. She watched him ram his few possessions into his bag.

'This is awful, Ed. We can't leave it like this. What about next weekend? Will you be up? Shall I ring you tonight?'

'No, I won't be up next weekend. I'm going climbing with Rob.'

'Oh of course. I'd forgotten about that. So what about the one after?'

Ed put a hand on each of her shoulders.

'The Saturday after next, which you have seem to have forgotten about as well, is Lambdale Show. I'm presenting the prizes for the horse section, local celebrity that I am. I had hoped and you had promised – something that you are very good at doing, but not quite so good at keeping – that you would be at my side, in a suitably long flowing dress and a floppy straw hat – well, something of that ilk.'

'Oh no, I *had* completely forgotten.'

'No surprise there then,' Ed retorted, unkindly. 'Will you be coming?'

He could see her thinking quickly.

'Of course. I wouldn't miss it for the world.'

Pausing, Ed gave her a look of disbelief before choosing to be diplomatic and opting to give her the benefit of the doubt.

'Good. I shall look forward to it. I trust you will too. Now, if you'll excuse me, I've a long drive ahead of me. Oh, if I'm not mistaken I can hear Sebastian drumming his fingers on his desk, awaiting your arrival. Better not keep him waiting.'

'Sarcasm doesn't suit you, Ed,' Hannah bit back but he had no reply for her.

With a quick peck on each cheek, he walked out of the house, not looking back and merely waving one hand out of the sun roof as he drove off, leaving Hannah watching him, part bereft, more irritated, before diving back inside to gather together her papers and hurry to the office.

10

'So that's how it was left,' Ed concluded, draining his pint and looking around to see if there was a long queue at the bar. 'Sorry to unload it all onto you but thanks for letting me. Another?'

Rob had listened quietly to all Ed had to say, giving him his full concentration and still had a glass over half full. He shook his head, wondering whether he ought to suggest that his friend might be better with an orange juice. Ed was drinking at a fairly alarming rate tonight, trying to exorcise the resentment he felt towards Hannah. Rob had watched him veer from anger to despair as pint after pint disappeared, barely touching the sides. Ed returned, drinking as he walked to avoid any spillage.

'Hasn't she rung since?' Rob inquired.

'Nope.'

'Have you rung her?'

'You must be joking. She knows where I am if she wants me. If I were to try ringing her, she'd be unavailable or in yet another meeting with Sebastian.' He pronounced the name with mockery.

'Hasn't she even sent a text?'

'She's not really into all of that. A phone's a phone, as far as she's concerned and nothing else.'

They sat for a moment, drinking. Ed wiped his mouth and swirled the amber liquid around in the glass, gazing into it as though it might give him a flash of inspiration.

'What should I do, Rob? It's obviously not working out, this long-distance relationship business. I feel it's me doing all the running and while I know I should be pleased for her and all that sort of stuff,

I feel she's cut me out of her new life and left no time for the two of us.'

'There's no denying it's hard work living apart like that. I once went out with a girl who lived in London, when I was in Leeds. When you're together, there's such huge pressure on you to have a good time. We lasted a few months, then it just fizzled out. What about Hannah, do you still care about her?'

'I care about the Hannah I used to know. I'm not sure if I'm so keen on this new, pushy, work-driven woman she's turned into. We used to have fun, Rob. I can't remember the last time we had a good talk or a laugh and as for sex – well, don't get me started. Talk about the return of the Ice Age.'

'Doesn't sound good, mate,' Rob commented philosophically.

Ed agreed. 'No it doesn't. I think we're on the way out, quite honestly. She's supposed to be coming down next weekend for the show but we'll see. If she does, then maybe we've a chance, if not, then I think I'm going to call it a day.'

'Shame, but maybe it's for the best.'

'Christ, I can't go on about it any more. I'm just going round and round in circles. It's boring me to death so God alone knows how you must be feeling. Let's change the subject. How's things with Faith?'

'Good, thanks. She's still got a problem with her eating but it's better than it was. It's stress and worry – as soon as that mounts up, she starts bingeing and vomiting. Daft, really as she thinks I don't know.'

'Tell her you do.'

'I've tried once or twice but she's very wary. As soon as I get near the subject, she's up and off on a different tack. Sad, really as I'd love to help her.'

'Women!' sighed Ed and sank the last dregs. 'Another?'

This time Rob accepted without hesitation but waved away Ed's offer to get them in saying that it was definitely his turn. It was proving to be a glum evening. Usually they laughed and joked their way through three or four pints, putting the world, in particular the NHS, to rights but not tonight. Ed, still smarting five days later from his abortive weekend was not good company and all of Rob's attempts to lift his spirits had fallen on stony ground. He knew Ed well enough to understand that the prickly exterior was a front and that underneath Ed was sad and felt rejected. Hannah, on the few occasions Rob had met her, had come across as a nice enough girl, quiet, perhaps rather plain in his eyes and very driven by work. Yet she had seemed genuinely attached to Ed, the looks she gave him were those of real affection and any old idiot could tell that Ed had fallen for her in a big way.

'Ring her, Ed. You'll feel better if you do. It's pointless holding a grudge like this. You just get angrier the more you think about it.'

Ed thought for a moment and acknowledged this was true.

'Perhaps.'

'Do it. Look, you and I are off camping this weekend and I want to have a good time. What's more, I want you to have a good time too. So get it sorted and ring her tonight when you get home.'

'You're exasperating, Rob, but you're also right. Okay, I'll ring her tonight. Now let's concentrate on this weekend.'

The phone rang repeatedly and Ed was on the brink of giving up when Hannah answered.

'Hi you,' he started, determined to be cheerful.

'Oh, it's you, hi, Ed.'

Was it his too-vivid imagination that made him think she sounded wary?

'How're things? I thought you might be out.'

'I was upstairs.'

'In bed? Sorry, I didn't realise what time it was.'

'I wasn't asleep.'

'I've just got back from the pub with Rob.'

Silence. She wasn't making this easy for him. Time to go in at the deep end.

'Look, Hannah – I feel wretched about last weekend. I was intolerant. Sorry.'

'Forget it. I have. It can't have been much fun for you.'

'No, it wasn't.'

Another silence. Help, thought Ed, this is like ploughing through treacle.

'So, you're okay then?'

'Yes, fine.'

'Good. Hey, Hannah, are you angry with me? You don't sound like your usual self.'

'I'm tired, Ed. It's been another busy week. I'll be working again this weekend.'

'Poor you. Rob and I are off to the Peak District. Should be great. We've just been out this evening, planning it all.'

'Sounds lovely. Have a good time.'

'It'll keep my mind off missing you,' he volunteered.

'You'll be able to think of me, up to my eyes in paper.'

He heard her yawn.

'You sound exhausted. I'll not keep you. It's just that we hadn't spoken for days and I was worried that I hadn't heard anything.'

Hannah said nothing. Change the subject, thought Ed.

'Are you looking forward to the show? Ellie's kids are going in the gymkhana events. It's their first show. She says they've been practising like mad but keep falling off.'

'That's nice. Look Ed, I think I'm going to have to ring off now, I'm falling asleep at this end and I've another early start tomorrow. You have a nice weekend and I'll speak to you on Sunday, or maybe early next week.'

'Are you sure you're all right?' Ed was worried. 'Have you eaten all that nice fresh food I got you?'

'Some of it,' she replied, crossing her fingers for in fact most of it had gone in the bin untouched. 'Speak later, Ed, night.'

'Love you, Hannah,' Ed whispered, but she had already gone. Not just from the other end of the phone but up to her bedroom where Sebastian, resplendent in his nakedness, was waiting for her to resume the love making that had been so thoughtlessly interrupted by Ed's call.

'Now, where were we?' he growled.

Hannah, ecstatic, cast aside her dressing gown and confidently straddled him, with not even a passing thought for the man who really loved her and who was sitting, stroking his cats, knowing that their relationship was over.

Rob and Ed had a terrific weekend, both determined to have some fun. Blessed with good weather, they went walking, climbing and caving. Staying on a camp site with like- minded individuals, they made new friends and met up with some old ones. They laughed a lot and relaxed. Just what the doctor ordered, commented Rob as they swapped stories of their outdoor pursuits while eating hearty meals at the nearby pub, washed down with tankards of the strong, dark local brew. For forty-eight hours, Lambdale was a world away, worries were left behind and as they drove home, refreshed and invigorated, happily tired, Ed realised that Hannah had rarely been in his mind, a fact that he found surprising but rather consoling. The decision he had to make was now quite clear to him.

Hebe and Toby seemed overjoyed to see him, jumping up onto the back of the armchair to be stroked as he put his bag down, purring loudly before hissing at each other and jumping down, hoping to be fed. Ed flung open windows to let in the cooling evening air and put on the kettle. Unpacking done, climbing gear sorted neatly and cleaned, he turned his attention to cheese on toast, watching it hungrily as it bubbled like thick lava under the grill. Barbara had left a cake, cherry by the look of it, so a thick wedge of this would do nicely to finish his meal. Sitting down with his plate, he checked the phone for messages. Just one, from his mother, nothing to worry about, just calling for a chat. He rang back and talked as he ate, telling her all about his weekend and listening to her tales of home. The familiar voice was soothing and made him feel as though he had been wrapped in a warm blanket. Despite not having lived at home for years and being thirty- two years of age, there was still no substitute for the reassuring tones of his mother, transporting him in an instant back to the dramatic landscapes of home and the cosiness of the house he had grown up in.

Ever tactful, she made no comment about Hannah, waiting for Ed to raise the subject. When informed of his plans, she was merely supportive rather than judgemental, keeping whatever feelings she really had to herself and encouraging him that whatever choices he made, she and his father were there for him, come what may. On a whim, he invited them over the coming weekend, guilty that he had devoted so much time to Hannah at their expense and wanting to make it up to them. The speed with which she accepted made him laugh and he went on to insist that it was to be a break for them both and the kitchen would be out of bounds. They were to behave as guests.

So that was sorted. Now there was just the rather more important matter of Hannah to resolve. It had not gone un-noticed that she had made no attempt to contact him and now, when he was starting to think about bed, he doubted she would ring. But he had decided what to do and the longer he put it off, hoping for a last-minute reprieve, the worse it would become.

She answered immediately, sounding different to their last ex-change, more friendly, more like Hannah. She asked about his weekend, about work, seeming genuinely interested, envious of his caving, bemoaning the fact that she had, yet again, been in the office most of the time. They discussed the weather. Edinburgh was hot and oppressive, apparently. She was longing for some fresh air. The perfect cue for Ed to mention the coming weekend.

The change was instantaneous. Out came a deluge of excuses, apologies, pleas for forgiveness. It was simply impossible. They were so close to finishing the work on this case that had commanded so much time and effort that there was just no way that she would be able to get away.

Ed listened to her flimsy and unimpressive speech, Hannah unaware that he was shaking his head. He took a deep breath.

'I think we should finish, Hannah. I've had enough of this.'

As soon as the words were out of his mouth, relief swept over him. Dutifully he listened to Hannah's reaction of shock but managed to be resistant to her powers of persuasion which tried to change his mind.

11

As the weight had been lifted from Ed's shoulders, with it had floated a small part of his soul. From the outside, no one could tell. He looked normal and behaved normally. His work was unaffected, his interaction with friends the same, his patience with Abigail miraculously intact. But Ed was internally shaken by just how much he missed Hannah, despite the fact that they had seen so little of each other of late. His thoughts strayed to her on an all too regular basis, so much reminded him of her, silly things really – his climbing gear, the green tea in his kitchen cupboard and of course, Toby. Late at night, when his loneliness was most acute, he was tempted more than once to ring her, make amends, offer to try again but he didn't, too aware that there had been no contact from her since the final call, no text, no voicemail, not even a conventional letter or card. He was curious that she had accepted his decision without a qualm, not asking for reasons why and trying to negotiate, a chance to put all her argumentative skills to the fore in an effort to win him back. That was certainly a relief in some ways, but it hurt to realise that he had meant so little to her after they had talked of love and, in their own way, commitment. Reliving her empty promises made him angry, partly with Hannah but more so with himself, for not having seen how shallow she was, wanting to believe that she observed the same standards as he did, sure that he had found a soul mate in whom he could place his trust completely.

As he tied his tie, dark blue with tiny multicoloured spots, on the day of Lambdale Agricultural Show, it was difficult not to remember that Hannah should have been there, on his arm, walking around with him, being shown off by him. He had assiduously avoided the two ties that she had given him.

His parents had arrived on the Thursday evening. Barbara had come up trumps and had polished, dusted and hoovered his house with alacrity, leaving it spotless and not in need of any input from his mother. While she had cleaned by day, Ed had spent his evenings in the tiny garden, weeding and tidying, feeding the patch of grass that was hardly big enough to be called a lawn, putting in some late bedding plants to add a splash of colour.

Alan and Ailsa Diamond had been speedy with appreciative com-ments. They had come laden with gifts, a gigantic home-made cake, scones and pies to go in his freezer and fresh vegetables from their garden. There was even a bottle of cloudy wine, made by a neighbour from the grapes in his conservatory. Alan hinted that perhaps there was no rush to drink it, winking as he did so, to ensure that Ed read between the lines and got the message that it was truly awful. Ed had hugged them both; there was something extra special about seeing them both on this visit.

The sunny weather had petered out on the Friday, clouds and blustery downpours charging in with no consideration from the west to replace it, bringing an associated significant drop in the temperature. Alan and Ailsa had a wet day exploring and returned bedraggled. Not the most promising forecast for the show but infinitely more pleasant for the animals that would be paraded, admired and competed, to say nothing of the stalwart members of the local Countrywomen's association who would be exhibiting their wares in the extensive marquees.

His parents were waiting for him when he came down. His mother brushed his collar with her hand, tutting at the cat hairs which had a habit of getting everywhere, including places the cats had never been. She nodded her approval at his clothes, a light blue shirt, dark blue trousers and a light beige jacket.

They set off shortly after ten, Ed keen to fulfil his role to the maximum by being there for as much of the show as possible, having a good look round and watching the classes as well as indulging in a sit down lunch in the VIPs' area. It had rained most of the night and now the sky was a heavy metallic grey, clouds scudding along with the occasional glimpse of blue, the latter not enough to patch a pair of sailor's trousers but perhaps – hopefully – a hint of things to come. Wisely stowed away in the back of the car were raincoats, Wellington boots and umbrellas. Nearing the showground, which was a large meadow just outside the town, they crawled to a standstill joining the end of the queue that was waiting to drive through the entrance gate.

'Nobody seems to be put off by the weather,' observed Alan, peering over the top of the newspaper he had brought to read to see why they had stopped.

'It's the local show. It's a big occasion,' explained Ed. 'Folk have been preparing for ages for this. Take Ellie for example, she's been making the twins' fancy dress outfit since Christmas, or so she says.'

'Whatever is it? It must be very special,' Ailsa asked, intrigued.

'She's refused to give anything away. We've kept asking and trying to guess but we've been told to wait until today.'

Finally it was their turn and Ed eased the car through the gate and was directed off towards the officials' car parking area. The car tyres spun ominously for a second, trying to grip the soft ground and Ed noticed gloomily that there was already a tractor on site, towing cars onto the field. It didn't bode well for going home by which time the ground would be well and truly churned up by massive horseboxes and cattle wagons. Strains of brass band music wafted in the gusty wind, interspersed with moos, baas and whinnies, together with the happy chatter of humans as the numbers started to swell.

Leaving his parents to wander around on their own, with arrangements to meet for lunch at one, if they hadn't bumped in to one another before that, Ed announced his arrival to the show secretary, received instructions of what his role involved and then, free for the morning, went looking for Ellie and her family. He found them with little difficulty. Lydia and Virginia were arguing loudly over some minutiae to do with their tack and Ellie, self-appointed referee, was trying desperately to concentrate their minds on the job in hand, that of getting the ponies ready for their first class. Excited by the new sounds and aromas around them, the two ponies, Smudge and Jester, were unusually restless, indignant at being tied to the trailer, tossing their heads, stamping their feet, picking up on the atmosphere that their little riders were creating with their bickering. The tack dispute resolved, Lydia's hat was then nowhere to be found, causing her to burst into tears and Virginia, not to be outdone by her sister, spotted a stable stain on the inside of Jester's back leg which had her in a similar state of distress a moment later. Ellie, still intent on being calmness personified, located the hat in the back of the car and stuck it on her daughter's head firmly before finding wipes in her handbag which made short work of the brown mark. Somehow, and Ed had to marvel at how she did it, Ellie had the ponies tacked up and the two girls mounted and ready to go by which time they were firm friends again and comparing notes on how nervous they felt. Spotting friends in the distance, they thanked their mother and trotted off, Jester bucking with joy because he was no longer tied up, causing Virginia to collapse on his neck and lose her stirrups but, remarkably, stay on, giggling.

'I hardly dare look,' breathed Ellie, watching them go. 'They're so fearless when it comes to those ponies. When they fall off, which they seem to do terribly frequently, they just bounce up and get straight back on again. I've lost count of the number of times my heart's been in my mouth. I think the Emergency Department know us all by our first names because we've been there so often. But you can't wrap them in cotton wool all day every day, can you? I'd much rather they were outdoors like this, having fun and exercise than be glued to computer screens in their bedroom.'

She paused and looked at Ed.

'Don't they both look adorable in those little hacking jackets?'

Ed nodded, momentarily envious of their happy family life. This could have been me and Hannah, he thought, before washing the idea firmly from his mind.

'Where's Ian?' he asked.

'He'll be along soon. He had to wait for an important phone call. I just hope he gets here in time for their first class – he'd be devastated to miss it.'

'And what's the first class?'

'Best condition and turned-out pony and rider. Hence the flap about the stable stain. You'd get marked down for something like that.'

'What else are they doing?'

'Bonny pony competition, fancy dress and the gymkhana this afternoon. They begged me to let them enter the junior jumping but I don't think my nerves could stand it, so we had to compromise on extra entries in the games. Come on, I'd better get to the ring side. Look! There's Ian!'

They both waved as they crossed the grass, Ed feeling his brogues sinking a little further than he would have liked into the mud. Finding an empty space at the ring side, he stood and watched with Ellie and Ian as the class progressed and a string of young riders of assorted shapes and sizes, mounted on an equally diverse selection of ponies, walked round in a large circle and then trotted. He noticed that Ellie was clutching Ian's arm tightly, both their faces flushed with pride as they willed on their daughters. Another moment when the spectre of Hannah took the opportunity to loom large.

The competitors were then subjected to close inspection by the judge, a lady of statuesque proportions who was taking her role exceedingly seriously. Were their boots polished, were their gloves clean? She peered behind buckles, checked manes and tails and stood back with a concentrated expression on her face, one hand clutching her chin to examine the whole general effect. She was wearing an ankle-length waxed coat, which flapped threateningly, upsetting a number of the ponies, and a wide-brimmed hat, the front of which was covered with feathers, giving the appearance of a pigeon that had crash landed. She deliberated for an age unaware that Ellie, and doubtless all the other mothers, was muttering at her to hurry up, finding the wait unbearable.

'Hooray,' cried Ian, turning to share a kiss with Ellie, 'Lydia's got a third and Virginia a fourth. That's fantastic! Well done, girls!'

All the ponies exited the ring with considerably less control than that with which they had entered. Lydia, red in the face with indescribable joy, slid off Smudge, hugging him as she did so.

'Mum, Dad, did you see that? I was third. Virginia was fourth. How great is that? There must have been hundreds of ponies in the class.'

'We won money, Mum. Can we spend it on ice cream please?'

Ed congratulated them all and left them to it, promising to meet up later for a drink, after the presentation of the trophies. He couldn't resist looking back over his shoulder at the four of them, well, six including Smudge and Jester, who were enjoying a group hug along with mutual admiration of the rosettes they had won.

Taking his time, for there was much to stop and look at, Ed wove his way through the now quite considerable crowd. His progress was hampered by patients coming up to him to chat, mostly expressing pleasantries and comments about the show, only one whispering some lurid details about his bowels and asking if he had his prescription pad with him.

He watched ferrets racing down large plastic tubes, some more enthusiastically than others, patted the sheep pronounced best in show and watched with appreciation while a local farmer with a chainsaw transformed a large log into an exquisite carving of an owl on a branch.

The heavens opened and he hurried towards the nearest marquee, squelching deeper and deeper into the mud. Too many others were of a similar mind and it was claustrophobic shuffling round to admire the delights of home-grown vegetables, flower arrangements and baking. The judging had taken place first thing and the comments were on show for all to view. Whoever had taken on this role had not felt any obligation to be diplomatic. Ed marvelled at the fact that a chocolate cake could be criticised as having 'not enough chocolate' and a deflated-looking Victoria sponge adorned with the words 'did you read the recipe?'.

Moving on there was an impressive photography display which Ed spent some time studying, envious of some of the techniques used and effects thus created. Perhaps he should have submitted one or two of his own. Perhaps next year, under an alias, just to be on the safe side. He had definitely picked up some ideas to use next time he was out. Taking a couple of backward steps to view one of the photos from a slightly different angle, he felt himself collide with someone and turned to apologise.

'I'm so sorry, please excuse me...' he started.

'Hello. How are you?'

'Why, hello there,' he replied, trying to keep his balance while a couple in matching raincoats and hats pushed past.

Tina was smiling at him, using her show catalogue as a fan, flushed by the steamy humidity in the tent. She still managed to look fresh and pretty, clad in the ubiquitous waxed jacket, jeans and Wellingtons.

'It's so busy, isn't it?'

'Very,' nodded Ed, having to stop himself from falling forwards on top of her as someone else paid little attention to his presence, intent on getting closer to the knitting display.

'What's in here?' she asked at the exact same moment as Ed enquired after her aunt, causing them both to laugh nervously.

'There's so much to see,' commented Tina. 'I hardy know where to start.'

'In here,' Ed informed her, 'there's photography, art, home baking, arts and crafts and the children's section. It's all fascinating but I'd maybe leave it until it stops raining and it gets less crowded.'

'That might be a very good idea,' she agreed, laughing as more people jostled them out of their way.

'Next door, there's a flower show and vegetables. But it's no less jampacked in there.'

'Oh, thank you. It's nice to see you. Are you here in an official capacity?'

'Only that of presenting some trophies this afternoon. I keep well clear of the first aid tent. This is supposed to be fun, not work.'

Tina nodded and he could see that she was struggling to think of what to say next.

'Anyway, I'd better get on,' he started, wondering how he could excuse himself without seeming impolite and looking around the tent for a reason to go.

Miraculously, he saw Clare and David, shuffling with the masses towards him, waving at him over the sea of heads.

'I'll see you later, maybe,' Tina, who had been following his eyes, suggested, ducking a little to avoid an umbrella. 'I think I'll get out of here while I'm still in one piece.'

Ed laughed with her and raised his hand to her as she disappeared from sight before pinning himself to the soggy wall of the marquee until his friends joined him.

'Ugh,' was Clare's greeting. 'What a day!'

'Let's get out of here and go and get a coffee or something,' Ed jerked his head towards the entrance and the other two nodded in agreement.

They splashed across the now widespread muddy terrain, David leading the way for Clare to follow. Ed noticed that she was wearing flipflops, a more inappropriate form of footwear he could not have imagined. Reading his mind, Clare put him straight.

'They're the only shoes that I can get on. My feet have started to swell. Well, actually that's the understatement of the year, in fact my feet and most of my legs have started to swell. I couldn't even get David's other wellies on and they're huge. I feel really daft wallowing around in this quagmire in these.'

'Then that's another good reason for you to have a sit down,' Ed judged.

'Thanks for that,' said David, 'she won't listen to anything I say.'

Ed pointed to the refreshment tent, which fortunately was not too far away and strode out leading the way. 'At least the rain seems to be blowing over. Do you want to sit inside or out?'

'Oh, out, please, if it's fine. Isn't there some sort of dare-devil motor bike display on soon?'

Clare fell heavily into her chair and heaved a sigh of relief. David tenderly put her feet up on a spare chair, whisking it away before it could be appropriated by anyone else, oblivious to the dirt and mud that had splashed up to her knees. Ed fetched cups of luke- warm coffee and glanced at his watch as he sat down.

'My parents will be along in a moment – they're joining me for lunch. Why don't you as well?'

'That'd be great, Ed, thanks. Clare needs to have a rest. She's so stubborn, she's determined to keep going and I'm forever telling her to slow down and think of the baby.'

David put his arm round his wife protectively.

'I get so bored,' explained Clare. 'I was really hoping that I'd be able to come back to work next week but then my feet turned into balloons so I'm back at the clinic in a few days for yet another review. Fortunately my blood pressure's normal and there's no protein in my urine, so they're wondering if it's just related to the hot weather we've had and the fact that I've put on a lot of weight really quickly – as you can see.'

She patted her swollen abdomen, pride in her voice.

On cue, the sun finally deigned to peep out from behind a cloud as they were joined by Ed's parents and a rather splendid lunch ensued

– barbequed Cajun chicken or salmon fillets with lime and coriander, a variety of salads and then profiteroles or strawberries and cream to follow. Clare ate all of hers and went back inside the tent, emerging with a generously portioned second helping, supplied by one of the caterers who had taken pity on her. Conversation was sporadically disrupted as their attentions were drawn to the antics of the motor cycle stuntman, Dave the Dynamo, who played to the crowd with a professionalism of many years' practice as he proceeded to accelerate up steep ramps in order to jump through hoops of flames and over a carefully lined-up row of cars. It said more than a considerable amount for his skill that he managed to stay upright at all times, despite skidding and sliding on the wet grass.

As he took his final lap of honour, standing tall on the pedals of his machine, one arm raised high above his head to wave, he received a rapturous round of well-deserved applause from everyone.

'I was convinced he was going to fall off,' breathed Clare to Ed. 'I'd been desperately trying to remember what the correct first aid was for a neck injury.'

David hugged her to him. 'Don't you ever stop worrying?' he pretended to chastise.

'No,' was her simple and honest reply.

'You're hopeless but I love you.'

'Oh look,' Ailsa pointed to the ring entrance, where a rather odd selection of ponies was coming into the ring, 'it's the fancy dress.'

'Brilliant,' cried Clare, moving her chair nearer to the ringside for the best view possible. 'Now we'll find out what Ellie's been up to all this time.'

Roars of laughter greeted the entrants as they made their way round the well- trodden ring perimeter. Leading them all was a Shetland pony, brushed to perfection and decorated in pink bows, ridden competently by a small girl dressed in a matching fairy outfit. Behind her were cowboys, Batman and Robin, a highwayman whose moustache kept falling off and a group of evil-looking pirates who brandished cutlasses and growled a lot. Then a white pony astride which a young boy clad in skeleton pyjamas clung for dear life onto the mane, a Humpty Dumpty and a Little Red Riding Hood. Last of all came a small pony, covered in green sheets, barely able to see where it was going, a glowing testament to its unflappable nature. On either side were two little figures, dressed as surgeons in gowns, with masks and gloves, one leading the pony, the other with a huge cardboard scalpel, liberally covered in what might have been blood but was more likely to be tomato ketchup, in her hand. On the pony's back, under yet another green sheet was an indeterminate figure, the long-suffering patient and a further generous helping of strategically placed ketchup.

'No prizes for guessing which entry is Lydia and Virginia,' Ed chortled, wiping his eyes as they all fell about laughing, sides aching, as a link of sausages, doubtless intended to mimic the patient's innards, fell off and lay dejectedly on the grass. One of the girls ran back to get it, tried unsuccessfully to fling it back onto her pony and ended up dangling it round her neck.

'Who'd want to judge that?' Clare commented. 'It's impossible. You'd not want to disappoint anyone.'

'I think they all get some sort of prize,' Ed reassured her.

'Those girls have just got to win,' Ailsa decided. 'I mean – just how much work and thought has gone into that!'

Win they did and the excitement was palpable from where they were sitting. Ellie waved a victorious thumbs-up, shrieking with delight and hugging Ian. Ed gesticulated wildly, inviting her to join them and she nodded furiously, indicating that she just had to sort out the twins first. She appeared some moments later, with the girls, who were already squabbling over who should have the cherished red rosette.

'Ian'll join us in a bit. He's just taking the ponies home. They've had a long day and I don't like leaving them tied up to the trailer in case anything happens. Stop it, you two. How many times do I have to tell you?'

Calmly, she extracted the red rosette from their clutches where it was in grave danger of being ripped into pieces and affixed it to her own blouse.

'I think I deserve this as it was my idea and I did most of the work.'

'But we thought of the blood,' insisted Lydia.

'And the guts,' added her sister.

Ellie quelled them with a look and the girls, who knew just how far to push their parents, capitulated, sat on the grass and spread out the array of second, third and fourth rosettes that were the total tally for the day after the gymkhana events and described to Ailsa, their captive audience, in minute detail and doubtless with some fanciful embellishments, just how each one had been won.

The rain held off and although blustery gusts of wind battered the trees and caused marquee walls to shudder, there was still an ambience of happiness and success. Ed, feeling good after a thoroughly enjoyable and relaxing day, a feeling facilitated by two glasses of wine with his lunch, presented the trophies with a flourish, congratulated all the winners, patting their mounts. It was after six when they finally decided to leave, Clare and David having left earlier, the twins determined to sit things out until the bitter end. Only the promise of pizza and ice cream for tea persuaded them to make a move.

Alan and Ailsa walked with Ed back to his car, chatting about the day's highlights. In the distance, Ed spotted Tina, wading through the mud carrying a large plant. She waved, an action that he returned, if a little self consciously. He could see his mother watching him as he did so.

There was no way that they were going to be able to drive straight off the field. The combination of the day's extra rain and the churning up of the ground by other vehicles made an easy passage impossible. Ed sighed as he listened to his wheels squealing as they tried to get some grip. Surrendering, he switched off the engine.

It was only as they were waiting for the tractor to come and tow them off the field that he realised, with satisfaction, that Hannah had not even tried to intrude on his thoughts for several hours.

12

One of the best things about a job like Ed's was that it required his total concentration and this proved to be an enormous blessing over the next month as the hurt inflicted by Hannah slowly but irrevocably started to heal. Time for complacency and despondency was not an option. Surgeries were full, often with extras, Clare had not been permitted to return and Abigail still required him to have eyes in the back and sides of his head. There seemed to be a glut of patients with serious problems, new cancer diagnoses, a rape victim and a desperate young woman who had just found out that her husband had been sexually abusing their two small children.

The partners made a point of meeting together each day, after work, in the corner of the local pub, needing to get away from the surgery, to talk and offer mutual support, each one of them aware of the mental stress that was involved in helping these people adjust to the tragedies that had decimated their lives. Ellie burst into floods of angry tears at the unfairness of life on more than one occasion and Faith looked pale and wan, worn out by daily visits to a terminally ill patient who had a variety of symptoms that were proving exceedingly difficult to control.

With no sign of the stress receding – the last telephone call of the day had been from the hospital maternity wing to inform them of a stillbirth and Ed had just told them of yet another cancer case, recently diagnosed but too advanced for any treatment other than palliative – John offered to cancel his annual leave, tinged with guilt at the thought of leaving his friends to cope with the emotive demands. In one voice, the others refused to let him consider it. He needed the break, they would get theirs with the passage of time, of course they would manage without him.

Previously, Ed's first reaction on reaching home would have been to ring Hannah, to pour out his heart to her and wait to hear her sympathetic and soothing but down to earth comments but now, the temptation to do so, or even to email was becoming increasingly resistible and he found more comfort sitting with a beer, stroking and playing with Hebe and Toby, waiting for his tea to cook.

Slowly but surely, he felt his usual enthusiasm creeping back into his veins. Subliminally at first but then he began to feel restless. Out came his bike, initially for solitary but therapeutic rides. Then he found he needed no persuasion to go climbing with Rob, loving the feeling of the wind beating around him, the hint of danger, the panoramic views, the necessity to focus on something completely different. He was waking in the mornings looking forward; Hannah was no longer his last thought before he fell asleep, nor the first he had when he opened his eyes. It felt good to feel free, unfettered, back to his old self and his energy was boundless. So much so that he decided that he needed to decorate, exorcise the tiny bit of Hannah that still haunted his house and he set about changing the bedroom completely. Appropriating a large box from the local supermarket, he filled it with what possessions of hers remained. Little of any significance, mostly CDs, books, including some recipe books and a few items of clothing that she could not have had any love or need for, not having approached him in some form to ask for them back. He noticed with some chagrin that amongst the latter was a nightdress and also a blouse that he had given her. He recalled being so pleased with his choices, positive that she would adore them but now they were evidence of how wrong he had been. Decluttered completely, he sealed up the box with an excessive amount of heavy-duty tape, making more than sure that the box would not be opened without some considerable wrestle and a sharp knife. He then stashed it away, in his bike shed, underneath a packing case and a cheap barbecue which he had never used and dusted his hands with satisfaction that it was safely out of sight.

With the arrival of pots of paint, brushes and rollers came chaos upstairs. The cats, delighted with their new adventure playground, wrapped themselves up the dust sheets, shot their paws out like lethal weapons from under the bed as Ed passed by and lithely scaled their way to the summit of the piled-up furniture, where they sat up on their haunches and had boxing matches to establish just who was the king of the castle.

Wanting to create an effect that was completely different, Ed opted for blues and cream. Light blue and cornflower blue, aiming for a seaside look that he had once seen in a Sunday magazine, clean, crisp and light. Up came the carpet and the floorboards were stained and polished. The result was stunning and as he sat back to admire his handiwork, Ed wondered why on earth he hadn't done it sooner. The days were long, the light evenings a bonus. As soon as he got back from work, he continued where he had left off the night before, not easing up at all until the room was finished, until he felt that it looked completely unrecognisable in all respects and there was nothing left at all to remind him of what had happened. A trip to Harrogate on his half day secured new white bed linen, blue checked material that, if he asked her nicely, Barbara would turn into some curtains and two bright yellow bedside lights that crouched like matching suns on their respective tables. He was momentarily tempted by, but then dismissed, a pair of wooden seagulls which might well have looked quite chic on the chest of drawers.

Job finished, he stood at the door and enjoyed the feeling of achievement. It looked just as he'd hoped and with Hebe and Toby, companionably curled up on the bed, he felt that a professional interior designer would have been pushed to surpass what he had done. Inspired, he set to downstairs, happy with the lounge, instead concentrating on the kitchen, which now looked dark and pokey. A week later, by which time he felt that he never wanted to see another takeaway as long as he lived, this room too was finished. More clean, refreshing colours, a blind to replace the dingy curtain and a stable door, the top half of which, when open, positively invited the light to flood in.

It was almost as though he had moved house. He liked that. It really felt like a new start. Coming home the first night after the work was completed, the smells of newly dried paint still the first thing to hit his nostrils, his home looked spotless. Barbara had been in and worked her usual magic. Her approval was evident as the bedroom curtains were finished and in place, plus she had put fresh flowers into a vase on his bedroom window sill and left a peach and raspberry crumble for him on the worktop next to the kitchen sink. Wallowing in his delight, Ed poured a glass of red wine and grilled lamb chops, boiled new potatoes and peas and then sat, eating and drinking, as happy and satisfied as he had been for as long as he could remember. Later, slipping between the new sheets, which felt crisp and unfamiliar against his tired body, he stretched out languorously before falling into a dreamless sleep.

Bizarrely, when John departed on his holiday – two weeks in Norway – with his wife Faye, work started to quieten down. Those remaining, Ed, Faith and Ellie, worked stolidly and hard but found time most days to chill out at lunchtime and catch up. Even Abigail seemed to appreciate the pressure they were all under and nobly offered to decrease her appointment times to fifteen minutes so that she could see more patients in each surgery and never moaned, well not audibly, when she was scheduled for emergency visits. With his days more manageable and his evenings now free, Ed made the most of his spare time, cycling into and around the Dales, stopping for a snack and a pint, pushing his fitness up a notch and feeling the benefit for it. There were still uncomfortable moments when Hannah was able to cause a twinge of pain but these were shorter, less severe and further apart. By now he could dismiss these more readily, divert his thoughts, refuse to be sucked back into unpleasant memories and feelings, confirming his belief that he was definitely, as one of the practice counsellors would no doubt refer to it, moving on.

One glorious early afternoon, he was sitting outside Delicious, enjoying an iced coffee and a slab of home-made cake (vanilla sponge with a filling of fresh blueberries and cream), spoiling himself as the end of another week of concentrated work approached. Ellie had left a few moments earlier, anticipating a telephone call from a consultant, needing to discuss a patient's bizarre blood results and Faith had driven off to the local undertakers to fill in a cremation form. Now alone, he was contentedly soaking up the atmosphere, listening to the rattle of cups on saucers and cutlery on plates, the appreciative murmurs of other customers as they bit into their food and the happy babble of conversation that floated on the warm summer air.

It had been a good week, he reflected, helped along by the sunshine, which inevitably instilled more positivism into everyone, staff and patients alike. Without a doubt the most memorable highlight of the week had been the arrival of a card for Abigail, thanking her for her care. Ed had so enjoyed giving it to her, watching her open it and read the words inside. She had been speechless, he could have sworn that there were the beginnings of tears in her eyes and he knew instinctively that this was going to be something of a turning point for her. She'd played it down of course, stuffing it back in the envelope and shoving it carelessly into her brief case. No way was she going to let her professional façade slip in front of the others, but he had caught her looking at it again when he had bounded into her surgery after her last patient of the day.

He was smiling as he reminisced, stretched out in his chair with one leg crossed over the other, enjoying the solitude and the chance to people watch and think. Sitting in the sun with a comfortably full stomach was proving to be soporific. He mused over the possibility of a short nap, for there was at least an hour before he was needed back at work. The weekend was looking promising. Tonight, he was meeting up with Rob and Faith for a drink and a bite to eat and tomorrow the two of them were off climbing while Faith went riding. If the weather continued in its present vein then anything short of a fabulous day was impossible.

He allowed himself to close his eyes.

'Is this seat free?'

He jolted back to being fully awake and hurriedly sat up in his chair.

'Yes, of course,' he replied, shielding his eyes with one hand to see who was speaking.

'Hello again,' he started.

'Oh!' Tina laughed. 'I didn't realise it was you. We're always bumping into each other, aren't we? Do you mind if I sit here, or were you working?'

Ed shook his head.

'I think it must have been fairly obvious that I was on the verge of nodding off. No, please sit down. You've done me a favour making me wake up. It was just so lovely and warm sitting here, contemplating, I couldn't help but doze a little.'

'I'm sorry to disturb you.'

Tina carefully decanted her cup of coffee off the tray before sitting down opposite him. Ed noticed that she had not succumbed to the home baking and wished that his will power was as strong. He also noticed that she was wearing an exceedingly skimpy top and a short skirt, revealing shapely, smooth, lightly tanned legs.

'It is the most gorgeous day,' she agreed, moving her chair a little to catch more of the sun. 'I'm so glad that I'm staying here at this time of the year. I feel like I'm on holiday.'

Ed agreed with her, taking a bite of his cake.

'I know just what you mean. Sometimes I have to stop and pinch myself – I'm really lucky to be working and living here. Don't you miss home? Wasn't it London? It's very different here.'

'You've a good memory,' Tina was impressed. 'Yes, of course I miss London. I love it there, there's so much going on but this here,' she gesticulated around the market square with one arm, 'is perfect for what I need at the moment.'

'And what's that?'

'I'm writing up my thesis. I need quiet and no distractions, so it seemed like a perfect opportunity when Aunty Kath announced that she had decided to move and asked if I would come up and help. And now that she's so well settled into Cherry Tree house, I just visit most days for an hour or so, maybe take her out, but the rest of the time is my own to work.'

'How's it going? Work, I mean.'

Tina paused to take a sip of her coffee, still really too hot to drink.

'Good. Slow but good.'

By now, Ed was wiping the last bits of cream off his plate with a fork. He'd eaten hurriedly, for some reason, feeling a little awkward that he was the only one with food.

'Your thesis,' he asked, smacking his lips appreciatively, 'what are you writing that on?'

Tina looked at him.

'You really want to know?'

'Absolutely,' he insisted.

'You'll be sorry you asked,' she promised. 'Anthropomorphism in early English Literature. I'm hopefully working towards a PhD in English Lit.'

'That sound impressive,' Ed decided to say, hoping that his answer sounded suitably polite and interested.

Tina smiled at him.

'Well done. Most people are left speechless. Not that it bothers me as I'm finding it fascinating and the research side of things is going fantastically.'

'Well, that's great,' Ed replied, with genuine feeling. 'And how are you feeling about your aunt now she's moved?'

'I can't begin to tell you how much of a relief it is. I used to come up and see her in that dreadful flat – did you ever go there?'

'It was pretty grim,' Ed agreed.

'I'd cry all the way home after a visit. I hated it. Especially when it was obvious that she was becoming less and less able to cope. First of all, I could see that she wasn't cleaning like she used to. There'd be a layer of dust everywhere and the bathroom was beyond description but would she have anyone in to help? Oh no, it would be an invasion of her privacy, she used to say. She couldn't see that it would have made her life easier. You know that she's enough to cope with, what with her brittle bones and the damage that's done to her body. But she was determined to carry on. Then I came up and found food rotting in the fridge. Ugh, green slime on an unidentifiable object and milk that had turned solid, it was so old. I was nearly sick as I tried to clear it up. That was the final straw, I think, along with a pile of washing that smelled of wee. Plus, she told me about the fall she'd had. I sat down with her and told her straight how worried I was about her and what might happen to her if she left things any longer.'

'She obviously listened to you.'

'Yes, thank the Lord. I was expecting to be sent away with a flea in my ear but she actually seemed grateful that I'd brought up the subject. I couldn't believe it when she decided then and there that she'd come and see you to ask your advice. Thank you so much for helping her.'

Ed held up one hand. 'I didn't do anything. She'd made her own mind up, which was the only way. It's just a miracle that Cherry Tree House had a vacancy.'

'I know. Have you seen her recently? Her room's looking really homely now.'

'No, but I expect it'll not be long until I do. She never forgets when she's due to have her blood pressure checked.'

Tina drained the last of her drink.

'They make good coffee here. I think I'll have another. Can I get you one, too?'

'Thanks, but no. I'm due back in surgery shortly, so I must be making a move. It's been nice seeing you. Enjoy the sunshine!'

Ed rose to his feet, extending his hand to shake Tina's. She hesitated then obliged, looking into his eyes as she did so.

'Thank you, Dr Diamond.'

'I'm Ed.'

'Well thank you, Ed, I don't know what we'd have done without you.'

Again waving away her platitudes, he turned to leave, taking care not to knock the table.

'Ed,' Tina called and he looked back over his shoulder.

'Yes?'

'I'd really like to say thanks properly. Perhaps I could buy you a drink after surgery?'

'There's really no need. But thanks anyway. Bye.'

Walking away, he felt as though he had been rude and churlish, both of which were inexcusable. He wondered why he had behaved in such a way. There was no denying that she was very attractive and Ed knew that he had definitely been tempted to say yes to the drink later on. She'd looked upset when he'd turned her down, or maybe his masculine pride imaged this. In reality he had plenty of time for another coffee but part of him wanted to be safe, back in the surgery. He wasn't sure if he was ready yet for that hint of desire, which he could feel was threatening to uncurl within him. Aware of its stirring and afraid, he knew he had to get away before it could take shape and take over. As he walked back to the medical centre, dawdling, going the long way round to maximise his time outside he tried to analyse his feelings.

There was no reason why he shouldn't be attracted to a new woman, it was only natural. It was a good sign, surely, yet more confirmation that Hannah was a thing of the past. Tina was unarguably gorgeous and her outfit today had left little to the imagination. What would it be like to stroke her soft skin, what would she be like in bed? Very different from Hannah, of that he was sure. She was advertising her sexuality in a way that Hannah never did, virtually offering herself to him – or was she? Was he just letting his mind run away with him, testosterone driven, leaving common sense behind? There was just something about her that made him feel uneasy. Indefinable and probably he was being grossly unfair. Perhaps it was his inner defences pulling together to save him from more upset.

Perhaps she was just a grateful patient wanting to say thanks. But therein lay the problem. Patients rarely offered to take the doctor out. For sure they arrived at the surgery with chocolates, bottles of wine, sometimes even a brace of pheasants or a freshly caught trout but apart from the occasional pint bought by a local farmer at an opportunistic meeting in the pub, arrangements that were tantamount to a date were strictly off limits, as of course were any relationships with patients. Whatever she thought of him, however beguiling she appeared to be, he knew that deep down his soul was unmoved, just as well as it was not allowed to happen and there was no way that he was going to make a fundamental mistake like that.

His surgery was good and his patients happy. He ran to time and finished with a flourish, diagnosing a case of pityriasis rosea in a young man who presented with the typical, scaly rash. He called Abigail in to see it and commended her when she recognised the condition without hesitation. Checking through his diary, he had only a couple of referral letters to do and then he would be free. Even better, a glance at his watch confirmed that there would be time for a quick ride out on his bike before he needed to get ready to meet Rob and Faith.

13

Abigail was starting to enjoy general practice. She had established good rapport with a number of patients, an achievement backed up by their requests to see her again on subsequent visits and she found that this continuity made a lot of sense, even though some of them had unfathomable problems that refused to go away no matter what she did. Her liking for esoteric diagnoses and a multitude of investigations still burned in her heart, but she had listened to what Ed had discussed with her on more than one occasion and tried to adapt, even though this left her feeling that there were too many chinks in her armour at times. The prospect of each surgery was now far less like a battle with a wild and unpredictable bear, more of a rough and tumble with a friendly dog and so she found that her free time was no longer beset with worry and anxiety as she had started to look forward to each day. Along with her change in mind-set came a softening of her personality. The partners warmed to her and in turn she let them see snatches of her real personality. Whilst she still dressed to impress, there was a definite suggestion of casualness about her now, cool short-sleeved summer dresses or swirling skirts, bare legs and sandals replaced the previously favoured severely tailored trousers, suits, tan- coloured tights and flat shoes. She wore her hair loose, held back by an Alice band so still under control, but a big improvement on the scraped-back bun.

This morning was proving to be no exception to the new-found rule. She had started off comfortably with the review of a patient with high blood pressure, followed by one who had been found to have a leaking heart valve and was awaiting the summons for an operation. Confident in her cardiology expertise, Abigail had no qualms dealing with either of these patients and felt that even Ed would have been impressed with the way she had handled their questions and considered the impact of their respective diseases on their daily lives. Two children followed, a one-year-old girl with acute diarrhoea, as evidenced by the accompanying aroma, and her three-year-old sister. It did not take a mastermind to come to the conclusion that the latter was just starting with an identical virus as she assumed a complexion of varying green hues and then vomited copiously all over the carpet.

Abigail cleared up as best she could, summoned help and was rewarded by the arrival of Joan, well practised in coping with such scenarios, complete with mop, bucket and can of oversweet-smelling air freshener, which mixed with the pervading pong rather than eradicated it. This cleaning operation took some time and Abigail found that she was running late. Subsequent patients had to be steered around the damp patch on the carpet and appeased with apologies for both the delay and the lingering odour but rather than criticism, Abigail found herself on the receiving end of understanding and commiseration, which surprised but delighted her. One lady, attending for repeat medication, even produced a bar of chocolate from her close to bursting shopping bag and pressed her to take it, saying that she'd deserve a treat with her coffee later on.

Sylvia Naden was forty-nine, but liked to think that she looked a lot younger. A neat cut to her dark brown hair, which had been skilfully embellished with highlights of warm blond, framed her worried face, her eye make-up had been put on with less care than usual, lipstick smudged in one corner. She bustled in, trying to look as though she was in control. Protectively clutching her capacious and extravagant handbag to her stomach, she sat down slowly, taking great care to balance on the very edge of the seat.

'I'm so glad you're a lady doctor,' she began and promptly burst into floods of tears before she could come out with any more information.

Slightly thrown off kilter as she liked to have the first word, Abigail reached for the box of tissues and passed them over. Sylvia accepted one with a gulp of gratitude and wiped her nose.

'I'm so sorry,' she wept.

'That's okay,' Abigail said. 'What's wrong? I mean how can I help you?'

'I'm so ashamed,' Sylvia sniffed.

Abigail waited to see what would happen next. Nothing, other than Sylvia weeping afresh.

'What are you ashamed of?' she prompted.

Sylvia cast a furtive glance around the room.

'This is confidential, isn't it?'

'Of course,' Abigail reassured her.

'You're sure about that?'

'Definitely. Anything you say to me will stay between you, me and these four walls.'

Sylvia's shoulders relaxed a little as she sighed. She mopped her cheeks and nose. 'I never thought that anything like this would happen to me. Me, of all people. My friends would be horrified.'

Abigail made what she hoped might be an encouraging noise.

'You see, I'm married. I have been for nearly thirty years. To Tony. Loving, caring Tony. First-rate father of our two children. But boring, predictable Tony. Gets up every morning and comes home every night at the same time. He's got a well-paid job and he never forgets birthdays or anniversaries. We entertain a lot and go out a lot. We take the same holidays each year, one in the Algarve, two in Cyprus at our timeshare and two in Southern Ireland where his family come from. We make love every Saturday night without fail and he trusts me implicitly. I have everything a woman could ask for. I don't have to work. I can spend as much as I want. I go to the gym or play tennis and meet girlfriends for lunch. People would give their eye teeth to be me, I'm aware of that. So why wasn't it enough? Why did I have to go and ruin it all?'

She looked at Abigail as if it were her fault.

'There I was, stuck in a rut. Same old, same old. Then along came this chap. He's a friend – huh, well I thought he was. Known him and his wife for years. It's the old story, I was flattered by his attentions, it was new, exciting, made me feel alive for the first time in years.'

Abigail raised her eyebrows.

'Yup, you've guessed it, we started an affair a few months ago. It was amazing! The sex was out of this world – we'd go to hotels or he'd come to my house during the day. The more I saw of him, the more I wanted him. I loved the danger. He made me feel like a teenager again. Oh I know that sounds as clichéd as it could, but I'm telling you the truth. It was as though I'd been in a deep sleep for years and then suddenly allowed to taste life. I was hooked, I couldn't get enough.'

'So...' But Abigail was not allowed to interrupt.

'He promised me so much. We were going to leave our partners and run away. We made elaborate plans, whispering in each other's ears after we'd made love or over a bottle of wine in some dark corner of a wine bar. Do you know how naïve that sounds now? Oh how could I have done this? Why has it happened to me?'

Sylvia crumpled before Abigail.

'Here, have another tissue.'

It was gratefully accepted, in fact Sylvia grabbed the box and helped herself to a handful, each one plucked out with a little more vehemence than the one before.

'I'm so angry with him now,' she sobbed. 'With what he's done to me!'

'He's left you, has he?' Abigail anticipated.

Sylvia looked up, mid sniff.

'No, no, no.' She waved a fistful of used tissues around. 'Far worse than that.'

Abigail was perplexed. She'd been sure that she had known what was coming next.

'Then what is it?'

'We made a pact. Never to give each other things. It would have been too difficult to explain them away to our other halves. I longed to buy him stuff, new shirts, cufflinks, sexy underwear...' she paused, embarrassed, 'but he made me promise never to do so and because he gave me all this tripe about how he wanted to shower me with diamonds but didn't dare in case Tony found out, I agreed. It was all part of our secret, you know?'

Abigail didn't but had the sense to nod her head.

'But now he's broken that rule and I hate him.'

The now-empty tissue box was replaced on the desk and then flattened with a furious clenched fist.

'Oh dear.' Help, thought Abigail, I really don't know what to say.

'We met a week ago. In a pub. One of our usual haunts. I knew something was wrong the moment he walked in. Looked all sheepish. Sat opposite me rather than beside me. We had a bottle of red wine and he pretended everything was normal, but I knew it wasn't. He wouldn't look me in the eye. So I asked him outright. He filled his glass to the brim and drank it all down in one. Dutch courage if I ever saw it.'

Anger raged in Sylvia's red-rimmed eyes, causing Abigail to feel distinctly uneasy.

'Told me he'd been seeing someone else as well as me! Bastard!'

This was said with such ferocity that Abigail jumped.

'Guess what, this floozy, whoever she is, has given him Chlamydia and now I think he's given it to me. What sort of bloody present is that?'

A string of expletives followed before the flood gates opened anew, now that she had finally confessed her reason for coming to the surgery. Tissues nothing more that crumpled damp balls, Abigail passed over paper towels, less gentle to sore noses but still useful in an emergency such as this.

'You poor thing,' she tried.

'I don't want your sympathy. I don't deserve it. What if I've given it to Tony? How on earth am I going to explain that one away? He's not an idiot. He'll put two and two together immediately and I can't bear to think how that will hurt him.'

'What about you? Do you have any symptoms?'

Sylvia shook her head, blowing her nose vigorously.

'Only that I feel dirty and tarnished.'

'Well that's a start. This is terrible for you,' Abigail consoled her, 'but you really need to have some swabs and you must have the treatment regardless of the results.'

'Okay, I thought you'd say that. I've been reading up about it.'

Abigail dreaded her next question. 'Do you think he might have passed on anything else?'

'Such as?' Sylvia looked alarmed.

Abigail was as gentle as she could be. 'Other sexually transmitted diseases.'

'Oh! I never thought of that. This just gets worse. What a bloody nightmare this is turning into.' She blew her nose forcefully. 'What should I do?'

It took Abigail a further fifteen minutes to negotiate a plan of action with Sylvia, as each of her recommendations were met with a new outburst of either rage or despair. They agreed that it would be best if she had a thorough check-up and screening and an appointment was secured for her later that day at the genito-urinary medicine clinic in Leeds, Sylvia having eschewed the offer of anything more local, for fear of bumping into anyone who might know her, however remotely.

Before leaving, Sylvia stepped over to look at her reflection in the small mirror above the hand basin.

'Just look at me. I look a wreck. I can't go looking like this.'

She made some tentative attempt to wipe away the mascara that by now was all over her face.

'You look fine,' Abigail heard herself lie. 'No one out there will notice. If they do, they'll just think you've a bad cold, or hay fever.'

Sylvia gave her the look of one who was unconvinced but sniffed, stood up straight and did her best to make a dignified exit, after expressing her thanks. Difficult though the consultation had been, apprehensive though it had made her feel, Abigail was left with the sensation of a job well done, she'd even remembered to suggest that Sylvia came back to see her in a week's time for a supportive chat, an idea that had been well received through the snuffles and stilted gulps that continued even as she left the room.

Quite worn out, Abigail uttered a silent prayer for the next patient, which was luckily also her last, to be something simple. Certainly as she was ushered in, the initial impressions were promising. A friendly young face, a smiling greeting, no hint of mental anguish – just the job. With any luck it'd be a sore throat.

'Hello, it's Christine Baxter, isn't it?'

'Yes. Hi, Dr Watson, I'm Chrissie. How are you today?'

Abigail laughed. This was a more promising start.

'That's what I'm supposed to say to you! Come in and have a seat.'

They both sat down.

'How can I help you?'

'I've just come for my smear.'

Excellent, thought Abigail. That's just about as good as a sore throat.

'Anything else I can do for you?' she asked, half dreading the answer in case Chrissie remembered anything else.

'No, just that, thanks.'

'Fine, well if you'd like to follow me through here, into the examination room, we'll have it done in no time.'

Abigail drew a cheery yellow curtain around the couch, allowing some privacy for her patient to undress in and started to fill in the appropriate forms in readiness.

'You're quite new here, aren't you?' asked Chrissie.

'Yes. I'm doing my training in general practice. I've had many years of hospital experience though before I came here.' She felt obliged to mention this fact; the word 'training' could not help but imply a novice status.

'Are you enjoying it? It must be very different for you.'

'I am, thank you. Are you ready for me?'

'Yes. I'm a bit nervous. My last smear was quite painful. I hope you don't mind if I just keep chatting. It helps to take my mind off what's happening.'

Abigail ventured behind the curtain. Chrissie was on the couch, lower half of her body covered with an unfolded sheet. Her clothes were neatly folded on the adjacent chair.

'No, that's fine. I'll try to be extra gentle and take things nice and slowly. Just tell me if you want me to stop so that you can relax more. There are just a couple of things I need to know in order to fill this form in completely. When was your last period, please, and when was your last smear. We don't seem to have any notes for you as yet.'

'I've not been a patient here for long. The date of my last smear is in my diary. I can get you that in a trice but as for my last period, I can't remember. I have one of those implants and I don't think I've had any bleeding at all since it was fitted. It's been great.'

'Okay, right now can you lie back and try to relax. Keep talking if it helps. Good, and now draw up your knees and then let them flop apart. A little bit more. Try not to be so tense. That's better. Thanks.'

'You must be pleased to have come to such a good practice,' Chrissie said, the pitch of her voice rising slightly as Abigail embarked on the procedure.

'I am. This next bit is going to feel a bit cold.'

'And in such a lovely part of the country. What a wonderful place to practice.'

'Yes.' Abigail was concentrating.

'Do you live in Lambdale? Ouch!'

'Sorry. I just need to move this a little bit to see your cervix more clearly. No. I'm staying with a friend who lives about ten miles from here.'

The sound of a plastic ratchet being turned made Chrissie feel nauseous.

'Okay. The other doctors here seem very pleasant.'

'They are.'

'I bet they all live locally, don't they? They'd have to, wouldn't they?'

'Yes – nearly finished.'

'Good. Whose is that neat little sports car in the car park? Is it yours?'

'Done! I wish! No, that's Dr Bonnington's.'

'Really? I was sure it would either be yours or perhaps I thought that young male doctor's. What's his name again? Can I get dressed now?'

'Of course. I think you must be meaning Dr Diamond. He's my trainer. His is the Golf. He cycles to work a lot of the time though. One of those keep-fit types. Not that he has to cycle very far. He only lives in one of those cottages down by the river.'

'Thank you so much. That was much better than last time. Those cottages are really pretty. Tiny though.'

'Well, he lives on his own, so I expect there's plenty of room for one.'

Abigail finished packaging up the smear. 'Your result will come to you in the post. It should be in about two to three weeks. If you've heard nothing within a month, then give us a call and we can chase it up for you.'

'You've been very kind. Apologies again for being such a wimp and gibbering on like a mad woman.'

'Don't mention it. We all hate having our smears done. All being well, that's it for the next three years but never hesitate to come back sooner if you've any abnormal bleeding.'

'I won't. Thanks again.'

'Bye,' smiled Abigail, thankful to see the last of her patients leaving the room.

All in all it had been a good surgery. A few issues to reflect on with Ed, something she now looked forward to. She scribbled a list, checking on the computer for names, so that they could review notes. Yes, she definitely wanted to discuss the heart valve patient. The child who had vomited would doubtless make him laugh. There was a prescribing query and a need for some advice about a referral. Then of course, she must tell him about Sylvia. She'd need plenty of ideas as to how best to conduct the follow-up appointment as the thought of it was already making her a little anxious. And that last patient, what was she called? Oh yes, Chrissie. She was just a smear so that was fine. She'd never stopped talking just for that simple procedure. She'd been quite nosy really. Goodness only knows what she'd be like if she'd had any other problems. Anyway, there was enough to discuss for two tutorials without her, let alone one.

Abigail slipped the list into her diary and packed up her bag. She was desperate for a drink and a piece of that chocolate.

Ed was waiting upstairs for her, standing at the window, watching John put his bag into the boot of his car before driving off on his visits. Ellie had departed on hers some time ago and Faith was covering emergency appointments and telephone calls, so he was alone, cradling a cup of tea in his hands.

'Hi, all well?' he greeted his registrar. 'Kettle's just boiled.'

'Fine. Sorry I'm late.'

'It's not a problem. That's what happens. Get a drink and then let's sit down and talk. The others are all out or busy, so we'll not be disturbed up here. What's that? Chocolate? Another grateful patient?'

Abigail blushed and explained, breaking off a chunk and offering it to him.

'Just the job,' he munched. 'Now, where shall we start?'

145

14

'Clare, there is absolutely no way that I am going to let you go back to work.'

Professor Corbett was writing in her notes as he spoke, carefully documenting his findings and recommendations. He snapped the top of his fountain pen back in place with an air of finality. It's now or never, thought Clare, plucking up her courage for one last-ditch attempt at a reprieve. She leant towards him.

'My partners are really understanding. I'm sure they'd just let me do some short surgeries. There'd be no pressure on me to do house calls or anything like that...'

Her words tailed off to nothing as he turned to her and peered over the top of his glasses that were perched on the very end of his nose. His look said it all. This was a non-negotiable situation. Taking off his glasses and twirling them around with one hand, he sat back in his chair and pushed her notes to one side.

'You are impossible, Clare. I know that you're a very committed and gifted GP and I admire your determination to work if you can. However, not for the first time, let's look at the facts before us. You are thirty weeks pregnant now. You've already had a fairly significant bleed. Your blood pressure is up and is higher today than it has been previously. You have oedematous feet and ankles and you've had to take your wedding ring off because your fingers are swollen also.'

Clare glanced down at the cheap costume jewellery ring that David had bought her to be a temporary replacement for her wedding ring. It was gold coloured with a row of large, imitation diamonds. She'd hoped the professor would not spot it.

'I've seen it all before,' he told her, reading her mind. 'Luckily there's no protein in your urine but there's no way that we're going to take any chances with you and your baby.'

Clare sighed. 'I know you're right. But I'm so bored just sitting at home on my own all day. Perhaps they could send some paperwork for me to do.'

'You're incorrigible. Perhaps they could send a few patients round and you could consult from the living room. Of course they can't. You've got to face it, Clare, and get used to the idea that you will not be going back to work before the baby's born.'

'What if my blood pressure comes down?' she asked optimistically.

'Then we'll be delighted and it will be proof that the rest is doing you good, so it must continue.'

Clare scratched her head and sighed, prepared now to capitulate.

'Okay. You're the boss. I'll ring and let them know.'

'Good girl. You've not that long to go. The time will fly past. Read all those books you've always wanted to read but never had time for.'

A look of disbelief fluttered across Clare's face and he laughed.

'It will. Make the most of it, when the baby arrives, you'll have plenty to occupy your every waking, and most of your sleeping moments. Right, now I need to see you in a week but I'll make sure your midwife – it's Marjorie isn't it? – comes and sees you at home in a few days. She can ring me if she's any concerns. Any questions?'

'Just one,' Clare began, 'can you recommend any good books? I've exhausted all the ones we've got at home.'

She levered herself out of the chair and rubbed her back. The baby kicked indignantly.

'I'm very partial to a good detective novel myself,' confessed the Professor. 'Take good care and I'll see you very soon.'

Clare stood at the open door. 'Thanks – sorry if I was awkward.'

He waved her away. 'I've forgotten already. Now off you go. If I see David at lunchtime, I'll give him a list of titles for you.'

'You're very kind, thanks again. Bye.'

The waiting area was still quite full and Clare tried not to make eye contact with any of the other women, some of whom were giving her impatient looks, wondering why she had been called in to be seen when she'd arrived after them and then had had the audacity to take up so much time. Music was playing softly in the background, melodic and gentle, supposedly soothing and calming but mostly difficult to hear as it was drowned out by the constant chatter of patients, the screams of toddlers as they disembowelled the toy box and the bustling of busy staff who kept scurrying past. There was a weary-looking lady waiting to take a tray of tea and coffee in for the professor. Clare smiled at her, hoping to cheer her up.

'I think you could go in now. He'll need a strong drink after seeing me.'

There was little reaction, simply a bemused look before she tapped softly on the door and then had to knock again, more assertively.

Clare made her appointment and then ambled off to the Department of Psychiatry to find David, who had promised her a lift home when he had finished his own clinic. He'd wanted to come with her, offering to cancel some of his patients, but Clare had put her foot down, assuring him there was no need, her secret hope being that she might just have been able to persuade Professor Corbett to let her go back to work if she was alone, there being not the slightest hope if David were there, backing up his every word. Still, she'd tried and if she were honest, she was actually glad that work had been vetoed as, though she would never admit it, she did feel extremely tired at times.

The aroma of chips met her as she rounded a corner, not far from the hospital restaurant, reminding her how hungry she was. In the distance, she saw Zoë Ferguson marching purposefully down the corridor towards her, but on recognising her stopped and greeted her warmly.

'Clare, how nice to see you again. How are you?'

'Fine, thanks. I've just come from the clinic. If you ignore the fact that my blood pressure's high and my toes and fingers have mysteriously been replaced by sausages then I'm in great shape.'

'You're looking well, anyway. So that's good. You're in good hands with the Prof – he's the very best, you know.'

'I do know that. I'm just a bit peeved that he's told me that I've to finish work. I've already been off what seems like a lifetime and it's really boring. Any way, never mind me, how are you? Are you enjoying your new job?'

'Clare, I love it. I'm so thrilled to have got the post here. It's busy, of course, but that's how I like it and I've lots of plans for the department that I can't wait to get started on.'

'Sounds great. I'd love to hear all about it. I know, why don't you come for supper on Saturday, if you're free? Nothing fancy, but it'd be wonderful to have some company.'

'Are you sure? I mean, I don't want to put you under any pressure.'

Zoë looked concerned and Clare was quick to reassure her.

'Please come. I promise I won't do a thing. David will be doing the cooking – he's very accomplished, so long as he keeps it simple. I'll sit with my feet up all the time and you can report back to the Prof just how good I'm being. Please?'

'Go on then, I'd love to,' Zoë accepted after a pause. 'But I'll ring on Saturday morning just to check that it's still okay to come.'

'That'd be great. I'll really look forward to it and I'm sure David will too.'

Feeling decidedly more cheerful, Clare walked more confidently towards David's office. Cicely, his secretary, in the throes of dealing with what sounded like a most complex telephone call, mouthed hello as Clare entered her office and motioned for her to sit down.

'Yes, I know that it's very difficult for you and of course I'll pass the message on to Dr Jennings as soon as he's free. Shall I ask him to ring you back? He might not be able to until this afternoon. Give me your number. Right, cheerio for now.'

'Phew,' Cicely scribbled furiously in her notebook. 'I really don't know how David copes with all this lot sometimes. Some of them are so demanding and rude when they ring up.'

She was a motherly sort of woman, with comforting curves to her anatomy that suggested homeliness rather than sexuality. With a fondness for grey, possibly to match her curly hair, today she was clad in a turtle-neck jumper of that colour and a slightly darker skirt, the only brightness in her ensemble being a large cameo brooch which she wore above her left breast and which wobbled incongruously as she took each breath. As a secretary she was largely very reliable but had a penchant every now and then for forgetting something rather important, which David, even with his endless patience, found infuriating and he would come home in one of his rare bad moods, only to be mollified the next day by her abject apologies and a return to her usual high standard of service. He was well aware that her attributes well outweighed her downsides and was content to keep her working for him. He also knew that she was a single woman, never married, with little money to speak of, working towards the day when she could retire on a full and reasonable pension after decades of working at the hospital. There was no way he could have been so cruel as to crucify this small ambition.

'Would you like me to make you a cuppa?' Cicely eyed Clare from around her computer screen, pencil stuck behind one ear, protruding like an antenna.

'I don't think so, thanks. Do you think he'll be long?'

Her question was answered by David's timely arrival. He bent down and kissed Clare on the lips and patted her abdomen, quite happy with this public demonstration of affection.

'Everything okay, darling?'

Clare felt a glow of love.

'Baby's fine, but I've to finish work completely.'

'Good.' David turned his attention to a pile of letters that Cicely was wafting in front of him, wanting signatures on them all and a clutch of papers riddled with messages of one sort or another. Clare carried on talking while he appended each letter with his neat italic writing.

'I met Zoë in the corridor as I was coming here. I've asked her for supper this weekend. You don't mind do you?'

'That sounds like a splendid idea. Why don't we invite the others as well. It'd give her a chance to meet a few folk. Right, I'm done. Let's get you home. Cicely, I'll deal with these messages when I get back. I'll not be above an hour at the most. If there's anything urgent, I've got my mobile.'

Marjorie deemed that Clare was fit to entertain friends when she visited on Saturday morning and spent a considerable amount of time drinking coffee and eating cake. She pronounced Clare's blood pressure to be a little better and expressed pleasure that her legs were less swollen. Having spent all of Friday virtually horizontal on the settee, planning a menu and writing a shopping list – it had been a challenge to get the Biro to work when upside down – Clare was grateful that her strategy had been a success. Ellie and Ian had been delighted to accept, offering to bring dessert. Ed too, had needed no persuading and nor had John and Faye. Only Faith and Rob were unable to come. They had set off on holiday the day before, heading for the west coast of Scotland. Originally, Faith had wanted to go somewhere abroad, with guaranteed good weather, where they could sit out in the sun, relax, read and swim. Rob had pleaded with her for an alternative destination. For someone like him, who liked to be active, the very thought of a sun lounger made him feel prickly. With the additional problem of a fair, freckly skin which burnt after the merest brush with the sun, a lie and fry holiday was just the worst thing he could imagine. At first, Faith had stood her ground but then surrendered without hesitation after seeing a patient who had a malignant melanoma, and agreed to his suggestion, placated by the thought of an hotel with an award-winning restaurant, leisure complex and swimming pool, to say nothing of the local scenic delights.

So there would just be the eight of them for supper and informality was the order of the evening. David was going to cook steaks and serve them with jacket potatoes and a mixed salad with a mustard dressing. He was more than capable of this, plus Ellie would need no encouragement to help out were he to run into trouble. For dessert, Clare had suggested he bought a cheesecake from Delicious to go with whatever Ellie brought – which would doubtless be creamy, unhealthy but simply delectable. Following instructions, he had done but then had fallen foul of temptation as he discovered that they were now selling local ice cream. Six tubs now sat squatly in their freezer, each one a different flavour and Clare's mouth watered at the thought of tasting them. Usually it was David who was the ice-cream fanatic but pregnancy had made her crave just about everything edible, particularly if it was sweet. As she watched David starting to make preparations, she felt ridiculously excited at the thought of the approaching evening. How sad was she becoming when having a few friends around seemed like the best thing that had happened for months?

David insisted that she went upstairs to rest in the afternoon, despite her promises that she could do so in the lounge and be near him in the kitchen if he needed any advice. He was having none of it. Gently but firmly, he accompanied her to the bedroom, pulled back the duvet and settled her beneath it, where, to her surprise, she fell asleep in no time, waking, much in the manner of the Sleeping Beauty, when he came and kissed her softly and told her that there was time for a shower and hair wash before their guests arrived. She settled on some smart-ish trousers and a smock top that did not make her look too balloon like, giving up on any sort of footwear as none of her shoes seemed to fit. She made a mental note to ask Ellie to come and paint her toenails, a job that physically was no longer possible. Barely able to see her feet when she was standing up, there was no way that she could reach them to perform cosmetic duties.

Everyone's so kind, thought Clare, as she gratefully sniffed a large bunch of flowers from John and Faye. Other gifts arrived in the form of wickedly delicious chocolates from Ellie and Ian and a pile of DVDs from Ed. A raspberry and kiwi pavlova had been delivered to the kitchen.

'The girls arranged the fruit,' Ellie explained. 'They'd just had a big argument. That's why one half is all kiwi and the other all raspberry. They thought it looked cool.'

Zoë was last to arrive, bearing a bag which turned out to contain a selection of detective novels. Clare burst out laughing.

'No prizes for guessing who you've been talking to!'

'Well, I did happen to mention that I was coming here tonight,' Zoë confessed. 'I've brought you this plant as well. Now that really is from me.'

'Oh, an orchid,' breathed Clare. 'How gorgeous.'

'It's really easy to look after and looks great. Thanks for the invite tonight. It's good to get away from the hospital. I've been working so hard, I think I've gone a bit stir crazy.'

'Please, come in and meet the others. What would you like to drink?'

It was simply the best evening Clare could recall having since she had fallen pregnant. Nobody seemed to be the slightest fazed by her lying resplendent on the settee, rather like an ancient Roman at a feast and Zoë was chattering away, full of self confidence before she had even finished her first glass of red wine. David was enjoying himself too, bedecked in a striped butchers' apron, wandering back and forth, topping up glasses and brandishing tongs as he took orders for how his guests would like their steak cooked. Plans to eat at the table were abandoned. It was easier to balance plates on laps, sitting round in a circle, conversation unbroken, laughter increasing. Halfway through pudding, when Clare was devouring a substantial helping of pavlova (two slices – well she had to try each topping), Ellie caught her eye and inclined her head minutely to one side, glancing that way simultaneously. Clare, following her gaze, saw Ed and Zoë deep in an animated discussion. They looked relaxed and happy. Clare and Ellie shared a conspiratorial half smile and returned their attentions to the equally important matter of meringue.

Their assumption was correct. Ed was having a really good time. He'd had no idea that there was going to be anyone else there apart from the usual suspects. Zoë was proving to be something of a revelation, the last thing he'd expected to find when he'd set off from home. She was easy to talk to, funny, intelligent and astute. A little like Hannah, but different. Her short hair was softer and the cut flattering to her heart- shaped face. And it wasn't just her hair that was more feminine; even in her casual clothes, he could detect that she had a good figure. These were differences Ed found that he approved of. Pretty too. No, not beautiful but definitely pretty and he liked the way she had dressed, jeans and a sleeveless top, the sort that really deserves toned arms, which Zoë had, thanks to years of tennis and lacrosse. When she took off her glasses to mop up the tears that were streaming down her cheeks after one of Ian's hysterically funny stories, Ed noticed that she had deep blue eyes and if he wasn't mistaken, didn't they sparkle just that little bit more when they looked into his? She was a good listener too, genuinely interested to hear about not just the practice but more personal details such as his hobbies and they discovered a mutual love of walking but her confession to a fear of heights made climbing, for her, a non-starter.

'I'm full of admiration for you, Ed,' she told him as he offered the chance to give it a try, 'but there's just no way that I could even try a practice wall in a gym. I can get vertigo on the first rung of a ladder.'

'We ought to do this regularly,' Ellie advocated as she rummaged through the chocolates that she had brought, looking for a soft caramel. 'Then it'll give Clare something to look forward to. My house next time.'

The proposal was carried unanimously and Clare beamed at them all, touched by their magnanimity. She felt exhausted but sublimely happy, full of good food. The baby had twirled and kicked the entire evening – obviously a party animal in the making – and Ed was looking more cheerful than she had seen him for a long time. As Ellie hugged her good bye she whispered, 'Let's keep our fingers crossed that Zoë and Ed keep in touch. Don't you think they look good together?'

Clare nodded emphatically.

Ed, sitting back in the taxi, was in complete agreement. Pleasantly light headed, but far from drunk, he was definitely determined to get to know Zoë better. It had been neither the time nor the place to swap contact details as they were leaving. He had not wanted to embarrass her in front of his partners and so he had simply kissed her on both cheeks, in exactly the same way he did with Clare, Faye and Ellie. A stranger observing would have thought he was doing no more than bid farewell to a group of close friends. Only Ed knew that when his lips brushed against the softness of her skin his stomach had performed an excited lurch of anticipation. As he got ready for bed – a quick shower and then a cup of tea while he stroked the cats, he found that he was unable to stop thinking about her. He could still smell the discreet perfume that she had been wearing and feel the touch of her hands on his arms as they had said goodbye. The dramatic effect she had had on him amazed and stirred him. The power of the emotion was both exciting and frightening, the promise of things that may be to come, the fear of failure if he was knocked back. Nothing ventured, nothing gained and he made a mental note to ring Clare in the morning, give his thanks for a splendid evening and then ask her for Zoë's number.

15

His plans were thwarted the next morning when repeated attempts to phone Clare were met with David's voice on the answering machine each time. Tactfully, but impatiently, having waited until almost midday before he rang, Ed became anxious, his desire to contact Zoë replaced by a fervent hope that nothing was wrong. A quick call to Ellie provided the answer. Clare was back at the hospital. She'd spent most of the night vomiting and a urinary tract infection was suspected.

'But she was on such good form last night,' Ed wailed.

Ellie concurred. 'I spoke to David briefly. He'd come back to pack a bag for her as she's to stay in overnight. He sounded worn out. I don't think either of them had any sleep.'

'Poor Clare, she's having a miserable pregnancy. Anything I can do?' asked Ed.

'I think everything's in hand, as far as I can tell. I'm sure David will ring me later, so I'll get back to you on that one.'

Thus Ed was forced to put his plans on hold and he spent his Sunday catching up with the boring necessities of home life, such as washing and housework, all the while trying to come up with a creditable Plan B that would get him in touch with Zoë. He slept poorly, still undecided as what to do.

Fate's more sensitive side must have been touched by his plight for the second patient on Monday morning was a perimenopausal woman who was on the waiting list for a hysterectomy, having been found to have a large mass of fibroids that were sitting on and irritating her bladder. She was worn out by nights disrupted by trips to the bathroom and days pervaded by a continuous low abdominal gripe. Desperate to know when her operation would be, she had come to see Ed and implore him to try to expedite her admission. Ed's heart leapt when he enquired who her consultant was and received the answer that it was the new one, Miss Ferguson. Whilst a letter faxed through to the secretary would have been perfectly adequate, Ed was champing at the bit to go one better and, being the concerned GP that he was, take the opportunity to discuss the case with the consultant in question.

He rang after racing through the rest of his surgery, eager to get to the end, his pulse accelerating. Switchboard informed him that Miss Ferguson was in theatre but that a message would be left for her to return his call at her earliest convenience. Barely able to contain his nerves, he slopped coffee all over his desk and gave Abigail free rein to pick which visits she wanted rather than vet them all himself first and choose those which might be educational for her. When his phone finally did ring, he snatched it up hungrily.

'Hi, Zoë, it's Ed Diamond.'

'Ed, how nice to hear from you.'

'Sorry to disturb you when you're operating.'

'No problem, I'm having a coffee between cases. What can I do for you?'

'Primarily, I'm calling about Mrs Halliwell. Do you remember her?'

'Forty-eight year old with huge fibroids.'

'That's the one.' Ed was impressed and went on to appeal for an earlier operation.

'I'll see what I can do. At the very least, I'll give her a ring and explain, perhaps offer to review her in the clinic. Would that be okay?'

'More than okay. Thanks, Zoë.'

He held his breath for a moment. 'Zoe?'

'I'm still here.' The tone of her voice suggested that she was smiling, he thought.

'I was wondering if you'd like to go out for a meal this weekend. There are some great restaurants around here that I'd love to show you.'

Her answer was instantaneous. 'Yes please. Look, they're calling for me to go back into theatre as the next patient's on the table, so here's my number. Call me tonight? I'll be home by seven.'

Replacing the receiver, Ed felt triumphant. She'd sounded as enthusiastic as he was. Where to take her? That was the next question. He'd found out some facts about her but not what she liked to eat and drink. The Golden Dog? That was certainly one of his favourites but also the last place he took Hannah. Too many memories. Better to opt for elsewhere, somewhere neutral for them both. He'd ask the others, something which doubtless would result in some ribbing when they found out who he was taking but between them they would come up with somewhere that would fit the bill.

A knock on his door and Joan's head appeared.

'Sorry to bother you, Ed, but there's another house call request come in. Would you be able to take it? You've already got one at Cherry Tree House and this one's just down the road from there.'

'Sure,' agreed Ed who at that moment in time would have happily offered to do everyone's house calls plus one on the other side of the world. 'Who's asked for me at Cherry Tree?'

'Kathleen Clarke. Back pain. Oh, and she wants her blood pressure checking.'

'Fine, print me off a list of them all and I'll be on my way.'

It was a dry day, with a mostly cloudy sky but enough blue to bring out the tourists who were determined to make the most of their holidays. The market square was packed and there wasn't a spare chair to be had outside Delicious where anorak-clad visitors, unfolding and studying maps of the locality, were planning their next moves. For once, Ed was not envious of their delicately iced but huge pastries the size of spades and cups of foaming cappuccino as he drove past. Nothing could better the way he felt and more importantly nothing could spoil it. There was no need to hurry for once, so he took his time, stopping to visit first of all a new mum with mastitis. As he made his way up the drive to the house, a detached new build in a small cul-de-sac of matching properties, he wondered why she had not come to surgery and thought about trying to challenge her on this subject, his own personal bugbear.

No sooner was he through the front door than the answer was obvious. Pandemonium reigned. Nearing half past eleven, she was still in her dressing gown, had matted hair which looked as though it had had no contact with a brush for days, vomit over one shoulder and a screaming red-faced baby being patted over the other. Sleep had abandoned her with the arrival of her son, her face was blotchy and her eyes were bleary and bloodshot. The floor of the hall, lounge and stairs was strewn with toys, books and discarded clothes, doubtless the possessions of the toddler who was sitting on the large black leather settee, alternately smearing pieces of banana into the cushions or joining in with the cacophony blaring out of the television.

Her apologies were profuse. She'd been up all night, trying to soothe the baby who had colic and when he had finally nodded off just before dawn, her other child had called her, wide awake and ready for the day, batteries fully recharged after over ten hours of unbroken sleep. So her day had begun, when yesterday had never finished – it had all rolled into one relentless slog. Despite nipples that were so sore that they were cracked and bleeding, she really, really wanted to keep on breast feeding because it was so important for the baby's wellbeing but she didn't know how long she could keep this up. Even using the breast pump was excruciating. He'd have to have a bottle that morning to satiate his frantic hunger.

Vince, her husband, had gone back to work, for some peace and quiet so he said and who could blame him – and she would give anything for a little time to have a shower, some sleep and feel human again. So saying, she dissolved into a mass of weary sobs.

Ed listened, checked out the mastitis and scribbled a prescription for antibiotics before contacting her midwife and asking her to call as soon as possible. When he left, he wondered if he could have done more but short of cleaning, entertaining the two children and phoning the husband and ordering him to be more supportive there was nothing that fell strictly within his remit.

Still buoyant, he made a quick call to an old farmer with gout in one big toe before steering down the narrow lane to Cherry Tree House. Mrs Barnabas greeted him warmly, her hands floury from baking, an unidentifiable stain on her trousers and a blob of something that looked very like raspberry jam in her hair. Strains of melodies, popular during the Second World War, greeted Ed as he made his way across the hall. Automatically he glanced into the day room where a group of residents were sitting, their chairs arranged in a semicircle. Three of the more able were standing, one of these optimistically gripping onto her walking frame. A dictatorial woman, in a badly fitting tracksuit and with a sweat band around her forehead, was commanding them to lift their arms and point their toes, bend their knees and rotate their ankles, all the while shouting encouragement and singing along with snatches of the music.

'It's keep fit morning,' Mrs Barnabas explained. 'That's Dorothy. She sounds very gruff, but they love her really.'

Ed had his doubts, if the looks on faces were to be believed but smiled politely and muttered words along the lines of how good it was that they were trying to maintain flexibility and agility as far as was possible.

'That's Ethel.' Mrs Barnabas pointed to a tiny sparrow of a woman who was fast asleep. 'She insists on going every week but nods off before they've barely had a chance to get going, bless her. At the end, she wakes up and always says how much better she feels.'

'I take it Kathleen Clarke's not joining in,' commented Ed as Mrs Barnabas made for the stairs.

'No, her back's very bad. It has been for a few days. I thought you ought to come and see her.'

'Of course.'

They made their way up the stairs. Mrs Barnabas knocked on and opened the door simultaneously.

'Here we are! Coo-ee, Kath, dear, it's the doctor.'

Sitting in a chair by the window, Kathleen formed a diminutive figure, her warped spine forcing her body into an even tighter ball than Ed remembered. She was watching something outside through a pair of binoculars but turned her head painfully to see her visitor.

'Dr Diamond, how nice to see you. Come over here so that I don't have to move from this chair. You can go, Mrs Barnabas. I want to talk to the doctor in private.'

'Most of the residents here like me to stay, in case they don't hear properly.'

'Good for them. There might be plenty wrong with me but my hearing happens to one system that's intact, so there's no worry. See you later.'

Mrs Barnabas was swatted away like an annoying insect might have been. She looked more than a little miffed to have been dismissed. Waiting until the door was closed properly, Kathleen kept silent and Ed pulled up a chair opposite her.

'So, how's it going?' he asked as an opener.

'Not much better,' was the terse reply. 'But I'm making the best of it. I've just been watching the birds on the bird table down there. Some days there's a woodpecker. It passes the time.'

'What about your Scrabble?' asked Ed, following her gaze out of the window.

'I've even started a Scrabble session. It was becoming very pre-dictable playing Doreen every day. A couple of the others are really quite good.'

'Well done, you. What's all this about a bad back?'

'Yes, it's been murder for three days. Here.'

She pointed to the lower part, wincing from the effort this required.

'Tell me some more about the pain.'

'Such as?'

'Does it come and go? Is it there all the time? What makes it worse or better? That sort of thing.'

Kathleen's eyes darted from side to side.

'Hard to say as it always aches, no matter what.' Kathleen beckoned for him to come closer. 'Don't tell anyone but I had a fall.'

'When?'

'Three days ago. Hurrying to the toilet. Didn't see my handbag and tripped over the damn thing. Took me an age to get back up, in fact I'd probably still be on the floor if it hadn't been for Tina arriving and helping me. I had to make her promise not to tell anyone. She wanted to ring you but I said no, I'd ask for you to come out myself.'

Shaking his head slightly, Ed examined her as best he could. She winced as he palpated the small of her back.

'You've probably fractured a vertebra,' he pronounced. 'Your bones are so chalky, it won't take much to squash one. That would account for all the pain. I'll send you for an x-ray to check.'

'No, no, I don't want to go anywhere. If it's broken, there's nothing anyone can do. I know that because it's happened before. There's no way I'm going anywhere near that hospital. Once they get you in their clutches, the only way out's in a coffin. Just give me some stronger painkillers and I'll be fine.'

She was defiant and Ed knew better than to irk her by arguing. He could empathise with her point of view and knew she was right. An x-ray would indeed be of academic use only. He could keep her comfortable here, where she was relatively happy and definitely well looked after.

'You win. But be very careful with these new tablets. I'll tell Mrs Barnabas to give you one at a time to start with. If you feel okay, but still have pain, you can double the dose. How are your bowels? These are bound to constipate you, so I'll prescribe a laxative as well.'

'Nothing that'll have me dashing for the bathroom because, quite simply, I can't.'

Ed patted her hand. 'No, just one that'll make your stools soft and easy to pass.'

'A likely story,' Kathleen retorted and they both laughed.

'What's going on?' asked a voice. Ed turned and saw that Tina had arrived. 'All this laughter – can I share the joke?'

'It's nothing,' Kathleen placated her. 'Lavatorial humour. Best you don't get involved. Grab yourself a seat. Dr Diamond's just about to check my blood pressure.'

As usual, Tina had taken a lot of trouble over her appearance. For someone who was apparently spending most of her time poring over books and a computer screen, her outfit of short fitted skirt, bolero jacket and low cut t-shirt seemed incongruous, thought Ed, but then remonstrated with his thoughts. For all he knew, she might be on her way somewhere special, probably to meet someone. An image of Zoë flashed into his mind. How many hours until he could ring her? How many days were there to Saturday? Perhaps they could make it Friday. Less time to wait.

Forcing himself to concentrate on the matter in hand, he finished Kathleen's checks, declared that he was pleased with her progress in all respects other than her back and started to make the sort of comments that wind up a consultation.

'Tina, had the keep fit class finished?' Kathleen inquired.

'Yes. They were laying tables for lunch when I came in.'

'Good, then it must be time for sherry. Dr Diamond, would you do me the honour of escorting me down?'

'It would be my pleasure,' he replied sincerely.

Progress was slow, even to traverse her room, punctuated by pauses while she got her breath back and took some brief respite from the pain. At the door, Ed turned to go in the direction of the lift but Kathleen pulled him the opposite way, exclaiming that she wasn't ready to give in yet. He protested, tactfully explaining that to take the easy route would not be an expression of weakness and she acquiesced, tightened the grip she had around his arm and crept onwards, taking minute steps, each one more painful than the last. At the lift door, she shooed him off.

'It's bad enough in this pokey lift as it is and I don't like to feel too hemmed in. Tina, see Dr Diamond to the door. I'll be down shortly, though this moves so slowly lunch might be over before it gets to the ground floor. Thanks for coming, Doc. You always cheer me up.'

'My pleasure, Kathleen. I'll pop back in a few days and see how you're getting on with the new tablets.'

Tina walked with him to the stairs, her arm brushing against his. Putting her hand on his forearm to wait, she cleared her throat.

'I'm so worried about her. She's been in such pain. She never complains but I can see it in her eyes.'

'She's feisty. She'll cope and I'll keep a close watch. So will Mrs Barnabas. She's very perceptive. Just be glad she's here now and not still in that awful flat.'

He moved on, towards the door. Tina overtook, blocking his way and catching hold of his hand.

'She's all I've got, Ed. She means the world to me.'

'The feeling's mutual. You're lucky to have each other.'

'I need to talk with you about the future. Please...'

'Of course.' A quick glance at his watch confirmed that now was not a good time. 'Make an appointment to see me.'

'There's so much I need to say though.'

'Tell the receptionists what it's for and they'll book extra time. Now I really must go.'

As he departed through the door there was a shout from the top of the stairs.

'The bloody lift's broken again. Well, I couldn't get it to work, so I've had to come this way. No, don't come and help, Tina, wait for me there. I've got my own way of doing this. Aaaaaagh...'

A missed footing and she folded, an unwanted marionette tossed to one side, and somersaulted down the stairs, slowly to start with then gathering speed like a glissando. Ed heard Tina's cry from the other side of the car park, where he had just put his bag back in the boot and raced back in. Kathleen was in a heap on the carpet, Tina crouching over her, afraid to touch her, having no idea what to do. Alerted by her screams, Mrs Barnabas shot out of the kitchen and made a bee-line for the telephone. Ed knelt down, feeling for a pulse, relieved to find one. Kathleen was moaning quietly, her eyes flickering, a hand shakily reaching out for Ed's.

'Is she dead?' shrieked Tina.

'No, but we mustn't move her.'

He made a cursory check, not wanting to cause any undue pain.

'The ambulance is on its way,' Mrs Barnabas contributed, full of efficiency. 'I'll fetch a blanket to keep her warm.'

'Has she broken anything?'

'I can't be sure but I think there's a fair chance she's fractured her left femur. See how her foot is rotated outwards?'

'Is she going to die?' Tina was fast becoming hysterical.

'Not if I've got anything to do with it,' Kathleen croaked.

'Try to stay calm,' Ed advised. 'Let's just get her safely to the hospital and then we'll know more.'

'Bugger, I said I didn't want to go to there.'

'I'm sorry, Kathleen, but you really have no choice now.'

Mrs Barnabas rushed back and gently covered up Kathleen with a fleecy blanket.

'Careful, don't put it over my head, I've not gone yet, you know.'

'Such spirit,' muttered Mrs Barnabas, with admiration. 'I'll go and make some tea for us all. Best thing after a nasty shock.'

'I'd rather have my sherry.'

'Kathleen, I'm afraid that you're not having anything to drink. It's best you stay nil by mouth for now.'

She had started to shake, despite the blanket's warmth, as the magnitude of what had just happened sunk in. Another blanket was placed on top of the first, then a duvet. Tina, who was shaking nearly as much, sat down beside her and stroked her hair, muttered words that she hoped were reassuring and looked helplessly at Ed, who was willing the ambulance to arrive. But they were more than halfway through their second cups of tea when it did but the crew were speedy and adept, scooping Kathleen onto a stretcher and into the back of the vehicle with well-practised ease, all the while keeping up a cheery banter.

'Anyone coming with her?' asked one, while the other ran round to climb into the driver's seat and start up the engine.

'Tina?' asked Ed.

She looked bemused, still in shock, shifting her gaze from Ed to Mrs Barnabas to the ambulance.

'Tell you what,' suggested Mrs Barnabas. 'I'll go with her. You finish your tea and then follow on in your car. Don't be hurrying or doing anything silly. We'll see you in the Emergency department.'

So saying, she managed, at the third attempt, to get into the back of the ambulance and the doors closed behind them. It disappeared from sight, apart from the flashing blue light that was visible above the top of the hedges as it started off on the journey to the hospital.

Tina flopped onto the bottom but one step.

'Oh, my goodness. I don't know what to say.'

'You look terrible. Here, keep drinking this tea. She's in the right hands now, so let them take care of her.

Trembling, she accepted the cup which jiggled in its saucer.

'What will happen now?' she managed to ask, teeth chattering in unison with the cup.

'The doctors will see her. I expect she'll have to have x-rays and some blood tests. If she's fractured the neck of her femur, then she might need an operation. Even if nothing's broken, I'm sure they'll keep her in overnight at the very least.'

'She'll hate it,' Tina sniffed.

'Right at the moment, it's what she needs. She'll understand that.'

They sat in silence as Tina finished her tea.

'I feel a little better now, thanks. I'd better get after her. I always seem to be thanking you, but again, I'm grateful.'

She stood up and took a couple of steps, her legs still wobbly like a new-born foal. Afraid she was about to fall too, Ed reached out to steady her and before he knew it, she had thrown her body up against him, her head burrowing into his shoulder, her arms around his waist. If she felt him stiffen, then she ignored it and snuggled closer. Gently he extracted himself from her embrace, uncomfortable with her proximity, disliking the way she had forced her way into his personal body space, uninvited. Holding her at arms' length he looked at her. There was more colour in her cheeks now, which he took to be due to embarrassment and he let go, taking a couple of steps back to regain his territory.

'You're looking better. Do you feel able to drive?'

'Yes of course. I'd better get off. She'll be asking for me.'

'You know the way?'

She nodded, picked up her handbag which had been thrown aside and had somehow landed under the telephone table and walked past Ed to the door, pausing momentarily to look deep into his eyes.

'I'll keep you informed of what's happening,' she promised.

16

Why am I so ridiculously nervous? Ed asked himself repeatedly as he went round and round in circles trying to decide where to take Zoë. Each time he came up with what seemed to be a pleasing solution, a larger negative thought popped up in his brain. His first and automatic option, The Golden Dog, ticked all the boxes but, and it was a but of enormous proportions, still had connotations relating to Hannah, which he would not be able to ignore and he would feel full of trepidation before the evening started. The Pelican and Boat was far too posh – overwhelmingly so with minuscule portions of beautifully arranged food, attentive waiters who lurked, waiting to pounce, and a price tag that left the unwary breathless. Harvey's was a possibility and one of Ed's favourites. Great pizza and pasta but it was very popular with families and consequently noisily frenetic. The perfect place for a raucous night out and somewhere he would love to take Zoë in the future, fingers crossed, but not what was required for two people in the very early stages of getting to know each other. No, something more intimate was required, but not overly so. The ambience had to be such that he would be able to talk to Zoë and find out more about her, rather than shout at her and struggle to hear her replies.

The two central pubs in Lambdale would be a vibrant crush of patients and holiday makers, all vying for the attention of the barmaids, plus their menus were limited – great if you wanted a generously portioned bar meal, each one served with a bucket of chips, but Ed wanted food that was a shade more eclectic. No, he needed somewhere out of town but not too far, good food but not too expensive. The last thing he wanted was for Zoë to be uncomfortable in any way.

Exasperated by his indecision, he finally asked John and Ellie on the Wednesday for their advice, the latter immediately throwing a spanner into the works by suggesting that they go for a picnic instead. The weather forecast was promising to be good, she'd read. What could be more romantic? She offered to lend him her wicker picnic basket and had all sorts of ideas of what eatables to take – delicacies she could have conjured up in a moment with her eyes closed but that were way outside the range of Ed's basic but limited cooking skills. The mental image, however, Ed found captivating. Sitting on a tartan rug, chilled bottle of wine, crusty French bread exploding into a million crispy crumbs when bitten into – yes, Ed had no difficulty in seeing the appeal of this scenario. Only when John, slipping into the role of devil's advocate, started to talk about wasps, flies and ants did his balloon of fantasy pop.

But then it was John who ultimately saved the day and came up with the idea of the Millbank Arms. It was ten miles away and rather off the well-beaten tourist track. Faye has been a while before with some girlfriends for lunch and had been so impressed that she had taken her husband for his birthday and he had rated the place just as highly. Relieved, Ed rang immediately and booked a table before he could change his mind and then sat back to ponder over his next dilemma, that of what to wear. A suit? Too formal. Jeans? Too casual. A tie? What would she be wearing?

Ellie, teasing him, offered to ring Zoë and find out.

'Calm down, Ed. You're a good-looking bloke. Just wear some something you feel comfortable in. Chinos and a nice shirt, that cool jacket you bought earlier this summer.'

'Do you think that would be good enough?'

'It'd be fine. I'd be impressed if I was going out with you.'

'Thanks, Ellie. I don't know why I'm in this state. I can't remember being like this with Hannah,' Ed confessed.

'Do you still think about her?' Ellie asked.

After a pause, Ed nodded. 'More than I thought I would. It's weird. In some ways I still miss her hugely, but I know she's not right for me.'

'It's always hard keeping a long-distance relationship going. She was obviously hell bent on her career. I don't think she'd have let anything or anyone come between her and it.'

'It's true, Ellie. I always felt that it was me making all the running. There's more to having a relationship. Look at you and Ian – you're so good together that you seem to merge into each other. That's what I want to find. I think that's why I feel this night out with Zoë is so important. Something about her, and I can't define what, touched me. I haven't felt this way for such a long time, I really want it to be a success.'

'Personally, I think it's rather sweet that you're all on edge. Just relax and go with the flow as they say. Remember how well the two of you got on at Clare's. It'll be a million times easier to chat when we're all not watching you. I liked her a lot, so did Ian and he's usually a very good judge of character. If your evening turns out to be a disaster, which I doubt that it will, then at least you'll have a good meal and if it's not then that's great. Have fun. You deserve some. Don't forget to ring me on Saturday morning to tell me how it went. That is of course, unless the evening together turns into a weekend together...' Her voice was suggestive.

He laughed.

'That's better!' Ellie congratulated him. 'Just enjoy, okay?'

'I intend to. Hey, look at the time, I'm going to the registrars' meeting at the hospital and I promised Abigail a lift. See you later?'

'Yes, sure. Are you popping in to see Clare? Call me anytime if you want some more fashion advice.'

Leaving the room, he ruffled her thick auburn hair in gratitude and she giggled. What a relief it was to see Ed looking more like his old self again. Since his break-up with Hannah, he had assumed a sort of haggard and haunted look, aged ten years and even his sense of humour had deserted him. From a personal point of view, Ellie, while finding Hannah a pleasant enough but scarily intelligent woman, had never thought that Ed had found a good match. Of course they shared common ground with their love of outdoor sports but there was something cold and almost clinical about her from the way she dressed to the way she conducted her strictly organised life. Nor had she never shown Ed any spontaneous affection in public. Ellie had lost count of the times she had seen Ed put his arm around Hannah's shoulders or kissed her on the cheek. He was that type of guy, open, honest and caring. Eager to give, but needing his feelings to be reciprocated equally. Not once had she seen Hannah take the initiative when it came to any show of fondness and for Ellie, whose life revolved around warmth, love and trust, this struck her as highly suspicious.

Ed sang along with the radio as he eased his car out of the rather tight space that some injudicious parking by a patient had left him with and leant across to open the door for Abigail. She kept up a steady diatribe about some house call that she'd been on, only to find that there was no one in, as they drove to the hospital which Ed, if he were truthful, would have to admit that he was only listening to with one ear. He was looking forward to the meeting and the drug company-sponsored lunch that would precede it. If he sneaked out just before the meeting finished there would be time to see Clare, who, he knew, would be tearing her hair out with frustration at being confined to a hospital bed. There was always the possibility, he mused, that he might just bump into Zoë... Not that this was in any way an ulterior motive for going to the obstetric department.

He found her as he predicted. Looking grumpy, Clare was whipping through the pages of a magazine, barely looking at its contents and sighing loudly. She was in a side ward, a privilege granted to her because she was a doctor but in many ways she would have preferred to be on the main ward where at least there would be other mums-to-be to talk to. An intravenous line was attached to her left forearm, leading to a bag of saline which monotonously dripped silently into the giving set. On the closet beside her bed were a photograph of David, an ultrasonic image of her baby and a vase full of flowers. On the table, which had been pushed to one side, lay a tray. A plate bore the remnants of a gravy-embossed main course and a pudding bowl which had been scraped clean. Back on the bed, beside her, was a half-empty packet of chocolate biscuits and a box of Maltesers.

Tapping softly on the door, he watched her look up and her face soften with pleasure at the sight of him.

'Ed, how wonderful! I didn't think I'd get any visitors until this evening.'

He went over and kissed her on the cheek.

'How're things? What's the drip for?'

'I've still got this stupid urine infection. The oral antibiotics didn't work and I started to have some contractions. Boy, was that frightening. I thought I was going into labour. I'm only thirty weeks. So now I've got to have i-v antibiotics. What a nightmare! I thought I'd only be in overnight.'

'Have the contractions stopped?'

'Yes, thank goodness. With any luck this,' she flicked the intravenous line with distaste, 'will be coming down later today. Then I've to have another scan, to check on the baby's growth. I must say this enforced rest has certainly made my ankles better.'

So saying, she produced one of her feet from under the untidy bedclothes and waved it around for Ed to admire.

'My blood pressure's been better too. I think I'm rapidly becoming Professor Corbett's worst patient as there's always something wrong with me. I don't know who'll be more relieved when this baby's born, him or me! Never mind all that, I'm sick of thinking about it. What's your news?'

She patted the bed, indicating for Ed to sit down.

'I've just been at the registrars' teaching session. It was quite good

– all about how to use the chemical pathology department. When to request investigations, how much they cost – stuff like that.'

'I hope Abigail was there taking notes,' Clare grinned, feeling better by the second for having someone to talk to. She offered him a biscuit, which he accepted.

'Yes, she was,' Ed replied, munching. 'She's been a lot better recently. Seems to be enjoying herself a bit, though she might not admit it. There's been some good feed back from patients about her.'

'That's great,' Clare enthused. 'Well done, Ed. It's all thanks to you.'

He shrugged modestly. 'I don't know about that. By the way, thanks so much for last Saturday evening. It was great.'

'I can't believe it was only a few days ago. It feels I've been stuck in this bed for a lifetime. I'm so glad you enjoyed yourself. You seemed to be getting on very well with Zoë.'

'I really liked her, Clare. I'm taking her out the day after tomorrow.'

Clare bit her top lip in an attempt not to smile.

'I know. She told me! She's popped in to see me a few times.'

'Really?' Ed was elated. He looked over his shoulder at the doorway, optimistically. This was surely a sign that she was looking forward to the meal as much as he was.

'Really,' Clare repeated emphatically. 'She sounded very excited. Where are you taking her?'

Ed described his dilemma and Clare nodded her approval at his final decision.

'I've never been there but there was an excellent review in the Yorkshire Post a couple of months ago.'

She pushed the box of Maltesers towards him, grabbing a handful first.

'I'm sure you'll have a great time. I'll be thinking of you – hopefully from the comfort of my own bed, or if I'm particularly lucky, I might be allowed to graduate onto the settee.'

'How's David?' Ed asked.

'Fine. Away giving a lecture today in Leeds, but he'll be in tonight. I feel so sorry for him. He keeps looking at me helplessly because he wants to make everything all right but can't. Thank goodness he's a psychiatrist. I don't think he'd be able to cope with obstetrics.'

'He's going to be a great dad,' Ed assured her. 'Just like you're going to be a brilliant mum. Hey, talking of new mums, I went on this visit the other day...'

Clare's face was screwed up with horror as she listened to his account of the patient with mastitis and she protectively cupped her hands over her own swollen breasts.

'Ed! You're supposed to be here to cheer me up!'

Chastised, Ed told her about Kathleen Clarke.

'You're joking! How dreadful! How is she?'

'She's on Flamborough ward. She did have a fractured neck of femur and had a hip replacement yesterday. I have no idea what her prognosis is. With bones as badly affected by osteoporosis as hers, I wonder if she'll ever walk again.'

'Will she be able to go back to Cherry Tree House? It's just a residential home, not nursing.'

'I know. She'd more or less settled there. Well, maybe I'll clarify that statement by saying that she was making the best of it. She'd be horrified if she had to move again.'

'Are you going in to see her while you're here?' Clare asked.

'I might,' Ed admitted, glancing at his watch. 'I'm a bit tight for time.'

'I don't mind if you want to go now. It's been great just having you here for a bit and hearing what's been going on in the real world.'

'Are you sure?' Ed was hesitant.

'Yes, of course. Have another Malteser to see you on your way. I'll ring you when I get home.'

She blew him a kiss and he waved, pausing at the door, feeling sorry for leaving her when he knew full well that she was just putting on a brave face for him. He could see through her bravado that she was afraid, hating the fact that she was the patient rather than the doctor, wanting to rebel but compelled to acquiesce for fear of putting the new little life inside her at any risk.

There was no sign of Zoë as he made his way out of the ward and he felt ridiculously disappointed. He even stood and skimmed through the leaflets on the notice board, hoping that she might just make an entrance if he waited a few moments more. Still no sign and common sense informed him that she was probably in clinic or operating so he contented himself with a quick mental calculation of how many hours were left until Friday evening.

He had five minutes before he was due to meet Abigail in the main foyer of the building and reckoned that this was just enough time to visit Flamborough ward and get the latest update on Kathleen. A ward round was just finishing. Gareth Pickering, consultant orthopaedic surgeon, was issuing final instructions to the sister in charge of the ward. Gareth was gigantic in height and width, the muscle from his rugby-playing days having been replaced by fat with the passage of time. His hair was all over the place and would have benefited from a good cut and his shirt, which had been hastily tucked into the front of his trousers, flapped loosely at the back, much in the manner of a truculent school boy. His chronic sinus problems, exacerbated by hay fever, meant that he sneezed repeatedly and punctuated his every waking moment – and probably those while asleep – with sniffs and snorts which were more than off putting on first meetings. Despite his unconventional appearance though, he was a brilliant surgeon and had an unexpectedly good bedside manner, an unusual mix of attributes which needless to say made him very popular.

Greeting Ed like a long-lost brother, he slapped him on the shoulder vigorously and asked in a booming voice why a general practitioner had plucked up the courage to enter through the portals of the orthopaedic ward. On hearing his explanation, Gareth pulled a face and led Ed down the ward and back into the corridor.

'We've just seen her on the ward round. Really tricky op that, bones like chalk. It was a real struggle getting the acetabular component in. Can't see that she's going to do well, I'm afraid. Sorry, Ed.'

'I rather expected that you'd say something along those lines,' Ed replied. 'Shame – she's such a game old lady. Can I pop and see her?'

'By all means but two minutes ago she was fast asleep. The physios had her out of bed for the first time this morning, so she'll be worn out. Their report wasn't good.'

'Poor soul, I'll leave her to rest then. Maybe come back another time.'

'Good idea. I'm sure she's going to be on the ward for a while. You'll have to excuse me, Ed, but I'm due back in theatre. It's good to see you. Let's have a pint or two sometime soon, eh?'

'Look forward to it, Gareth. Take care.'

They shook hands and Gareth strode off towards the operating theatre, Ed convinced that he could feel reverberations each time his massive foot came into contact with the floor. The news about Kathleen was far from good, if not unexpected. Hurrying back to the main foyer, Ed found Abigail waiting impatiently for him. She was standing outside the shop, which sold everything from flowers to spare pairs of pants, reading the newspaper headlines.

'All set?' Ed called. 'Right, let's get back to work.'

17

'Crab bisque, please, then the sirloin steak.'

'How would you like that cooking, madame?'

'Medium rare, thank you.'

Zoë closed the menu and handed it back to the waiter, a young lad, perhaps not yet sixteen, who had introduced himself as Adam and was taking his duties extremely seriously. He had what looked like a table cloth tied round his waist to make an ankle- length apron and his hair stood up in freshly gelled spikes.

'And for you, sir?'

Ed was spoiled for choice.

'It's hard, but I think I'll plump for the scallops with pancetta and then the rack of lamb.'

'A very good choice, sir, if I may say so.'

Zoë and Ed shared a smile.

'Can I get you any more drinks?'

'Zoë?' asked Ed.

'I'm fine at the moment.' Her glass of red wine was still three quarters full.

'And so am I. Thank you very much.'

'Very good, sir. Enjoy your meal. I'll be back in a moment with the bread basket.'

Adam backed away from the table, bowing subserviently before disappearing into the kitchen.

'He's after a big tip,' Zoë predicted.

She took a sip of wine and looked around her, approvingly. Impressed by Ed's choice, she appreciated the tasteful way in which someone had made the room feel up to date while at the same time doing justice to the original features such as the low ceiling with its thick dark beams. The walls were painted with warm, bright colours and the carpet, rather than the ubiquitous deep red that has a distinct tendency to feature in country pubs was dark beige with a subtle stripe of white. There was no sign of horse brasses or pieces of old farming equipment hanging from rusty hooks, no Toby jugs or pewter tankards, not even a burnished copper jelly pan playing host to a potted plant. With just ten, perhaps twelve, tables, the room was not large and consequently felt homely. The sound of merry chatter and clinking glasses from the other side of the bar added to rather than subtracted from the welcoming feel. Several other couples were already eating and a party of four, who were at a table decorated with balloons, seemed to be between courses.

'I love it here, Ed,' Zoë announced. 'Do you come here often?' she followed on with and then laughed at her hackneyed question.

'I've never been before,' confessed Ed, before explaining how he had chosen this venue.

'All of those places sound good,' agreed Zoe. 'Perhaps you'll take me to them as well.'

'I'd love to,' beamed Ed, suddenly relaxing.

He'd been so nervous before picking her up that he had even considered resorting to some sort of dutch courage. A quick slug of whisky, a diazepam tablet – there were some in his doctors' bag. Choosing what to wear had been a nightmare. His bed had been strewn with clothes that he had tried on and then rejected. Toby and Hebe, initially asleep, had objected so violently to a pair of trousers landing on top of them that they had stretched, given him a glare of piercing intensity and then stalked off in high dudgeon, tails straight up in the air, in search of some peace and quiet to resume their snoozes. Finally having decided on exactly what Ellie had suggested, he had rammed all the clothes back into the wardrobe, hanging them up untidily and then had spilt cologne over his shirt because his hand had been shaking so much, which necessitated a further change for fear of smelling too much like a car salesman. He had given thanks for the fact that he was male and had short hair. How he would ever have coped if he had had a hairstyle and make up to contend with in addition just did not bear thinking about.

Thinking that he was ready, he had got into his car, only to find the remnants of wrappers from sandwiches and chocolate bars on the floor by the passenger seat and even an apple core which must have been there for an age as it was brittle and broke into pieces when he had picked it up. So there had been that to tidy up, then the petrol gauge had been on empty and a stop at the garage had been called for and all the while the clock had been ticking, making him late for picking up Zoë.

Not that she had minded in the slightest. At the prearranged time, she had not even been close to being ready. Unbeknown to Ed, her room had the appearance of having been hit by an identical bomb, possibly worse as she had not bothered even to attempt to tidy up before she left. It had been hopeless. That dress had made her look fat, that skirt was too frumpy, the trousers that would have been perfect had mysteriously developed a stain on the front of the left leg, rendering them unwearable and that other dress – well, she was sure that all the buttons had fastened easily the last time she had worn it. Thoughtless washing must have shrunk it. The blue top was too revealing, not a good thing for a first date, the green one might be too cold, the pink needed ironing and there was no time for things like that. She had really wanted to wear those chic new sandals with the wedge heels because she thought they made her ankles look slim and feminine and she had spent an age doing her toenails as soon as she'd finished work. So that had effectively eliminated the possibility of the pleated skirt, which would have clashed with the nail polish and the same problem applied to that cute little checked dress which, okay, was on the short side but she could just about get away with it.

Miraculously, she had strolled down the path from her flat looking quite divine in a calf-length navy skirt, which swirled attractively as she moved and a white top with little capped sleeves and a scooped-out neck. This outfit matched her sandals perfectly. She was greeted by Ed, cool in his taupe chinos and a shirt which he would have described as dark red but purists would have called burgundy, and each had the same instantaneous thought – that this was something very special.

Their drive to the pub had been full of polite conversation and silences just too long to be natural. The subject of the weather had been dissected and examined in detail, followed by similar treatment of the lovely countryside and whether Ed was pleased with his car or not. It was a relief to arrive at the Millbank Arms, go inside and settle down with a glass of wine. Little did Adam realise how he had helped them, acting as a catalyst and providing them with a laugh to share and thus relax and start to enjoy each other's company.

'What's it like living in a hospital flat?' asked Ed, tearing his bread roll into pieces and applying a generous helping of butter.

'Grim. Well, I suppose that's unfair. It's clean, relatively quiet, except for when the nurses in the next block have a party and of course very convenient for work. I'm going to buy somewhere but I've been so busy settling in from a work point of view that I've hardly had a chance to look around or visit any estate agents. When I see all this gorgeous countryside, I'd love to find somewhere out here.'

'What about your on call?' Ed wondered. 'Surely you'd be too far out for that?'

'Oh yes, but I think I could manage to live in an on-call room one night a week, especially if it meant having a home somewhere beautiful to come back to. It's not a bad rota at all. Oh, here are our starters. Wow! That looks good.'

It took all of Adam's concentration to place the bowl of steaming hot bisque in front of Zoë without spilling any and he looked decidedly happier when he returned but a few moments later with Ed's scallops, elegantly set out on a transparent rectangular plate. They tucked in, each one running out of superlatives to describe their food. A common love of seafood was discovered along with a mutual hate of reaching over the table to eat off other people's plates.

Ed asked about Clare.

'She's home. The Prof let her go this afternoon, finally. But she's back in clinic on Monday for a check. The baby seems a little on the small side, so she's having to have serial scans to check on the growth. It's turning into a very long and drawn-out pregnancy for her. I'll probably be seeing her myself after next week, as he's away on holiday for a couple of weeks.'

'I just hope everything will work out okay for her. She's had a rough time over the last couple of years and could do with some good luck.'

Zoë raised her eyebrows but was tactful enough not to ask for more detail.

'I'm sure she'll get it.'

Starters completely eaten, they leant towards each other to talk, Zoë filling Ed in on her path to consultancy, how she'd hated working in central London but it had served a purpose in that she had gained some unique experience on an assisted conception unit, working for a hot-headed Egyptian, with hair and a beard like wire wool who expected nothing short of perfection from his juniors and let rip in his native tongue at the top of his voice, regardless of where he was, if anyone failed to come up to scratch. Hard work it had been but the time and effort she had put in had resulted in a first- class reference and a M.D. which put her head and neck in front of most of her rivals.

'So why come here?' Ed was curious. 'By the sound of it you could have had your pick of any job in the country, or the world. A top teaching hospital for instance.'

Zoë drained her glass and Ed gestured to Adam to refill it.

'I wanted the patient contact. I missed talking to them, the hands-on stuff. It's all very well being in an ivory tower, at the cutting edge of research, but I felt isolated from reality most of the time. And I wanted a life outside of work. A nice home, friends, interests that weren't medical. So I made the big decision to come and work in a good district hospital and so far I haven't regretted it for a second.'

'What about time for relationships?' Ed heard himself asking about a topic that he had been longing to explore.

'Not a lot to tell really. Work has tended to take priority. Nobody serious for a while, let's put it that way. How about you?'

'I was seeing someone,' he began, 'until a few weeks ago. She was called Hannah. She moved to Edinburgh to some high-powered job as a solicitor. We kept on seeing each other for a bit.'

He was surprised to feel a lump develop in his throat.

'It still hurts, doesn't it?' Zoë said perceptively.

Ed looked into her eyes and then studied her face, which was equally pretty whether she was serious or laughing. He felt indescribably safe in her presence and wanted to tell her everything there and then. Instinctively, he knew that she would listen and understand, say all the right things and mean them. He'd had no plans to even mention Hannah this evening, there was no way she was invited to join them when they were just in the first throes of discovering each other.

'Yes. I'd be lying if I said anything else. I thought we had a future together and was prepared to try. She wasn't, so I can see now that it would never have worked out. I'm well on the way to recovery. In fact, it's getting better all the time.'

'Good.'

She reached across the table and took his hand and squeezed it gently. Ed liked the feel of her soft skin and stroked her short but well-manicured nails with his thumb. A subtle cough from the diplomatic Adam heralded the arrival of their main courses and they let go of each other with some reluctance to make way for the separate plates of fresh vegetables and potatoes dauphinoise. Ed inhaled the delicious aroma of wine, garlic and rosemary from his rack of lamb and sighed with contentment. The meat was pink, just as he liked it. His knife glided through it as he composed his first mouthful which simply confirmed that it was tender and sweet.

Zoë, wisely, once she had helped both of them to vegetables, moved the conversation on. She could tell that there was more she needed to find out about Hannah but now was not the time. Deftly she steered the subject to his family and childhood. In turn he learned that she was the youngest of three children, her older sister living on the east coast with a husband and rapidly expanding family, currently numbering four with one on the way.

'And she's nearly forty. I feel I should be taking her to one side and giving her a short lecture on reliable contraception.'

Her brother was a microbiologist, in Devon, a keen surfer when he got the opportunity and a confirmed bachelor.

'You'd get on well, Ed,' she told him. 'He's into outdoorsy things. He cycles everywhere and has done a bit of climbing in his time.'

'Does he have a girlfriend?' Ed asked, wishing that he hadn't eaten all his bread so that he could soak up the rich gravy.

'It's not a question of "does he have a girlfriend" but more how many does he have?'

Ed raised his eyebrows.

'He's, I'm afraid to admit it, outrageous. He has no sense of loyalty to any girl and is a love 'em and leave 'em type. But girls don't seem to be put off by his reputation, which I can assure you precedes him. They think he's amazing when he's strutting round the hospital being all brainy with his sun-bleached hair and tanned skin and literally fall at his feet drooling when they see him in his wetsuit. Poor Mum and Dad can't keep up with his conquests. The last one he took home, they confused with her predecessor and called her by the wrong name, so you can imagine how well that went. Their dream is to see him settle down with a nice girl, get married and then produce two more grandchildren for them. It's weird how he can be so different from Jilly – that's my sister. She's been with Dom since they were both sixteen. Like Siamese twins. As far as I'm aware they've never looked at anyone else, let alone had a relationship. And now they seem to be determined to produce enough children to sink a battleship. The adorable thing about them is that they are besotted with each other, even now.'

'And which one are you like?'

'Me? Neither. I'm strictly monogamous when I'm in a relationship. I'd like to believe in happy endings and finding the right bloke and having a small – note that please – family one day.'

'Good for you. I do too. I mean the believe in happy endings bit, not finding the right bloke.'

They sniggered and Ed boldly reached out for her hand again.

'This is so nice,' he whispered and she smiled happily back.

'Have Sir and Madame finished?'

A little voice appeared at Ed's shoulder. Adam was hovering.

'Yes, thank you. It was delicious.'

'Oh good. I'll tell Mum, I mean, I'll pass on your compliments to the chef.'

With a considerable degree of skill, Adam stacked the empty plates and dishes into a teetering pile and wobbled into the kitchen. Ed and Zoë cringed expectantly as they waited for the crash which they felt sure was inevitable but none was forthcoming, merely Adam returning, wiping his hands on his apron and then reaching into his back pocket for his order pad.

'Would you like pudding?'

'What is there?' Ed inquired.

Adam cleared his throat in preparation for a recitation, reminding Ed of Abigail in some of her tutorials. There was something infinitely more endearing about Adam though, decided Ed.

'Chocolate fondant, fresh fruit salad, sticky toffee pudding, ice cream and an apple and blackberry meringue-y thing, which I can't remember the name of. Oh and cheese, of course.'

'Sounds fantastic,' Zoë told him. 'Which would you recommend?'

'Easy,' Adam, quick as a flash, replied. 'Sticky toffee pud. It's gorgeous. Specially if you have it with ice cream.' He quickly glanced around and then leant forward. 'I had some earlier – it was yummy.'

'Well?' Ed looked at Zoë.

'No contest,' she held up her hands. 'That'll do for me.'

'And me as well.'

'Won't be long,' promised Adam.

'I don't really need pudding,' confessed Zoë. 'I'm already quite full. But he made it sound so tempting and I've always been a pudding person. It's so great to be out eating proper food. I've tended to rely on the hospital restaurant most of the time and it's passable but doesn't begin to compare with this.'

How satisfying her honesty was, Ed thought, watching her while she arranged her spoon and fork in readiness and then reached for her glass.

'Another drink?' he asked.

'Are you having one?'

'Nothing alcoholic.'

'Maybe coffee then.'

'I'd wondered if you'd like to come back to my house for that,' Ed hesitated. 'We could have a drink as well.' He began to panic, thinking that he'd gone too far and tried desperately to regain control of the situation. 'But say if you'd rather not. I don't want to put you under any pressure at all.'

Zoë stood up. Ed's heart sank. He had definitely said the wrong thing, been too forward.

'I'm just off to find the ladies'. Coffee and another drink sounds perfect.'

So saying, she kissed him lightly on the cheek before threading her way between the tables to the other side of the room. Ed's ability to relax deserted him once more and the butterflies and galloping pulse that had accompanied him on the journey to the pub returned with a vengeance. He was wondering about having another glass of wine and trusting to luck that there were no police around as he drove them back to his house but then Zoë returned, sat down and looked at him. Instantaneously he felt better, trepidation having given way to anticipation. They lingered over their dessert, savouring the moment now that the rest of the evening's plans had been agreed. Having barely noticed just how good the sticky toffee pudding was, Ed asked for the bill and paid. He then took Zoë by the hand and led her to the car, leaving behind an incredulous Adam, stuttering his thanks as it sank in just how generous a gratuity they had left him.

Ed held open the car door for Zoë, but before she made a move to get in, barred her way, wrapped his arms around her and kissed her passionately on the lips. Rather than surprised by his spontaneity, she was thrilled and returned the kiss with equal intensity. Thinking back, he wondered what on earth had made him act in this way. His normal regime for chatting up a woman was slow (almost to the point of tedium, one unsuitable girl had commented), verging on the timid. He always found it difficult to read the signals, interpret them correctly and act accordingly. The female species might be deadlier but it definitely was a curious entity. They led men to believe one thing and then exerted their prerogative to change their minds. They liked to dress alluringly and flirt shockingly, safe in the knowledge that they were in the public domain and on show. How could he, a mere man, fuelled by testosterone over which he had no control, fail to be aroused by such behaviour? How could he possibly be expected to realise that this performance was more for all those around them, in particular those of the same gender? No sooner did they seek some privacy than a metamorphosis took place and a completely different character came into being.

Consequently he rarely made the first move unless he was as sure as he could be that this was what was expected of him. Initial dates were for fact finding, putting out feelers, toes in the water, describe it what ever way you want, basically analysing whether this was a good experience or not and did he want it to go further. Perhaps this was mortifyingly old fashioned – plenty of people seemed to assume that the date would end in sex, probably drunken and not a lot of fun, with recriminations in the morning when you looked at each other and struggled to think just what it was that you had seen that was even vaguely attractive. None of this was appealing to Ed. Perhaps it might have been some ten or fifteen years ago, when he had been at medical school and his peers were behaving in this way but the fact was that conduct of this ilk had never been for him. Jeered at by his student friends, he held fast to his belief that sex should not be casual but part of a more meaningful relationship.

A little embarrassed therefore at his actions, he started to pull away, albeit reluctantly. Zoë had other ideas and refused to relinquish her grip, coaxing him back into her arms to continue where he had left off and Ed was more than happy to oblige. Inside the car – finally – more embracing took place, hands inside clothes, short breathy gasps as they ignored the discomfort and interference of the gear lever and let their animal instincts take over. It took all his will power to extract himself from the moment, pausing for a last kiss before gasping,

'Let's get home.'

He drove shakily – how could he be expected to do otherwise with Zoë's hand on his thigh, stroking it rhythmically, suggestively, straying nearer and nearer to his groin? Occasionally she stretched across to caress his cheek, his ear, his neck. An outbreak of goose bumps exploded all over him. Quite how he got them both back safely to his house will forever remain one of life's mysteries and from the moment they fell through his front door, all thoughts of coffee and drinks were discarded when Ed suggested that perhaps the first room that Zoë might like to become intimately acquainted with was his bedroom.

18

Monday morning's surgery came too soon. After an idyllic weekend with Zoë, who did not leave until the very last thing on Sunday evening, Ed would have given anything to have more time with her. From start to finish, as he relived each moment, he had never been happier. She proved to be a good conversationalist, reasonably adept in the kitchen and astonishingly compatible as a lover. Loath to make comparisons, Ed was unable to prevent a brief moment where he recalled making love to Hannah, a passive and unimaginative partner and then thought of Zoë. After only forty-eight hours, he found her both physically irresistible and emotionally a joy. What made it even better was the fact that she made no attempt to hide that the feeling was mutual. When they talked, neither had any wish to be anything other than completely open and honest. Their senses of humour were so similar it was uncanny and whilst some of their opinions matched, others clashed violently but this worked just as well for it sparked off lively debate. When in bed Zoë's enjoyment and satisfaction were enchanting and her desire for Ed to feel equally pleasured touched him deeply.

On dropping her off at the flat, he kissed her tenderly and they planned to meet mid week. He was not even out of the hospital grounds when he received his first text message from her and screeched to a halt at the side of the road, much to the annoyance of the car behind him, to read it and reply. By the time he got home – a further three text messages later – there was an email waiting as well.

The weather was being typically Monday-ish. Rain was falling heavily from the moment he awoke with the clouds low lying and set for the day. Huge puddles decorated the surgery car park and the market square, coalescing into lakes as the rain continued to fall. Outside Delicious the tables and chairs looked forlorn and unwanted, water dripping off them sadly. Only a few folk were brave enough to be outside and skipped to one side as cars coursed by them through the wet, creating tidal waves of muddy brown water which crashed at their feet.

On any other day, Ed's first view of the waiting area would have caused his heart to sink like a stone; the seats were all full and the faces that greeted him were as dismal and lacklustre as the weather. No one was in particularly good humour. Phlegmy coughs, despondent sniffs and weary sighs bore no comparison to the friendly chatter and sharing of symptoms that came with the warm weather. Glum expressions and dripping umbrellas, plastic rain hats and Wellington boots had been substituted for the sandals, shirt sleeves and sunny dispositions of the past few weeks. All sure signs that autumn was knocking on the front door and sweeping the last, lingering vestiges of summer out of the back.

Nothing today could dent Ed's happiness. Today, come what may, the patients would be able to enjoy a doctor whose heart wore the biggest of smiles and whose beneficence knew no bounds.

What better start to his day than a call from Zoë? Short but immeasurably sweet, she was, like him, counting the hours until their next meeting. She had missed being next to him last night. He had hardly been able to ring off but it was comforting to know that she was thinking of him as she went off to do a ward round followed by clinic. It was all a bit too good to be true. Wonderful though she was, Zoë was not the usual sort of girl he would have chosen.

At medical school, Ed had made a secret vow that he would try to avoid relationships with other doctors, or indeed anyone connected with the profession. Not for him the archetypal union of doctor and nurse, the choice of so many of his male colleagues. He felt that this was too blinkered an approach to life, verging on the incestuous and wanted a partner with diverse interests that would make sure that they always had plenty to talk about and share. He had started off with the best of intentions and dated a psychology student, who made him take part in one of her experiments and then dumped him when his personality score did not come up to her stringent expectations. Nonplussed, he went out with a girl studying languages but she fainted the first time he told her about how he had dissected a dead body. She was followed by a physicist, who two-timed him and then, fed up with anyone on campus, he met a sales rep at a night club and enjoyed an undemanding but uninteresting few weeks with her.

His studies necessitated his full attention and meaningful relationships were forced onto the back burner. It was difficult to find someone who understood the pressure he was under with his exams and then, after qualifying, why he had to work such ludicrous hours. His outdoor pursuits became increasingly important as a means of escape. Switching off from work was vital and what better way to do it than slither up a rock face, wrestle against the wind on a hard cycle ride or trek up and down some hills miles from any sign of habitation?

On paper, Hannah had seemed to be the perfect solution at the time, combining professional commitment with a joint love of their hobbies but look where that had got him. Maybe a professional dating agency would have matched them as the perfect couple but the reality was that they were poles apart and now that the relationship was over he could stand back, be objective and acknowledge that this was the case.

And now, here was Zoë whom he should have dismissed instantly if he were to abide by his rule book. But what are rules, if not to be broken and Zoë certainly ticked all the right boxes. She and Ed had no difficulty identifying with each other's work. More to the point they could discuss it, bounce ideas of each other, sympathise and, perhaps, most importantly, understand the pressure and the strain.

It felt so right to Ed that he wondered why on earth he had been so against it earlier.

Beaming, he checked through the long list of patients who made up his morning's surgery without flinching in the slightest and went to invite the first one to come in. He was destined for a wealth of men's problems and spent the next two and a half hours examining testicles, discussing prostates and listening to the most personal and intimate details of those beleaguered by erectile dysfunction. By the end he felt that he had acquitted himself with credit and that there were a number of the male population of Lambdale who were, hopefully, considerably happier and better informed than they had been. Adding to his own contentment was the absence of interruptions from Abigail, who, although she was very much more confident and competent than she had been, still liked to have Ed's advice by telephone or his opinion in person on more than one occasion during each of her surgeries. This week and next, she was away which meant that he could luxuriate in the comfort of having only himself to worry about for all that time. Whilst the positives of being a trainer far outnumbered the negatives, there were times when the responsibility weighed him down and Abigail had been a particularly heavy millstone to bear. She was off to Spain with some friends to stay at a villa, soak up the sun and forget about work ostensibly but Ed suspected that she would not be far from a medical journal when she was sitting on the poolside, splashing her toes in the water or dipping into her tapas.

Upstairs, Ellie had already finished and was making a start on her post. Working hard, she didn't notice Ed coming in. Beside her was a mug of steaming coffee and a carefully arranged tower of custard creams, a sure sign that her morning had been far from ideal and sugary replenishment was necessary. John too was there, searching on the computer for the details of some rare syndrome that a newly registered patient had just admitted to having, bemoaning the irony of the fact that the one day that Abigail's vast knowledge might have come in useful, she wasn't there to help. Faith was back, concentrating fiercely on a telephone call that sounded from her end as though it was a negotiation about a patient who she thought ought to be admitted and who the doctor on the other end of the line did not.

None of them seemed to be aware that Ed was emitting some sort of radioactive glow of happiness as he entered the room, with only Faith barely looking up and giving him a quick wave. Nonchalantly, he sauntered over to the kettle to reboil the water and make a drink. Love might have done many things to him but it had not dulled his appetite and he chose a selection of biscuits to dunk and keep him going until lunchtime. He sat down.

'Hello, everyone,' he started.

'Hi, Ed,' replied John, not looking round. 'I don't suppose you know what Flanders-Foster-Costigan syndrome is?'

'I haven't a clue.'

Ellie suddenly realised he was there.

'Ed! Hello!'

She examined him quizzically, as though possessed of x-ray vision. 'Well?'

Ed smiled benignly and reached for a folder, opened it and pretended to be very interested in the contents. Ellie reached over and snatched it away from him and he burst out laughing.

'Well?' she repeated.

John swivelled around on his chair and looked equally expectant. No doubt Ellie had filled both him and Faith in earlier on Ed's plans for the weekend.

'Yes, very well, thanks. Good surgeries, you lot?' Ed decided to be annoying.

'No, terrible,' confessed Ellie. 'My patients used up a whole box of tissues between them and one of them had a list of thirteen problems they wanted to discuss. John's had someone collapse in mid-consultation and Faith knelt down by someone's bed on a visit and the carpet was soaked with urine, so now she smells too. That's why we desperately need you to cheer us up. Please don't keep us in suspense any longer.'

He gave in. 'I've had a fantastic weekend,' he admitted.

'Oh, that's great,' Ellie sighed. 'Now just tell us all the details. Well, perhaps not all of them. We'll allow you to omit the more personal moments – too much information and all that, but we'd like to know as much as possible.'

'There's really not that much to tell,' Ed began, only to be interrupted by Ellie saying that she was quite sure that there was and suggesting he start at the beginning with Friday evening.

So he did and apart from repeated slight deviations as Ellie wanted more pertinent facts such as what did he wear, what did Zoë wear, what did they eat and drink, he provided them with a short but accurate account of what a splendid time they had had. Yes, Zoë had stayed for the whole weekend and of course he was seeing her again, as it happened that would be Wednesday, when she had promised to drive up and see him for supper. John was politely delighted, Faith – now off the phone having been successful – was excited and Ellie positively enthralled.

'I'm so happy for you,' Ellie gasped, clapping her hands together. 'I wonder if I should ring Ian. We've been talking about you all the time. When you didn't ring on Saturday morning, we were so hoping that that was a good sign. He virtually had to drag me from the phone as I wanted to call you. I can't wait to tell him. You'll have to bring her round for supper. How about this weekend? We'd love to get to know her more.'

'Hang on,' Ed tried to calm her down. 'She's on call this weekend. Let's just give it a bit of time. I don't want to count my chickens. It's early days but if the current omens are anything to go by then the future's looking pretty damn good.'

'Ed, I'm speechless. That's brilliant. You have cheered us up,' Faith told him.

'Which is excellent,' agreed John, 'because there are rather more house calls than usual, and there are only three of us to do them, as Faith is in surgery, so who wants to do which ones?'

They perused the requested calls and decided that the best way forward was to divide them up geographically. None were urgent and some looked possibly unnecessary but it was often impossible to assess exactly what was going on from the message left by the caller. All of them could recall visits which had sounded innocuous and then turned out to be life threatening and conversely ones where they had dropped everything and dashed, only to find the most trivial of problems waiting for them. There was no reliable way to educate the patients. For the rest of time there would be those who did not want to bother the doctor and so diminished their symptoms and those who knew just the right words and phrases to use to generate immediate attention, usually when it was not needed.

Unfazed by the prospect of two local nursing homes, a family notorious for the unimaginable filth in which they lived and a chronically constipated elderly gentleman who rang for a visit several times a week to discuss his bowels, Ed turned up his collar and ran to his car, skipping between the puddles effortlessly. Nothing could dent his good humour. Today, no matter what life were to throw at him, he was impervious to stress and worry, protected by the impenetrable armour that he had acquired since falling in love.

Which turned out to be an exceedingly good thing as his last appointment of the afternoon was Tina, who had taken him at his word and had persuaded the receptionists to allot her three times the normal amount of time, oblivious to the needs of others. Outside the rain continued to fall. There had not been the slightest let up in the weather all day. The same weighty clouds clogged up the sky over Lambdale and what daylight they had experienced was already threatening to disappear. Ed was tiring, worn out by his hyperactivity, looking forward to going home, having his evening meal and ringing Zoë. He needed to hear her voice telling him all about her day, reinforcing her existence in his life. It was ludicrous that after so short a spell of time, he could feel such need for her and miss her so acutely. He had to force thoughts of asking her to move in with him to the very back of his mind. It was far too premature even to contemplate a major event like that, however much he wanted it. Having only ever had a whimsical belief in love at first sight, he was now a committed disciple to that philosophy and he hoped and prayed that Zoë's feelings for him were the same. Instinctively, he knew that they were.

Tina was dressed in a long waxed coat which came down to her ankles with matching hat, the epitome of country class. Ed closed the door behind her and heard the rustling of the coat as it was removed. Beneath, she had on a very short leather skirt, knee-high boots with toes pointed so acutely that they could doubtless inflict an unpleasant injury on anyone if called upon to do so, and a fine wool jumper with a plunging V neck. No attempt had been made to hide her extremely fine figure. Rather the opposite, her outfit had been chosen to accentuate and highlight, so much so that cynics would have gone a step further and described it as provocative.

'What a dreadful day,' she moaned, removing the hat and shaking her head. A fine mist of rain droplets fell to the ground.

Ed concurred and motioned for her to sit down, which she did with an unnecessary amount of leg crossing one way then the other before she appeared comfortable.

'I'm so grateful to you for your time. I know how busy you are. Firstly, I've something for you...'

Reaching down into her bag, she produced a bottle of champagne and a colossal box of chocolates.

'...and before you say anything, these are from Aunty Kath. She wanted you to have them as a thank you for that day when she fell. Oh, there's a card as well, somewhere. Oh, here it is. Sorry it's got a bit wet.'

Ed opened it, throwing the soggy envelope straight into the bin.

A cute array of baby animals holding flowers spelt out the words 'thank you' and inside, in decidedly wobbly, spidery writing were some touching words from his patient.

'There wasn't a great deal of choice at the hospital shop,' Tina explained. 'But she did write it herself.'

'I'm very flattered. It's so kind of her. There was no need for all this. Please pass on my thanks in return.'

'Sure. I'll be going in later.'

'How is she?'

'Cross. She hates being in hospital.'

Ed chuckled. 'That sounds as if she's getting better.'

Tina pulled a face. 'I'd agree – emotionally she's nearly back to normal. Otherwise, she's a disaster. I can't believe how much weight she's lost. It's so much more obvious when she's just got her nightdress on. There's nothing left of her. Her arms are like twigs. It's little wonder that she can't do anything. She just doesn't have the strength even to do really simple things like pull herself up the bed.'

'That's very sad,' Ed sympathised. 'Have you had a chance to speak to anyone about how she's doing?'

Tina uncrossed her legs, bent down to scratch her ankle – a difficult feat to pull off when wearing boots but one that produced a display of voluptuous bosom – and then resumed her original position.

'Yes. I've had a word with the ward sister. I'm afraid she's probably the most pessimistic person I've ever met in the world, apart from the physiotherapist that is. Full of doom and gloom. They both say Aunty Kath will never walk again and that she'll need to go into a nursing home.'

'I'm very sorry to hear that. But, if I'm honest, I'm not surprised.'

Ed explained gently about the softness and fragility of her bones, her lack of muscle and how her age was against her.

'But couldn't she go back to Cherry Tree House? She loved it there.'

Ed was diplomatic enough not to contradict her.

'I doubt it very much. She needs full nursing care now by people trained to do that. Cherry Tree's great, I agree, but there's no way that they could meet her needs now. It sounds as if you should be starting to look around for a place in a nursing home.'

'That's what the ward sister said. I wanted to talk to you first, because you know Aunty Kath so much better.'

'There are several homes that would be suitable for her. I'll give you the names.'

He turned to his desk and started writing. 'Here you are. What's wrong?'

Tina had seemed to shrink and was sobbing quietly into her hands, her shoulders drooping, her damp hair falling around her face. Sniffing, she peeped through her fingers at Ed.

'It's all so unfair. What a miserable end to someone's life. She hates being so totally reliant on other people.'

'Most of us would feel exactly the same. Loss of one's dignity is a hard and harsh reality to face up to.'

'How am I going to break it to her? Every day I go into see her and she clutches my hand as if she's expecting me to make her better. She keeps asking me when she's going back to Cherry Tree House. I can't look at her because there's such a pitiful look in her eyes and it hurts me so much to see it. I feel I'm letting her down.'

The intensity of the sobbing increased. Automatically, Ed leaned forward and placed a comforting hand on her shoulder, just as he would have done with any patient that was upset. She responded by putting her head on his chest. Ed allowed her a moment and then drew back. Tentatively, Tina sat more upright, her shoulders still hunched up despondently, her hands clasped in her lap. Mascara dribbled down her face creating a grotesque, clown-like appearance.

'Look,' Ed started. He cupped his hands around hers and pressed them together. 'I know this is hard for you but it's way harder for your aunt. She needs you to be strong for her at the moment, to be positive about the move, to know that you're going to be there for her, visiting, cheering her up, helping her settle in. Her bones may be weak but her mind isn't. One of her strengths is her common sense and no-nonsense approach to life. This won't be what she wants but she'll come to accept it and cope with it. Remember how she knew that she had to move from that flat. I bet she knows now that she can't go back to Cherry Tree, without having to hear it from anyone. She's nobody's fool and you must acknowledge this. Be honest with her. Feeding her false hope is a non-starter. Tell her the truth. She'll thank you for it at the end of the day, believe me.'

Tina let out a huge sigh. 'I guess you're right. Well, I know you are. I don't suppose you'd visit her and tell her about the nursing home?'

Ed shook his head and sat back in his chair.

'No, I think that's for you to do. The nurses and Mr Pickering will back you up. What you can tell her is that I'll be in to see her as soon as she moves from the hospital.'

'Oh dear.'

'You're better doing it sooner rather than later. What's more, you'll feel better when you've done it. It must be difficult going in at the moment, making small talk and trying to avoid the subject.'

He handed over a box of tissues and Tina pulled out a handful. She got up and went over to his sink, perusing her image in the mirror above it and blotting, as best she could, the smudges and smears of dislocated make up. It was some minutes before she was apparently satisfied with her repair work and Ed was becoming a smidgeon impatient, the prospect of getting home far more tantalising than being where he was at the moment.

Resignedly, Tina sat down again, having first paced up and down in a rather histrionic manner suggesting that she was in the throes of making a momentous decision.

'Ed,' she announced, 'as ever, you're right. I'll tell her this evening when I go and see her. Tomorrow, I'll go and visit these places. I hope they've got room for her. I get the impression from the nurses that they'd like her to move sooner rather than later.'

'Good for you,' Ed congratulated her. 'I'm sure it'll be easier than you think.'

'Fingers crossed.' Tina looked unconvinced. 'Shall I let you know how I get on?'

'For sure, keep in touch. I'll do whatever I can to help.'

Tina rose to her feet and, with relief which he hoped she did not see, so did Ed. She picked up her coat and hat. He walked her to the door and before opening it, gently put one hand around her shoulders and patted her lightly. She looked up at him and smiled.

'Thank you so much, Ed.'

'Good luck. Don't forget to say thank you for the gifts.'

'No of course not. You enjoy them. She'll be so pleased you liked them.'

She backed her way across the reception area and waved. Ed smiled and nodded encouragingly before retreating into his room. He spared a brief thought for Kathleen and her miserable prognosis before writing up the last of his notes, logging off and packing his bag with alacrity. Not much more than seconds later he was in his car, music turned up to full volume and well down the road on the way home, concentrating entirely on the evening ahead.

19

Wednesday morning and the rain finally stopped. There were small chinks in the cloud which permitted dramatic rays of harsh sun and whilst there was no blue sky on show, the general feeling was one of much greater brightness and optimism. With the fine weather came a rise not just in temperature but in everyone's hopes for an Indian summer. The square was busier than ever. It was market day and bright stalls were neatly set out in rows selling everything imaginable from comestibles such as chutneys, cheeses and olives to ironmongery and sheepskin slippers. Rows of colourful skirts and pashminas floated in the breeze opposite hats for every occasion, powerful binoculars and dog beds. Business seemed to be brisk. There were still enough holiday makers prowling around to swell the numbers of locals shopping and stall holders were anticipating a busy and profitable day.

The rush of the early part of the week had calmed and the partners at Teviotdale felt rather less stressed. Except for Ed of course, who was bouncing around like a small child after a can of pop, giddy with excitement and unable to sit still. He raced through morning surgery, flew round his visits and then headed for the shops where he spent an inordinate amount of money on expensive ingredients, the best champagne he could find and enough flowers to hold several weddings and still have some left over. He found that he couldn't stop once he'd started to spend, his mind jettisoning off at tangents. Zoë might like some hors d'ouevres, she might adore some chocolates after the meal, she might not like roses, so better to get plenty of different flowers to be on the safe side. For the first time ever he stopped to consider which aroma of air freshener might appeal to her more rather than grabbing the first he saw. Aware he was being quite irrational considering that he was catering for one simple meal and, hopefully, one breakfast which would probably amount to little more than a hurried piece of toast, he didn't care. He was having the time of his life and Zoë would laugh and laugh when he told her all about it.

After handing his credit card over to the checkout girl without a qualm at the amount she asked for, he steered his trolley erratically back over the bumps in the car park and packed his purchases into the boot, which only closed after some persuasion, which made him worry for the survival of the flowers. On reaching his house, he saw that the windows were wide open and the strains of a popular radio station were blaring out, a sure sign that Barbara was in and doing one of her big cleans. There she was, in the lounge, sashaying from side to side in time to the music as she hoovered, singing along in a loud voice. Her assistants, Toby and Hebe, were draped across the back of the sofa, like mirror images, immobile save for the most distal part of their tails which were curling and uncurling softly, their wide eyes watching her every move. They blinked and cast a cursory glance at Ed before resuming their observation of Barbara who was infinitely more interesting.

'Hi!' yelled Ed, wanting to announce his presence without making her jump.

The vacuum cleaner was switched off.

'Hello, Ed. I wasn't expecting you. Is anything wrong?'

'No, no. Far from it. I've been shopping. I've got a friend coming round for supper and I just wanted to drop things off. You carry on – don't mind me.'

Barbara, about to pick up where she had left off, halted in her tracks, mesmerised by the cornucopia of purchases which was making its way into the house. Ed, barely visible behind armfuls of flowers, peered at her between two scarlet gerberas.

'I don't suppose you'd arrange these in some vases for me,' he begged. 'I haven't the first clue how to do it.'

'Of course I will. Are you sure you've enough though?' Barbara's sarcasm was lost on Ed.

'I hope so. Do you think I need more?'

'No, certainly not. Who's coming for supper? The president of the Royal Horticultural Society?'

'My new girlfriend.'

'Ah,' Barbara hummed, meaningfully. 'Now all this is starting to make sense. I hope she doesn't have hay fever.'

'I never thought of that,' wailed Ed. 'Do you think she might have?'

'I'm joking, Ed. Don't be so nervy. Now then, what are you cooking?'

'I've got chicken, but I'm not sure what to do with that either. Probably just stick it in the oven and roast it... Perhaps...'

Barbara was quick on the uptake. She was very fond of Ed and loved looking after him.

'Ed, sweetheart, why don't you just leave everything in the kitchen and I'll sort it all for you? I can whip up a pudding as well if you like. I've nothing else planned for this afternoon, so it's easy for me to stay on and give you a hand.'

'Barbara, you're a life saver. Thank you so much.'

'She means a lot to you, I take it. I mean, let's face it, nobody goes to this much trouble for just anyone.'

'I can't begin to tell you, Barbara. I mean, she's pretty, she's got the happiest smile, she's intelligent and she cares – about life, about her work and hopefully about me as well.'

'She sounds a veritable paragon. I can see you're completely smitten. I never saw that look on your face when you talked about Hannah. Good luck to you. I think the world of you, Ed, and you deserve the best. I'll look forward to meeting her.'

'You'll love her. I know you will.'

'Off you go then. I'll ring if there's a problem but I can't imagine there will be. I'd better get cracking. I've the cleaning to finish first. See you later.'

She gesticulated for him to leave. Dismissed, Ed rummaged in his wallet and handed over her wages, plus a generous bonus for the work she would be doing that afternoon. Cheap at the price. It was a weight off his mind to know that the culinary part of his evening was bound to be a success. Doubtless Zoë would completely understand if he had cooked and it had gone wrong but, as far as he was concerned, Ed wanted everything to be perfect.

So, while Ed juggled with snotty noses and irritating skin complaints in the young and the reluctance of the elderly to accept the natural ageing process, Barbara turned up the volume on the radio even louder and danced around the kitchen, chopping and frying onions and garlic, whilst simultaneously executing the cha-cha, as a preamble to conjuring up chicken cacciatore, which she envisaged being served with jacket potatoes and sugar snap peas. Close inspection of Ed's fridge, which could do with a good turn out, she made a mental note, but that could wait until next week, unearthed ingredients for an orange and melon starter – nice and light – and a chocolate mousse for dessert, which would be thick, sinful and rich.

Like the good soul she was, she washed and cleared up, leaving the kitchen spotless, laid the tiny table and then set to work on the flowers which she had been keeping fresh in a row of buckets of water, just outside the back door. As Ed had only one vase and that was not large, she found it necessary to call on her more inventive side and make use of other receptacles such as a large saucepan, a measuring jug, the bowl from the food mixer and a row of empty wine bottles.

It was nearly six by the time she had finished and was writing a list of instructions for Ed on last-minute preparations. A deliciously tempting smell was emanating from the kitchen, one that Zoë could not fail to be impressed by. The lounge looked welcoming and warm, if rather overdosed with flowers and the cats, by now full of their own tea, were snoring gently on the hearthrug. Barbara was adding up in her head how long the potatoes would take when there was a knock on the door. She glanced at her watch, astonished to find how late it was.

Opening the door she saw a young woman. Eyeing her up and down, Barbara could see that she certainly ticked all the boxes that Ed had described. She was more than pretty, stunning even, hour-glass figure wrapped up in a belted coat and a smile that would melt the hardest of hearts. She looked taken aback to see Barbara.

'Oh, I'm sorry, I was looking for Ed Diamond. Have I got the wrong house?'

'No, dear. Come on in. He'll be home soon. The surgery closes at six but I expect you probably know that.'

'Do you think he'd mind?'

'Don't be daft. He'd be cross with me if I didn't let you in to make yourself at home. Don't tell him I told you, but you've made quite an impression on him.'

'Have I? That's great news. I think he's the most wonderful man I've ever met.'

'I'm Barbara by the way. I do his cleaning. Normally I wouldn't still be here, but – between you and me – I've been helping him out with your tea.'

Barbara stood to one side to let her come in.

'What a lovely room. What a delicious smell. Oh, cats! I love cats.'

'That's Hebe on the left and the other's Toby. Sit yourself down. Would you like a cup of tea?'

'Thank you. I don't want to put you to any trouble though.'

'Kettle's just boiled. Milk? Sugar?'

Barbara was already in the kitchen, looking out a mug. Conscious of the time, she was eager to get off but wanted to make sure that Ed's evening got off to a good start. She admired his taste in women. This one was a definite improvement on Hannah, whom she'd always found quiet and rather reticent. Good clothes sense too. About a hundred years ago she'd had long, flawless legs as well. But four kids and a family history of varicose veins had put paid to that.

'Just milk, please.'

'Better not offer you a biscuit. You've got a lovely meal to come, so you mustn't spoil your appetite. Here we are. Now, get comfy on that lovely sofa. I'm sure Ed wouldn't mind if you were to put the TV on. I must dash. Lovely to meet you and hope to see you again very soon.'

'Lovely to meet you too.'

Alone, she wandered around the room, studying all the photographs in detail, taking in all the books, picking up and stroking the cushions. She steered clear of the cats. Attracted by the mouth-watering garlicky smell she peeped in the kitchen, sneaked a look in the fridge and then wandered up stairs. Was it always this neat, she wondered? Or was it just because the cleaner, what was her name again, had been in that day and Ed had had no time to sully the perfection. She loved the bedroom, the cool colours, the seaside look, the wooden boat on the chest of drawers. So coincidental that she would have chosen these colours and accessories for her own room. Their harmoniousness was verging on being spooky. Kicking a cat toy to one side, she looked into the bathroom, enviously spotted the power shower and picked up each of several bottles on the shelf by the washbasin. Unscrewing the caps she sniffed the contents in turn. Eau de cologne – mmm, expensive, aftershave, even some moisturiser. It was good that he looked after himself, cared about his appearance. She admired that in a man.

She jumped as she heard the front door opening and the sound of Ed's voice greeting the cats. Suddenly nervous, she walked back across the tiny landing, her footsteps obvious on the wooden floorboards.

'Zoe?' Ed's voice floated upstairs. 'Is that you? Sorry I'm late but at least Barbara was here to let you in. I met her at the surgery as I was leaving. Her son works there as one of our receptionists. You certainly seem to have impressed her. I'm going to open some champagne –

come and have a glass. How's your day been? I can't wait to see you again. I missed you so much it's ridiculous.'

Heart in her mouth, heart thumping at an increasingly alarming rate, she made her way back down to the lounge and sat on the settee listening to Ed wrestling with the champagne bottle before hearing a satisfying pop and then an alluring gurgle as it was poured into two glasses.

'Here we are! Bloody hell! What on earth are you doing here?'

'Hi, Ed,' said Tina. 'You've a beautiful house.'

'That's beside the point. I asked why you were here.'

'You said I could talk to you any time. I thought it would be easier to talk away from your work. We can relax more, get to know each other better.'

'How did you know where I lived?'

'That doctor of yours, the one who did my smear, told me. Well, she gave me a rough idea and then I drove over here one night and watched which door you went into.'

'Are you saying you followed me?' Ed was incandescent, not just with Tina but with Abigail, who would be hearing some extremely harsh words on her return from holiday.

'No,' Tina replied innocently. 'I knew approximately where you lived, so I came and waited.'

'You have to leave,' Ed remonstrated with her, trying to keep cool and in control. 'You should not have come here.'

'But you said you'd do anything you could. And you held me in your arms when Aunty Kath fell. I felt your heart beating alongside mine and I knew you and I had a future together. And this week you put your arm around me and took my hands. I know you find me attractive. I've seen the way you look at me.'

'I'm sorry,' Ed began. 'You've got this all horribly wrong. I've never even considered having any sort of relationship with you other than professional. Of course I'll help you if I can with your aunt but that's where it ends.'

'You don't mean that,' Tina tried to sound beguiling. 'You need to unwind after a hard day at work. Come and sit next to me and I'll help you realise how you feel.'

'Tina, for the last time, please leave. You're not welcome here. I'm expecting my girlfriend any minute and I'd rather you were gone before she arrived.'

'We can tell her to go,' suggested Tina. 'Leave it to me. I'll talk to her. I'll tell her you've made a mistake and that it's me you really want. Don't worry, it'll be fine and then we'll have the rest of the evening and the rest of our lives together.'

Ed put down the two glasses he was still holding and walked to the door. He opened it.

'Go, now,' he ordered, the tone of his voice rising with impatience.

'Don't be silly. Get the drinks and come here.'

'Tina, how can I spell this out for you? I am not attracted to you. I have never given you any reason to think that I am, so I'm sorry if you've chosen to misinterpret my actions and twist them to suit your own ideas. I insist that you leave.'

'No.'

She was sounding more sullen, anger creeping into her words, her usually attractive mouth adorned with an ugly curl.

'You've led me on every time we've met. Even that first time when I came into the surgery with Aunty Kath and I looked like I'd slept in a rubbish bin, you couldn't keep your eyes off me. Then when you saw how well I scrubbed up, boy, did your eyes come out on stalks.'

'This is all in your imagination. Sure, I've treated you with respect and compassion, as any doctor would have done, but there has never, ever been anything more. What's more, there never will be.'

'What crap you talk.' She was getting really venomous now. 'Don't think I don't know about you doctors and how you walk around with this sanctimonious air as if you never do anything wrong but you do. Plus I know that you shouldn't have a relationship with a patient but you still do. You drink too much, you take controlled drugs, you behave abysmally but you nearly always get away with it because the public hold you in such high regard and refuse to believe that you'd put a foot wrong. Well, not me! I'm not so stupid. I know what trouble you could get into, Ed, if I say you've been coming on to me. I can be very good at making life difficult for people and I think that a not too discrete letter to the General Medical Council might just turn your oh so perfect life into a living hell. I might have to liven the details up a bit – like we had sex in your consulting room and in your car in between visits because you were gagging for it and how you asked me to wear nothing at all under my coat when I came to see you. Just like I am now in fact.'

She stood up and started to undo her belt.

'Get out,' shrieked a voice from the door. 'Get out now and never dare to come back.'

'Zoë,' breathed Ed.

'I'm waiting,' Zoë continued ominously. 'I'm witness to all that you've said, you evil, conniving little bitch, so you haven't a leg to stand on. And as for being a patient of Ed's, I think you'll find he'll have put you off the list by first thing tomorrow morning. You should be thoroughly ashamed of yourself, behaving in such a puerile way. Now go!'

'You haven't heard the last of this,' Tina spat, grabbing her handbag.

'I think we have,' Ed retorted. 'Best leave it that way, too.'

Zoë shut the door firmly behind Tina and turned to face Ed. She was shaking and more than happy to fall into his open arms. When she finally felt that she had had enough hugs and kisses to settle her anxiety – which actually settled very quickly but she was enjoying the affection and so allowed herself to wallow in it – she looked up at him.

'And what was all that about?'

Surprisingly, Ed and Zoë managed to resurrect what was left of the evening. The bottle of champagne helped without a doubt and it took most of it for Ed to explain. He felt appalled by what had happened and fearful for the possible ramifications, which, if Tina conspired adroitly, would make his life exceedingly uncomfortable for a long time. He could imagine the front pages of some of the seedier Sunday tabloids, outrageous headlines and photos of Tina, probably wearing nothing at all apart from a supposedly hard-done-by pout. Involvement with the General Medical Council would rock the very foundations of his vocation, regardless of his total innocence. All he'd done was try to be nice, to be understanding, to be a good doctor. How terrifyingly fragile was the line between empathy and affection.

It took all of Zoë's patience and objectivity to help him see that Tina was the owner of a very dubious personality and that the likelihood of her doing anything other than disappearing in a puff of smoke to try her luck elsewhere was remote.

'I'd be amazed if you ever saw her again. Even though you're still looking after her aunt,' was Zoë's opinion.

Gradually Ed calmed down. His upset had first to turn to fury before he finally accepted what Zoë was saying and knew that she was right. He also realised just how happy Tina would be if she knew that she had ruined their evening and there was no way that he was going to let that happen. Hadn't he been anticipating these precious hours with Zoë for three days? Exactly, time to get back on track.

Consequently it was later than planned when they started to eat, but by that time, Tina had been swept under the corner of the carpet in their minds and Zoë was regaling Ed with an account of one of her patients in labour.

'She and her husband had written a very precise birth plan. They wanted no pain relief, no drugs at all. They just wanted soft music playing in the background – you know the sort of thing – whales singing and flutes playing random notes – and he was going to massage her abdomen with some potion that he'd made up that morning. Well, of course, her contractions started to get stronger and more painful. He was being very supportive, helping her breathe through them, holding her hand and to start off with she coped quite well. Anyway, five hours later and she's still in labour, contracting every two to three minutes, whopping contractions, not far off being fully dilated but not quite there either. She's beside herself, sweat pouring off her, nightdress round her neck, wet through, hair stuck to her face. He's sitting in the corner of the room eating sandwiches and drinking cocoa from a flask and she's screaming out with the pain. He told her to calm down and she simply screamed at him and demanded an 'effing injection for the pain'. He tells her she doesn't need one and she banishes him from the room and won't let him back in, even when she delivers the baby an hour later. Best bit of all is that they call the baby Mars.'

'Mars?' echoed Ed.

'Yes,' Zoe was desperate to deliver her punchline. 'And their name is Barr. How thoughtless is that?'

'Mars Barr – poor kid,' Ed laughed. 'I don't know how you managed to keep a straight face.'

'One of the benefits of having a mask round your neck. You can just slip it over your face in moments of need – such as that.'

'Zoe, you're amazing. I'd never have got through this evening without you. I dread to think what might have happened if you hadn't turned up.'

'Forget her, Ed. Let's just think of us. What did you say was for pudding? Why don't we take it upstairs?'

20

Time, in its role of good healer, also restores and rebuilds confidence and a fortnight later, with not so much as a whisper from Tina, Ed was feeling immeasurably better in many respects. He had, however, been more shocked than he cared to admit by her appearance at his house and there were still moments, though admittedly these were becoming less intense, when floorboards creaking made him jump and the sound of the doorbell tempted him to hide behind the sofa. He tried hard not to imagine what might have happened had Zoë not appeared, like the cavalry, loud and sufficiently intimidating to save the day. What would he have done if Tina had followed through with her threats and made lewd and character-damning accusations? The thought made bile fizz up into his gullet and goose bumps trickle over his limbs.

He was aware that he had started to practise in a different way, defensively, keeping his distance from the patients, physically and emotionally and it felt alien to him to behave like this, especially with the ones he knew inside out. He might feel safe but he knew there was something missing, his instinctive ability to achieve a rapport and reach deep into the darkest corners of the souls of those who had chosen to come to see him. His new approach left him less satisfied and he wondered if the patients had noticed, feeling guilty that he was letting them down. Doubtless his usual consulting style would insinuate its way back into his everyday life as he lowered his guard but for the time being, he preferred not to take any chances.

There was an awful moment when he was asked to visit Kathleen Clarke, now moved to The Aardvark, a curiously named place but one which ensured that they were first in the business section of the phone directory under the category of nursing homes. He had a high opinion of the nursing care they provided and was pleased for Kathleen that she had been lucky enough to go there, for a bed to become available was a rarity. He shared his worries with Ellie and John, both of whom offered immediately to do the visit for him. Thanking them, he declined, still feeling obligated to see Kathleen himself. None of what had happened was her fault and he doubted that she had any idea at all of what was going though her niece's mind, beneath the disguise of caring relative.

He rang Zoë before he left surgery and was lucky to catch her.

'Just go and be your normal wonderful self,' she told him. 'If you worry about it, then you're giving into that foul-mouthed termagant. Don't lower your standards to those of hers. And if she is there then be polite but make it obvious you don't give a damn. She'll feel far more uncomfortable than you do.'

Easier said than done, he mused, deliberately driving the long way to the nursing home on the pretext that he needed to stop at the garage for fuel, despite his tank being nearly half full.

He arrived and looked around the small parking area for Tina's car. No sign – a good start. Unless of course she had walked there. Or taken a taxi. Or parked on the road round the corner. Doing his best to exterminate such fanciful thinking he rang the bell with panache and walked inside.

The nurse in charge, who hailed from Nigeria and was blessed with the smoothest of skins and a smile that would negate the need for a night light, was vociferous in her welcome before telling him in hushed tones that Kathleen was having difficulty settling in.

'They think she had a small stroke the day before she left hospital,' she explained. 'She's very withdrawn and barely eating a thing. She only drinks if we stand over her and encourage her. I'm afraid that she's now doubly incontinent. We've catheterised her to make her more comfy.'

'It sounds to me as though she's given up,' Ed diagnosed.

'I agree with you, Doctor. We'll do all we can, it goes without saying but I'm not holding out a lot of hope.'

'Er, what about her niece? Is she spending a lot of time here?'

'We've not seen her at all,' shaking her head. 'It might cheer Kathleen up if she did. She knows her aunt's here but since she came to look round in the first place, she's not been back.'

'That's a shame. They always seemed very close.' Ed hoped he sounded genuine but was secretly relieved for selfish reasons. 'Lead on, let's go and see her.'

Kathleen's room at the Aardvark Nursing home was as different to the one she'd enjoyed at Cherry Tree House as it could be. Square and purpose built, it smelled of a mixture of air freshener and furniture polish, neither of which quite masked the unmistakable hint of urine and faeces. There was a standard, oblong dressing table and a built-in wardrobe, carpet and curtains identical to every other room in the building, not unpleasant but functional rather than fashionable. None of Kathleen's possessions were on show, nothing to identify her as an individual, nothing for her to look at or touch that might give her cheer or hope.

Looking uncomfortable, propped up on a pile of pillows, Kathleen looked vacant and wan. Around her wrist she still wore the plastic identity bracelet with her name and hospital number on. Beside the bed a tube drooped morosely, leading to a catheter bag which contained a small volume of light yellow liquid. Her dull eyes moved fractionally to take in who had just entered but there was no reaction on her sad, furrowed face, the asymmetry of which left Ed in no doubt about the recent stroke. Edentulous, her lips were puckered, her jaw sunken. A small trickle of dried saliva made its way down her chin from the drooping corner of her mouth like a snail's silvery trail. Gone was the sparkle, the hint of mischief, the sheer determination to keep going. It was as though her soul had already departed and her body was marking time, agitating to follow.

Forgetting his resolve to keep his distance from patients, Ed went to the side of the bed and took her hand, expecting the usual grip of welcome but feeling nothing. He talked to her regardless, chatting as he would normally have done, in the hopes that she might be able to hear and understand but was simply unable to reply. There was no recognition whatsoever. Not even a flicker of a response.

'Do you think she's in any pain?' he asked the nurse who was busy adjusting Kathleen's pillows and pouring some over-diluted squash into a beaker. Ed was struck by its resemblance to the contents of the catheter bag.

'None at all, Doctor. She's got a fentanyl patch on and it seems to be working well. We're watching her carefully, especially when we turn her but she seems settled. Come on, darling, have some squash for me. It's a lovely orange flavour.'

Scooping her arm behind Kathleen's head to bring it forward, the nurse tried to coax her to drink. Kathleen permitted the spout of the drinker to slip between her lips. Just how much she actually swallowed was hard to tell as a considerable amount ran down her chin and onto her neck, quickly mopped up by the nurse who was expecting it to happen. A second attempt produced an identical outcome.

'It's so sad,' Ed said, as he walked back to the front door with the nurse. 'She was a tremendous woman – strong and resilient. I hope she's not aware of what's happened to her as she'd hate it.'

'I'm afraid I don't think she'll be with us for long.'

A statement with which Ed could not help but agree.

'Please continue with all the good care you're giving her. Let me know if there are any problems, but I'll pop in again in a few days.'

He left with mixed feelings, relief at Tina's absence, anger at Tina for not being there for her aunt when she probably most needed her and overwhelming wretchedness for Kathleen's plight.

'Shit!' he swore, banging both his clenched fists against the steering wheel.

Not a good start to his day and now there was Abigail to face after late-morning surgery. She had returned earlier in the week, minimally tanned but looking refreshed. Rather than being pleased to be back, Ed had noticed a disinclination to work and a somewhat robotic performance which he was prepared to accept for a day or two, knowing that many people found the transition from holiday into routine work difficult. But now, mid week and she was still the same. Fair enough, she was seeing her patients, completing all the necessary tasks after surgery, getting round her visits but it was all being carried out with weariness and a dreary acceptance that it was a chore that had to be done, rather than a stimulating experience which ought to be enjoyable – well most of the time. They had had one tutorial, going through some case histories of patients she had seen and Ed ended up cutting it short, for she was monosyllabic at best and he was exhausted from his attempts to crank her into action. He wondered if there was perhaps a personal problem and for this reason had hesitated before talking to her about Tina and the revelation of his home address, not really wanting to kick her when she was down already. She had though, committed an inexcusable sin and needed to be admonished. Lucky for her that she had been away when it happened for to be in receipt of Ed's tirade at the height of his anger would not have been a pleasant experience for either of them and he knew that he would have said things in a way that he would have regretted later and jeopardised the relationship with her that he had worked so hard for.

Now, though, he had to speak to her. He knew more or less what he was going to say and how he was going to phrase it. A few minutes at the end of the day seemed an appropriate time, giving her the evening to reflect on her actions and then he would carry on as normal tomorrow.

He was ravenous. Surgery had been awkward and involved innumerable floods of tears and it took all his will power not to reach out to his patients in any other way than to hand them the tissues. It had been particularly hard when one elderly lady, grieving painfully for her husband of fifty years, had opened the consultation by stating that she had come to see him because she knew he would listen. After she had gone, he was left feeling frustrated and impotent. Even the cakes at Delicious failed for once to lift his spirits.

To his surprise, Abigail was up in the staff room having lunch. She was sitting on one of the comfy chairs, one leg swinging over the other, whilst delicately picking pieces of a chopped salad out of a plastic container.

'Hi,' she greeted him, rooting around with her fork for a chunk of celery.

'Hi. How's your morning been?'

'Okay. I'm glad you're here though.'

'Problem?'

'No, not as such. But I need to have a word with you.'

'Sure. Now?'

'That'd be good. Thanks.'

'Do we need to go somewhere private?'

'I don't think so. It'll not take long.'

'Let me just make a drink then and I'm all yours.'

He continued to make superficial chat while he did so, the kettle taking longer than normal to boil, or so it seemed. Wondering what she was about to tell him, fearing that she was on the verge of admitting some dreadful gaffe with a patient, he poured water onto the muddy mess of instant coffee and milk in his mug, picked up his sandwich and went over to join her.

'Fire away.' He took a huge bite of ham salad with mayonnaise in a granary roll.

'I'm handing in my notice, Ed. General practice isn't for me. I'm not cut out to be that sort of doctor.'

Most of the filling of Ed's sandwich fell out onto his knee.

'What?'

'Please don't think that this is any criticism of you. You're a good trainer, this is an excellent practice and I've had some invaluable experience that I will take with me but I can't do this any longer.'

'I'm so surprised, Abigail. You've come on enormously in the last few weeks. I know you found it really difficult when you first joined us but we all agree that you're now a valuable member of the team.'

'That's very flattering of you but you'll not change my mind.'

'Why don't you see the job out and make a decision then? Surely that's the logical path to take. A year's general practice will always look good on your CV.'

'I'd made my decision before I went on holiday. So much so that I came back early and went to see my old consultant at the hospital. He's offered me a post back with him, which includes time for research and I can start more or less immediately.'

'Are you sure this is want you want?'

Abigail nodded emphatically.

'Well, I'm very sorry to hear it. Genuinely.'

'Thanks, Ed. It's not your fault. With hindsight, I made a mistake leaving the hospital, but it seemed like the right decision at the time.'

Ed reconstructed his sandwich and ineffectually mopped at the residual mess on his trouser. He cursed and then sighed.

'When do you want to leave?'

'As soon as possible. I've checked my contract and I'm supposed to give a month's notice. I've still some holiday due, so I'd like to use that if I could.'

'You'd better have a word with Elliott. See what he can sort out for you. You can't just drop everything and go. You'll have appointments booked. There are patients who are very attached to you. I wonder if you realise that.'

'They'll soon attach themselves to one of the rest of you.'

'I still think it's a crying shame.'

Abigail shrugged. 'Thanks, Ed, for trying to understand. I'll go and find Elliott now.'

She bustled out of the room. Ed noticed for the first time that she was back in her suit, looking officious and announcing to all she came into contact with that she wished to be kept at arm's length. For a moment he wondered if she had dressed in it on purpose, to symbolise her departure from general practice in more ways that just words. He felt a failure. In the history of the practice taking on registrars for training, there had never been anyone who had wanted to do anything other than forge a career in general practice. Colourful characters had come and gone, originally with John, who had established the training ethos within the practice, then with Clare who had assumed his mantle. The standard of the registrars had always been very high. It had been clear that some of them would not have fitted in at Teviotdale on a long-term basis but that was a personality issue, nothing more. There had still been that common bond between them. Even Sam, who was one that they would all rather forget, in particular Clare, was intent on becoming a general practitioner. What would the others think?

It turned out that he would find out sooner rather than later as he was shortly joined by Ellie, John and Faith, back en masse to write up notes on their house calls. Ever perceptive, Ellie knew something was wrong and came to sit beside him.

'You look a bit shell shocked, Ed. What's happened? How was your visit to Kathleen? Tina wasn't there was she?'

He managed a pathetic smile.

'It's not been one of my better days,' he summarised.

'Tell all,' Ellie encouraged him. 'You know you'd make me do the same.'

She was right, she usually was.

He described his visit.

'I felt so upset for her. I should be able to stand back and not get involved, but there's something about her.'

'Ah,' agreed John. 'The eternal question of why is life so cruel at times.'

'Ed, it's the fact that you care that makes you such a good doctor.

Don't ever stop feeling about the patients the way you do. That's why they love you. Yes, it makes it bloody hard at times like these but remember all the good sides to the job too.'

'I know, I know,' Ed muttered. 'You know what it's like. Every now and then it gets to you and you feel so fallible and useless.'

Ellie started on a string of consolatory comments but he interrupted her.

'There's more. Abigail's handed in her notice.'

'You're joking!' Faith gasped, looking round from the computer screen. 'Why?'

'That's great,' John commented through gritted teeth. 'I know these registrars are supposed to be supernumerary but we'll be stretched to the limit without her.'

'I feel I've let her down,' Ed told him.

'Never. You've done a great job. You've taught her all about how to be a good general practitioner. We've all shown her a cohesive and friendly practice that achieves excellent standards of medical care. If she's now decided that this job is not what she's cut out for then you've helped her. What a disaster it would have been if she'd just carried on, ended up in some practice hating every day and being miserable. No, you must look on this as a success. Thanks to you, she has realised where her heart lies – no pun intended as I know she wants to do cardiology – and so she should be very grateful to you.'

'Perhaps you're right,' Ed nodded slowly, wanting to believe him.

'Of course he is,' Ellie emphasised. 'We'll cope without her. We always do. Anyway, there might be another registrar that we can take on, or there might be one who's just finished their training and would like to do some locums for us.'

'I so love your perpetual optimism, Ellie,' Ed said admiringly.

'Thank you.' She gave him a hug. 'Now what IS that mess on your trouser leg?'

Uninhibited by the wet material clinging nastily to his left knee where Ellie had set to and sponged off the residue of his sandwich, Ed spent the afternoon covering for requests for urgent house calls and seeing a handful of patients who turned up at the surgery insisting that they needed to be seen that day. It turned out to be a gentle afternoon as nobody actually fell within the definition of urgent, for which he was grateful as his mind was still churning over the morning's revelations and regurgitating the details. The countryside was looking promisingly autumnal and he stopped once, at a remote spot, got out of his car and walked for a short distance just drinking in the fresh air and luxuriating in the beauty of the countryside in which he was lucky enough to live and work. The rolling hills and pastures were an amalgam of colours, heightened by the sunshine, nothing short of glorious.

It helped and feeling more positive, he sent a text to Zoë, whom he knew was in theatre all afternoon and looked forward to speaking to her later. She was on call overnight but usually there was time for a good chat which went some small way to making up for not seeing her. The prospect of the weekend, which was only two days away, was one to treasure. She had promised to come up immediately she finished work on the Friday and then they would have a whole two days and three nights together – utter bliss. The aim was to forget about work, replace it with some worthwhile leisure time and bask in each other's company.

Before leaving for the night, Ed made a point of seeking out both Ellie and John, to thank them both for their unerring support. John suggested a quick drink to round the day off with a flourish and a pint of local brew later had Ed feeling relaxed and content. He stopped on the way home for a pizza, appetite whetted by the alcohol and too lazy to cook. There was a cake that Barbara had left which would fill up any empty spaces in his stomach and the combination of this meal of fatty, stodgy comfort food, something unchallenging on television and some cat stroking would surely be the perfect remedy for a bad day.

Stuffed to satiety, further unwound by a glass or two of red wine, he was crashed out on the sofa, Hebe balanced perilously on his legs and Toby curled up like a hibernating squirrel on the cushion beside him. True to her word, Zoë rang and they shared details of their respective days. Hers had been busy but uneventful. Surgery had gone well and now, apart from a few women who were in early labour and ought, if they obliged and obeyed the rules, to be straightforward and not involve her, there was nothing pending and she was heading for bed, optimistic of a reasonable night's sleep, always allowing for the unexpected. He loved to hear how her voice softened when she told him she missed him. How amazing was this whirlwind coupling turning out to be? Already it was as if he had known her for years. Their minds were so similarly attuned they instinctively knew what the other was thinking. They made plans for the weekend, which involved being outdoors a lot and an alternative one for if the weather was impossible. Ed was determined to make it a weekend for them both to remember and to cram in as much as possible, for the subsequent two weekends Zoe was due to work, covering for Professor Corbett while he was away. He hadn't actually told her but Ed was planning to drive down and visit her while she did both these duties, knowing that not seeing her for such a long time would be agonising for him and he would be quite happy sitting reading, or walking locally if she was busy. A few minutes in her presence was all he needed to keep going, a touch of her skin, better still the caress of her lips on his which would lead on to an even greater sensual experience if there was time.

She was so relieved that Tina had not been evident at his visit, interested to hear about Abigail and made the passing comment that she was glad that she hadn't decided to give obstetrics and gynaecology a go instead. Envious of Ed's pizza, she informed him that while he had been tucking into that, she had been to the hospital restaurant and made do with corned beef hash with chips and cabbage. He immediately promised her the pizza of her choice at the weekend, if that's what she wanted, to which she replied that she didn't care a jot what they ate, all she wanted was to be with him.

On ringing off, her words echoed in his head and he wanted to call straight back and tell her that he loved her. On second thoughts, he preferred to do this when he could gaze into her eyes and see her reaction, which hopefully would be one of unbridled ecstasy.

Heaving his body off the sofa, to the disgust of Hebe, who narrowed her eyes with distain before settling down again on the cushion he had obligingly warmed for her, he went over to the computer to check his emails. Yawning and deciding that he was ready for bed, he clicked onto new mail and saw something that made his heart miss a beat.

21

Out of the blue, an email from Hannah.

Shaking a little, he vacillated over whether to open it. It was probably something simple, that she realised he still had some possessions of hers and wanted them back. Well, that was okay, he could post them on. For an awful moment he hoped that they hadn't gathered any mildew where he had stashed them away. It could get a bit damp in his shed. Even if they had, whose fault was that? Definitely not his, as she ought to have taken them with her when she left for Edinburgh.

He clicked to open the mail which he saw immediately was short.

'Dear Ed, Could you ring me? I need to speak to you. Love Hannah.'

Typical Hannah, brief, to the point and giving nothing away.

Not what he wanted to read. He hadn't envisaged any further contact with Hannah and was unsure whether he wanted any. Electronic contact was one thing, it was sufficiently impersonal, distant and controllable for him to cope with. His reflex reaction was to delete the message, sending it disappearing who knew where and pretend it had never happened. One solution yes, but one that was embarrassingly immature. He tried to pull himself together and don his sensible head. Having been involved with each other once doesn't mean that we can't stay friends. Other folk manage it, so it must be possible. He re-read the words, trying to discover some subliminal message.

Probably, she wanted some medical advice for herself, or more possibly a friend and couldn't think of anyone else to ask. Well, that was fine. Were the boot on the other foot, he could envisage that he might be in contact with her for legal advice. The alternative was their mutual love of climbing. That might be it. Perhaps she had finally organised a better work–life balance and was finding time for outdoor pursuits again. His mind shifted around irrationally.

What about Zoë? Would she mind? I'm getting this all out of proportion, Ed remonstrated with himself. There's absolutely nothing wrong with phoning her and maybe it would be nice to speak to her after all these weeks, show her there were no hard feelings, be of assistance if he could.

Irrespective of the lateness of the hour, he dialled her number, knowing well from experience that she would still be up and more than likely working. He could picture her concentrating furiously over an enormous pile of papers, a pencil behind one ear, ready to write notes in her minuscule handwriting that was illegible to many, whenever necessary. Predictably, she picked the phone up immediately.

'Hello?' Her voice sounded tired and wary.

'Hannah, it's me, Ed.'

A pause. Was she crying or was it interference on the line?

'Ed, thank you for ringing. You got my email obviously.'

'Yes. How are you?'

'Not too bad. How about you?'

'Good, thanks. Work's as busy as ever.'

Another pause. Ed felt nervous and his mouth had gone dry. He wanted Hannah to hurry up, make the first move and reveal why she needed to speak to him. How strange that talking to her felt so awkward. They never used to have that problem and she was having as much difficulty as him by the sound of it. Pleasantries were passed in a typically British way about the weather. Ed asked about climbing but Hannah had done none, which scotched that theory of his as to why she wanted to be in touch. She asked about the practice and the cats and he wondered how he might casually drop Zoë's name into the conversation, such that it was, so as to indicate that he had moved on from their time together and there was someone new and important in his life.

'How's work with you?' he asked.

'That's partly why I need to speak to you. Ed, I can't do this over the phone. Could we meet please? There's so much I want to talk to you about and explain but it'd just be too difficult like this. I'm back in Harrogate next weekend, staying with some friends. Can you come over?'

Ed was taken aback. He had assumed that she was safely many miles away, far from reach. Not for a moment had he thought about seeing her in the flesh.

'Er, I don't know.'

'Please, Ed. I need to speak to you urgently.'

'I'm not sure if it's a particularly good idea, Hannah,' he wavered.

'Please,' she implored. It was not like Hannah to beg. If he wasn't mistaken, she did sound on the verge of tears. More uncharacteristic behaviour – she was usually so tough, so resolute, so independent. With hindsight, that was one of the things about her that he found so attractive. Suddenly he felt sorry for her and agreed to see her. He would be driving over anyway to see Zoë, so, even though it did mean a rather roundabout route, it was not as if he would be putting himself out unnecessarily. He could just pop in, see Hannah for a few minutes, find out what all this secrecy was about and then head off for where he really wanted to be.

She sounded overly grateful, thanking him effusively, promising to email him with a time and place nearer to the day before ringing off, leaving Ed curious as to what on earth it was all about. He tossed about in bed, still wondering until the early hours, disturbed that his thoughts of Hannah had replaced those of Zoë who usually had the exclusivity of his emotions before he went to sleep.

Zoë was waiting for him when he got home on Friday evening. She'd been lucky enough to finish early, having called in a favour with one of the other consultants and thus had missed the worst of the traffic and made good time with her journey. Having been presented with a key at their last meeting, she had let herself in and was making a pot of tea when he arrived. Still in her work clothes, she was wearing a smart skirt and blouse, a little reminiscent of Abigail but somehow on Zoë, completely captivating. They clung to each other and kissed, every nerve in Ed's body thrilled to see and touch her again. Cuddling up on the sofa proved not to be enough for Ed, who needed the ultimate proximity and he led her up to the bedroom to show her just how much she had been missed. Tousled and sexually replete, they fell back on the bed, moist limbs still entangled while they got their breath back and descended from the heights of passion they had just attained. Ed, unable to keep his hands still, continued to stroke her gently, outlining her contours with gentleness and love, marvelling at her perfection, wanting more all the time.

'I love you, Zoë,' he whispered in her ear and then moved his head to watch her face.

She didn't even hesitate. She smiled.

'I love you too, Ed.'

'Move in with me.'

'Are you sure?'

'I've never ever been so sure of anything.'

'Then I'd love to.'

The happiness he felt was indescribable. He lay holding her, feeling her arms and legs wrapped around him, inhaling her perfume, a heady mix of something expensive and post-coital contentment and wishing that he never had to move. Bizarrely, Hannah rudely interrupted his reverie. He could not remember ever having felt like this with her. Their sex had never been such fun, or so sensitive. Hannah behaved as though it was a function that she was obliged to fulfil but that didn't mean that she necessarily had to enjoy it. What he had now was just so much better. He hugged Zoë fiercely, trying to squeeze away any remnants of Hannah.

'Go easy, Ed. I can hardly breathe,' Zoë laughed.

'Sorry to sound corny but you are simply the best thing that has

226

ever happened to me,' silencing her reply with a lascivious kiss and rolling over on top of her, ready to start again.

It was half way through Saturday when he finally decided to tell Zoë about his contact with Hannah. They had woken late, he'd made her breakfast in bed, they'd made love and then showered, both of them shoe horned into his tiny shower cubicle before being forced to admit that the only way they could wash properly was one at a time. Then, taking advantage of a fine day, they'd bought bulky sandwiches from Delicious and then set out, initially in the car but with plans to leave it, walk up into the Dales and leave the rest of the world behind. For once, Ed was happy to go at the rather slower pace that was Zoë's, her fitness level nowhere near the same as his. With anyone else, he would have been agitating to go faster, but whilst it took them considerably longer to reach the spot he had earmarked for their picnic, it provided him with more time to hold her hand.

She pretended to collapse dramatically onto the grassy floor.

'Phew, I'm so unfit.'

'We can soon put that right,' Ed promised her. 'Some regular exercise and you'll soon see an improvement.'

'That's fine,' she warned him. 'I need it. Just as long as it's walking. Don't even think of trying to get me up a rock face as there is no way that I could do it. I'm not even sure if I could watch you climb up one either. I'd be so afraid that you'd fall.'

He hugged her.

'Don't worry, we'll stick to walking. Or we could get you a bike. Here, have something to eat.' He opened his rucksack. 'There are drinks in here as well. Orange or apple juice?'

'Apple, please.'

They chewed approvingly, ready for sustenance after all their energy expenditure, gazing out at the exquisite panorama, Ed pointing out a kestrel, hovering motionlessly in the blue sky, waiting to swoop and pounce on unsuspecting prey.

'I saw Clare this week,' Zoë said, swallowing.

'How is she? I feel a bit guilty. I've not been in touch for a while.'

'A bit better, I think. Counting the days, as you would be by this stage. Her blood pressure's still a little high but her legs aren't quite as balloon like as they were, so she must have been taking our advice and keeping her feet up.'

'That's good news. How much longer has she to go now?'

'About six weeks. I think the Prof planned his holidays so that he'd be back in time to deliver her. I'll be seeing her again next week anyway in the clinic, hoping that I can get her through the next bit until he returns.'

'I'll try and pop in on her. I'll have to be careful how I tell her about Abigail or she'll probably volunteer to come back and help. You know what she's like.'

'Work is strictly off limits,' Zoë advised him sternly. 'You can tell her from me to cancel any ideas along those lines.'

'Don't worry, I will.'

He passed her a banana.

'Here, a good source of slow release carbohydrate. You'll need it as we've still a good way to go.'

She laid back, head in his lap and closed her eyes.

'Not just yet, please. I'd heard it was beautiful up here but I'd no idea just how amazing it was.'

'This is just one of my favourite places. I've loads more to show you, and I'm sure there are still plenty left for us to discover together.'

She nuzzled against him.

'I can't wait.'

There was no need to talk, just being there beside each other was sufficient.

He waited until she sat up and they were scrunching up the paper bags and screwing the tops back on to the empty bottles, in readiness for moving on, before mentioning Hannah. Zoë, if she was bothered, did not let Ed see.

'As you say, very curious. All very cloak and dagger. I wonder why she wouldn't say over the phone.'

'I haven't a clue,' Ed answered, throwing some crumbs as far as he could hopeful they would be found by some passing birdlife. 'I won't go and see her if you don't want me to.' He looked directly at Zoë.

'I don't mind, Ed. Go and see what she wants. Like you say, she maybe needs some medical advice.'

'I just wanted to tell you, Zoë. I'd hate us to have any secrets. I thought I'd go and see her then come over to you, if that's okay.'

'That's more than okay, you know it is. It'll make my weekend on call something to look forward to. Let's hope it's nice and quiet then we can spend most of it together. If you were serious about what you suggested this morning and weren't just in a post-coital fugue state, then I could pack up some on my stuff and you could bring it back.''

'Perfect,' Ed agreed.

Happy now partly because she knew, but more because she was serious about moving in with him, he stood up and pulled her up too, flung on his rucksack and then, taking her by the hand, set off across the brow of the hill at a spanking pace before descending sharply on a rough track which led down through a dark copse of huddled trees to the river below.

22

Clare was nesting. Well, that was according to David. Her own interpretation of the situation was rather different, that she was restless, bored, excited and most of all, scared stiff. Prepared to admit to the first three emotions, she was reluctant to come clean about the other, worried that she would be thought to be abnormal or, worse still, suspicions would be raised that her depressive illness was returning.

On a weekly basis now, for her pregnancy was surely the longest ever recorded, she sat in the waiting area at antenatal clinic, silently making comparisons with the other women and every time finding herself lacking in some way. She found it incredulous that, true to tradition, most of them did literally bloom, they managed to make the last trimester chic, as though they had just stepped off the front of a magazine cover. Lucky, lucky women who did not put an ounce of weight onto their thighs but merely developed a symmetrical and stylish bump, a unique fashion accessory that was priceless and enviable. On them, jeans and leggings looked flattering. Figure-hugging jersey tops were worn with pride, cardigans and jackets left open on purpose for the world to fully appreciate what lay beneath.

Much as she tried to emulate them, she never quite managed it. She tried hard. Admittedly she had some nice clothes, for David had insisted that she have not just whatever she needed but whatever she wanted but they never seemed to cling to her in quite the same, artistic way. Instead they looked as if they were a couple of sizes too small and accentuated her swollen abdomen in an ugly way, her now convex belly button attracting attention like a flashing beacon. She had given up on trousers long ago and as for the leggings that she had worn at first, well forget them, there was no way that she would be seen in public wearing those now.

She felt horribly bloated, uncomfortably so. It had to be unnatural to have assumed the proportions that she had. Last week she'd been faced with the ultimate in insults when a well-meaning nurse that she had never seen before had come over and asked her if she was having twins. With her expansion came problems that she had never dreamt of. The car seat had had to be pushed back so far that her feet no longer reached the pedals, thus driving was out, which meant she was dependent on David to be transported hither and thither, unless Ellie or one of her other friends had time to help out. Eating at the table was clumsy to say the least, unless she sat sideways, which was hardly practicable and made anything with sauce or gravy a nightmare as it usually ended up down her front. And sleeping was impossible. Like many her preferred position was to lie on her stomach, head resting on her folded arms, anything else had her fidgeting, restless, disruptive to David who had to be up and at work each day, so the spare room became a frequent haunt when she could bear it no more. At least there she was able to thrash about to her heart's content, fling pillows this way and that and get up and walk around to ease the cramps in her calves which had a habit of waking her just after she'd finally dropped off. Frequently, she tiptoed into the nursery, now ready and waiting, freshly decorated, a mobile of wild animals with smiling faces floating above the cot, a small herd of stuffed toys, sitting within, keeping it warm for the new arrival. Clare would take each one out in turn and show it to her baby, waiting for a kick or a squirm in response. This was really what kept her going – the reminder that there was someone there, alive, moving about, getting into the correct position to come out and meet her.

The prospect of motherhood alarmed and intrigued her. She had seen plenty of patients struggle but then again, some of the new mothers she had had the most concern for had turned up trumps and made it look easy. She wondered how she would cope. Would she over analyse everything, as was her wont at work, or were there natural mothering instincts waiting to be born, along with the baby? Would everyone expect her to be perfect because she was a doctor and had more theoretical knowledge than most?

With regard to David, she knew that he would be fabulous. He was blessed with endless patience and benignity, his ability to cope with what life threw in his direction was unerring and regardless of all they had been through, he still loved her unconditionally and already felt just the same about his first child. Each time she thought of David as a father, her heart quickened. The last thing she wanted was to struggle and let him down. Even though he showed no signs of bearing any grudges over their past history, Clare felt at times as though she was still on trial and compelled to be on her best behaviour whenever in his presence.

She knew that because her antenatal notes had been flagged up with her psychiatric history the midwife was on the alert for any signs of depression and would be watching her like a hawk post-natally. Though she had never said as much, Clare was confident that Ellie would be on her guard as well. Ditto Ed, John and of course, David. Such a diagnosis had always been hard to live with. She felt ashamed of what she had done and the events leading up to it. Personally, she was confident that she was cured but knew that when the baby arrived, she was sleep deprived and her hormones were bouncing in all directions that she would be at risk of a recurrence. Grateful as she was for those looking out for her, she wished passionately that there was no need and vowed silently to prove them all wrong.

Time for yet another visit to antenatal clinic. It was chilly outside but she had to make do with the same flip flops that she had worn all summer as it was impossible to prise her feet into any ordinary shoes. She chose a loose top and ankle-length skirt, hoping for a gypsy effect, cringed at her reflection and ripped them both off, settling for the same shapeless dress which had been her most frequently worn garment for the last few months. Dark navy blue, she hoped that it diminished her silhouette somewhat. Boring, but it would have to do. The addition of a necklace made of jingling coloured stones went some small way to brighten it up. She felt obliged to put on some make up, partly for the other women who would doubtless be scrutinising her appearance just as she did theirs and partly for Zoë, whom she knew she would be seeing and whose gimlet eye would be searching for the least indication that she was unwell.

The sound of the doorbell heralded the arrival of the taxi that she had ordered to take her to the hospital. She waddled downstairs, puffing, picked up her bag and a shawl which she hoped to drape decorously around her and went outside, taking care to lock the door behind her. David, up to his eyes in work, was out on a domiciliary visit sectioning someone under the Mental Health Act. He had promised to meet her at the clinic if he could and then deliver her home afterwards, staying for lunch, time permitting. Years of experience meant that Clare knew better than to expect him to turn up. Sectioning rarely went according to plan and getting two doctors, an approved social worker and the patient in the same place at the same time was a feat that required utmost patience and planning.

Shuffling into the waiting area, normal walking forbidden by her sloppy footwear, Clare was relieved to find it relatively empty. Marjorie spotted her and pounced immediately, checking her blood pressure – which caused a few noises of disapproval – and her urine – which resulted in the raising of her left eyebrow. Clare tried to read her face and hoped that one eyebrow was a better sign than if it had been both. Her ankles were poked and the indentation of Marjorie's finger took a while to resolve. Rather than say anything, she wrote frantically in Clare's already copious notes and disappeared with them, presumably to find Zoë.

'You can come in now,' she called, returning and leading the way into one of the consulting rooms.

'Clare, how nice to see you again.'

Zoë, ever optimistic, stood up to greet her friend and patient, motioning for her to take the chair nearest the desk. Clare gently lowered her bulk.

'Hi, Zoë. It's quiet out there today,' she commented, referring to the waiting area.

'Yes, great isn't it? The clinic's really small. Mostly women booked for midwife delivery, so hopefully there's nothing for me to do, unless there's a complication. Well then, how are you?'

'Good, thanks,' Clare was economical with the truth.

'Really?' Zoë gave her a long, penetrating look while Clare continued to smile at her. 'That's great. Your blood pressure's about the same as last week and there's no protein in your urine, so both of those things are good. I'd prefer your blood pressure to be down a bit, but at least it's not gone up. Now, is the baby moving a lot?'

'Yes, definitely,' Clare answered with certainty. 'Mostly at night, unfortunately.'

'Mmm, it's hard but think positively. An active baby is a good sign. Jump up onto the couch and let me feel your tummy.'

'Jump?' Clare was sceptical.

Zoë laughed. 'You know what I mean. Here, I'll give you a hand.'

She went over and helped Clare onto the couch and then to get comfortable when she lay down. Clare couldn't help but notice with envy how nice Zoë looked in well-fitted dark green trousers, a pretty white blouse with short sleeves and a frilled collar.

'I love your top,' she said admiringly. 'I can't wait to have some sort of figure back and be able to get into some proper clothes.'

'Not long now, Clare. Hang in there for these last few weeks. Hey, that's great, the baby's head down and he or she feels a good size. Couldn't be better. Excellent. Let me just listen to the heart and then we're about done.'

Even Clare's spirits could not fail to be lifted by the rhythmical beat picked up by the sonicaid, sounding a little like a galloping pony.

'Isn't that just the best sound?'

Zoë agreed.

'All's well, Clare. Up you get.'

'Are you sure?'

'Certain. The only slight concern is your blood pressure but I'm very happy that the baby seems to be growing well now and that's supported by the scan you had last week. You're going to have to come back next week though. You'll be due another growth scan and Professor Corbett will be back. I know he'll want to see you himself.'

'Okay,' agreed Clare. 'I'd rather not take any chances at this stage.'

'Very wise,' nodded Zoë. 'Do you need any antacid mixture or iron tablets?'

Clare shook her head, thinking of the packets of said tablets which were accumulating dust in the cupboard as just one of them made her hideously constipated. Rather than take them, she was eating as many iron-rich foods that she could think of and hoped that this was having the desired effect.

'We're done then. Hey, do you want a cup of coffee? I've nothing to do for half an hour or so and it'd be lovely to catch up a bit.'

'Sure,' Clare responded, very pleased at the thought of someone different to talk to.

'Come on, then. We'll go to the new coffee shop they've opened. It's next to the restaurant but does drinks and snacks. It's good. My treat.'

Sending a text message to David, while Zoë finished writing her notes up, Clare then gladly walked alongside Zoë down the endless corridors, which today seemed even longer than usual. Out of breath and relieved at having reached their destination, she then settled, perhaps unwisely, into a rather deep, squashy chair, which Zoë promised to lever her out of if necessary.

'Here we are. Two cappuccinos and I've got us a Danish pastry each. They're really good and I'm starving.'

'That's lovely, thanks, Zoë. I'm perpetually hungry. It probably goes quite a long way to explain why I'm the size of a barrage balloon.

I've put so much weight on, it's disgusting!'

Zoë smiled sympathetically.

'It's weird how women respond physically to pregnancy in such different ways.'

'Do you know, there's a woman I sometimes see in clinic who's about five weeks ahead on me and she says she's still wearing her usual jeans. I don't think I could even get mine as far as my knees.'

'Never make comparisons, Clare. We're all different, think of it like that. It'd be really boring if we were all the same. Isn't that one of the reasons you like general practice so much – the variety and the unpredictability?'

Clare pulled a disgruntled and unconvinced face. She bit into the feathery pastry, seeking solace in its sweetness and smacked her lips. Zoë watched her friend, more than a little worried. Clare had put on quite a credible performance during her consultation but there was just a nuance about her that hinted all was not quite as rosy as she would like to portray. She looked pale. When she smiled, only her mouth moved, there was no reciprocal wrinkling of the little lines around her eyes which in turn were devoid of much emotion. Sitting in the chair now, her shoulders hunched, her handbag on her knee in a half-hearted attempt to hide her pregnancy, she looked defeated.

'What's worrying you, Clare?' Zoë ventured.

'Nothing!' Clare was too quick to reply. 'I'm fine.'

'Are you sure? I'm asking as a friend, not your obstetrician.'

'Really, nothing. Well, maybe a few little things, like going into labour and the delivery. I'm not sure that I'll cope.'

'That's so normal,' Zoë reassured her. 'And when it happens, you'll be fine. Everyone worries beforehand. Especially with their first baby. It's a big step into the unknown and it doesn't matter how much you've read up on it, how many people you've discussed it with, it's still a huge adventure that's unique to you. But remember, women have been having children since the beginning of time. What's more, they don't just have one child but they come back again and have a second. In some cases they come back three, four and more times. If it was really that bad, we'd all be only children.

'You know as well as I do that we all worry about things that are going to happen and that's often the worst part because you've too much time to imagine what can go wrong. When what it is you're worrying about actually happens, it's never as bad as you think because you get swept along by it.'

Clare pondered on this wisdom and was forced to agree.

'This pregnancy is taking for ever though. Each day seems to drag more than the one before.'

'Poor you. It can't have helped having to give up work so early on.'

'Exactly. I'm so used to being busy with work and having no time to think about myself that it's been like a form of purgatory. Much as I love my home, there have been times when I've wanted to scream and run away.'

'You're over the worst now. You've six weeks to go. If your blood pressure stays up, Prof might induce you earlier than that. I doubt that he'll let you go beyond your due date. I know I wouldn't. This is the downhill slope now. Honestly! The end is in sight and it'll be here before you realise.'

'If you say so. I'll try hard to think of it like that.'

'Are you ready for this baby at home, I mean? Have you got everything you'll need?'

'And more,' Clare actually laughed. 'Thanks to David. He's been unstoppable. The nursery is beautiful – he did that himself. He's not usually one for decorating but this was different. I wanted to help but couldn't do very much because of having rest so much. You must come round and see it. Bring Ed and come for supper.'

'Lovely,' Zoë thanked her. 'But there's no way we're making any extra work for you.'

'Believe me, it'd be no work for me at all. David'll be in charge. We could even have a takeaway if that makes you feel better. Just the four of us, please?'

Zoë thought for a moment.

'I've a much better idea.'

Clare looked interested.

'What's that?'

'We will pop round and have a look at the nursery but one day when we're passing. You and David will come round to us one night next week. You can lie just as resplendently on the sofa there as you can at home and David will get a night off too.'

'That sounds a lovely idea. Thank you.'

'I'll let you into a secret as well....'

Zoë leant forward conspiratorially, Clare instinctively mirroring her.

'What?'

'I'm moving in with Ed.'

'That's fantastic,' cried Clare, causing one or two faces to turn in their direction. 'When?'

Zoë shrugged excitedly. 'As soon as I can. I'm seeing him tomorrow night and he's suggested that I bring the first of my stuff over then. Clare, I can't tell you how thrilled I am. He's the most wonderful person.'

'I'm so pleased for you both. Can I tell David?'

'Of course. It's not really a secret. In fact quite the opposite, I feel I'd like to make a public announcement and let everyone in the whole world know.'

Clare put her hand on her tummy and gasped.

'The baby's pleased too. He or she is turning somersaults!'

Clare left the hospital feeling a little happier. Not so much about herself but she was still upbeat about the news Zoë had shared with her. She even felt a little smug as, after all, she was the one who had introduced them to each other. Not surprisingly, there was no sign of David and imagining him to be up to his eyes in dealing with his patient, she knew better than disturb him with a call or text. She knew he'd be in touch as soon as he could, anxious to know the outcome of her check up and she would be able to be the bearer of the good news when he did so.

As the taxi rumbled along the roads, taking her back home, Clare reflected on the impact of Zoë's words. She was right; Clare did need to focus more on the positives. One – that she was over two thirds of the way through the pregnancy, over three quarters in fact, which sounded even better. Two – that her blood pressure was holding its own. Three – that the baby was very active and growing well and four – when she did finally go into labour, she would be surrounded by help and excellent care. Zoë had also promised her that she was available twenty-four hours a day for Clare, to answer any queries, calm any minor concerns, and provide reassuring advice. This was comforting to know but Clare suspected she would be reluctant to take up on her offer, fearful that she would be a nuisance, not wanting to disturb either Zoë or Ed while they were busy turning his house into theirs.

The house felt still and quiet but warm and cosy when Clare let herself in, made heavy weather of picking up the post and then made a bee line for the kitchen to search for some lunch, the Danish pastry having done little to assuage her hunger. Thanks to David's supermarket visit on the way home from work the previous evening, there was plenty of choice and Clare salivated as she prepared a substantial sandwich of prosciutto and ripe brie with salad. An apple and peach would be a healthy follow-up to this and a giant mug of hot chocolate would surely be a good source of calcium and protein.

Carefully she carried her lunch into the lounge, ready to put on the television and watch a daytime soap opera which she secretly had become quite addicted to but would never admit this to anyone. Sitting down and stretching over for the remote control, her breath was taken by a sudden, piercing abdominal spasm. Over in a fraction of a second, it immobilised her and left her terrified. Reflexly she put both hands on her belly, cautiously moving them around, seeking tender spots but finding none. She waited for the pain to return but there was none. As the minutes ticked past, she slowly started to breathe more regularly. A comforting kick inside soothed her and she exhaled deeply. It couldn't have been anything to do with her baby. It must have been a pulled muscle. She shouldn't have leant out like that. It was nothing, it had gone, she must take more care about doing things gradually and gently.

Settling to the television and her lunch, she was soon immersed in the marital disharmonies and hitherto unknown illegitimate children of her favourite characters, marvelling at how something so bad could at the same time be so riveting. The sandwich was good, but then anything edible tasted good at the moment, the larger the amount, the better. The hot chocolate slipped down like velvet and exerted a soporific effect which she felt obliged to give into, once her programme had finished. Lifting her feet up, she wriggled into a comfortable position and quickly drifted off to sleep.

Another shaft of pain woke her. Identical to its predecessor, it was gone as quickly as it came. Because she had experienced it before, it felt less threatening. She must have moved while dozing and pulled that same muscle again. She rubbed the area in the hopes that would help and tried to sleep again, managing only to doze on and off, restlessly, which left her, frustratingly, feeling more tired than she had originally. Her baby however was quiet – lucky thing, she thought, at least one of us is getting some rest.

David was home on time, an unusual but welcome event. He was profuse in his apologies for missing the clinic appointment. His day had turned out to be far worse than he'd anticipated. The police had had to be involved as the extremely disturbed patient had, in a bid for freedom, run out of the back door, leapt over the garden fence and sped off down the road, before finally being run to ground at a local pub where she was entertaining the regulars with a striptease dance performed on top of one of the tables.

Needless to say, David was delighted to hear that all was well with Clare and suitably pleased to hear about Ed and Zoë. What comforted him most, though he kept this to himself, was that Clare, although she looked shattered, sounded brighter and more animated than she had for some weeks. It was doing her good seeing Zoë. She was someone Clare could chat to and confide in. Professor Corbett was an excellent obstetrician, supremely skilled in his craft but David could tell that Clare was intimidated by him, always quiet in his presence, accepting his advice without question.

She never mentioned the pain to him. When it happened for a third time, half way through the evening, he was out of the room, washing up, talking to her from the kitchen, so he never saw her face contort and the tears well up in her eyes. By the time he returned to her, she was back to normal and the fact that she announced that she was off to bed was nothing out of the ordinary. He promised to be up to see her shortly and then sat back in his chair, rightly deciding that after the day he'd had, he deserved a beer and half an hour with a rather good football match.

The following day, Clare felt well. She took things quietly to the point of extreme slowness. A lie in bed until almost lunchtime, some worthwhile snoozes from which she woke actually feeling refreshed, a long soak in the bath all helped, for she was still unnerved by the ferocity of the pain she had experienced. A new book arrived that she had ordered on-line, the latest by one of her favourite authors and she was more than happy to sit for the afternoon and be engrossed in this. A crime novel, in the traditional who-done-it manner, it was just what she needed. With no sign whatsoever of either a doctor or a pregnant woman throughout the entire two hundred plus pages, Clare revelled in the intricacies of the plot enjoying it enormously and failing to spot until the very end – just as the author had intended – who the murderer was.

23

Ed woke on the Saturday morning and stretched sleepily. Rolling over, in his half- conscious state, he was optimistic of finding Zoë beside him but of course she was at the hospital, on call for the weekend and so had to be within easy distance of the wards, in case of emergency. Still, when he opened his eyes and looked around, there were signs of her presence on show. Perfumes on the dressing table, a jumper hanging on the back of a chair and through the half-open wardrobe door, he could see more of her clothes, neatly arranged, looking as if they belonged, next to his.

Outside the sun was shining with the promise of a fair day. The trees that he could see from his window were definitely adopting some stunning autumnal tints, particularly the horse chestnuts and his little garden was looking tired and ready for a rest.

Having heard nothing from Hannah – thank goodness – Ed had structured his day around seeing Zoë. He knew that her morning would be busy, so the plan was for him to drive over after lunch some time and then, emergencies permitting, they would be uninterrupted. There were plenty more of her belongings to bring and with some judicious packing it ought to be possible to cram a goodly amount into his car for him to bring back to the house. He planned to stay overnight. It was apparently rare that Zoë had to get up during the night, there were the middle grade staff who could manage most problems so he was looking forward to cuddling up against her and luxuriating in her smell and touch. Then tomorrow, he would drive back, first thing, leaving time to unpack the car before meeting up with Rob for a day out climbing. He hoped the weather would hold.

The weekend was looking decidedly promising.

Spurred on by the sunshine and his euphoria, he put on some running clothes and spent an energetic hour pounding down the lanes and up grassy tracks, leaping over stiles and sprinting back down rocky paths. It was good to be alive. The air was magical to breathe in, it felt sublime as it tantalised the deepest part of his lungs and his whole body became rejuvenated and invigorated. Back home, gasping and rehydrating with tap water, he pondered on the wisdom of a cold shower to energise him even more but wimped out and spent a far more enjoyable time letting the deliciously warm water needling over his toned body, relaxing the muscles he had just asked so much of.

Waiting for the kettle to boil and the bacon to crisp under the grill, he checked his phone, hoping for a message from Zoë, which there was but would be too embarrassing to recount verbatim. Smiling, he shook his head slightly, both amazed and excited by its content, marvelling how the words she chose exuded such eroticism and sensuality. He replied, wishing that he could equal her message, making do with just three very powerful words and lots of kisses. Turning back to the bacon, which was curling at the corners, his phone trembled and pinged. Zoë was obviously not very busy at the moment if she had time to reply so immediately.

It wasn't from Zoë, it was from Hannah, simply saying, ring me.

Ed sighed a little, his joy dissipating somewhat.

Better sooner rather than later. He had the presence of mind to turn off the grill.

Hannah was brief, on the verge of being abrupt. She passed on her address, gave Ed some directions to help him find the house where she was staying and he promised to meet her there in the afternoon. Any earlier would not suit her as other people would be in the house. Apart from impressing upon him that she needed to talk to him alone, she gave nothing away that provided Ed with any hint as to what she wanted.

Ed was a tinge irritated. This meant he would have to change his plans. He bit into his bacon sandwich angrily. Hebe and Toby appeared, lured by the smell of cooking and sat side by side, like book ends, fixing him with their inscrutable looks, willing him to share until they were rewarded with a piece of bacon fat each.

He washed up, some dishes from last night's supper also waiting to be done, then tidied around, feeling new responsibilities to keep his house well groomed now that he was sharing it with someone, even though she wouldn't be back until Monday night by which time Barbara would have been in and re-created order out of chaos. The remainder of the morning passed slowly, as time has a habit of doing when you'd prefer it to speed up and Ed clock watched while reading and writing emails, scanning some articles in a journal – though little of what he read sank in – and playing Solitaire on his computer.

Exasperated and wanting to get going, he grabbed his jacket and wallet and set off, planning to stop on the way to buy treats for Zoë. He had managed to get hold of her before he left, to explain his rearranged schedule, to promise to see her as soon as he could and phone when he was on his way.

The traffic was typical of Saturday. An eclectic mix of locals out shopping, tourists out making the most of the autumn sun, a couple of coaches on sight-seeing trips and the vital ingredient, some lumbering tractors effectively holding everyone else up. There was no quick way to Harrogate and the usually exquisite winding lanes which Ed loved so much were today an annoyance. He switched on a CD which he knew was one of Zoë's favourites. He wanted to feel as close as he could to her. She was there with him in spirit but he also could tell, by an uncharacteristic, momentary wobbliness in her voice that she was a little fearful of his meeting Hannah. He'd offered without hesitation to go to see Zoë first but she'd sounded back in control, claimed to be busy with someone about to deliver twins and told him to keep to his original plan, ending up by reminding him that she loved him so much.

The music kept him going to the outskirts of Harrogate, where he pulled over to set the postcode into his sat nav before being led this way and that down some little roads which were crammed with symmetrically terraced, but not unattractive, houses.

Hannah answered the door. She looked smaller than he remembered, more vulnerable. He kissed her on one cheek in a companionable manner and then followed her into a small living room, dominated by a large fireplace which would not have looked out of place in a stately home. Some fronds of palm were neatly arranged in a large vase to one side, a coffee table in front, the top of which invisible owing to the untidy mass of magazines which engulfed it, some spilling onto the floor. A mug containing what looked like a very old and very cold drink was on the carpet. He picked it up, for fear of kicking it over, and looked around for somewhere safe to put it but all available surfaces were occupied by something, be it books, newspapers or more magazines. Even the mantelpiece was awash with candlesticks, ornaments, pine cones and a piece of driftwood, all acting as paperweights for the wealth of letters and envelopes rammed underneath or behind them. What little carpet was visible was an uninspiring purple. It was probably best that it was hidden for there was no way that it complemented the deep red walls, which only made the room seem even tinier than it was.

She noticed that he was looking around.

'Sorry about the mess. This house is Jasmine's; she's a secretary at the solicitors' where I used to work here. We kept in touch when I left. Thank goodness. Sit down. Do you want a tea or coffee?'

Shaking his head, Ed settled into an armchair, covered with a variety of throws, which proved to be agreeably comfortable. Hannah was perched on the edge of the only other chair, transparently nervous, unable to keep her hands from fidgeting. He was still able to appreciate her muscular little body, perhaps rather less fit than it used to be, but she was wearing clothes that were loose fitting and it was hard to tell. Her short hair was longer than it had been and more messy. He suspected that she had not brushed it but simply run her fingers through it repeatedly, a habit she had of doing when stressed.

'What's all this about, Hannah?'

She pulled an apologetic face.

'I'm sorry, Ed,' she began and he was hit by a blast of déjà vu.

He waited for her to continue.

'Everything's gone wrong.'

'Such as?'

'I've left Edinburgh.'

'No! Why? I thought you loved it there.'

'I did. I take all the blame for my predicament. I've been totally stupid. So stupid that I can't honestly believe that I behaved like that. It was so unlike me.'

'What are you talking about?' Ed probed.

Hannah took a large breath.

'I blew it, Ed. I had the chance of a lifetime and I blew it.'

'But you're so good at your job. How could you? You were working like a... a...'

Ed's voice tailed off, not knowing quite what to compare her with.

'There was nothing wrong with my work, at least I don't think there was.'

'Then what was it?' Ed was becoming exasperated. As always with Hannah, it was akin to pulling teeth.

'I had an affair with one of the partners. You might remember him, Sebastian. I can't lie to you, Ed, I was seeing him while we were still together. I'm sorry. I shouldn't have done that. But it was so exciting. I'd never experienced anything like it before in my life, which sounds really corny, I know, but it was true.'

'Thanks a lot,' thought Ed.

'The senior partner found out. Not a problem in itself you might think until I tell you that he is Sebastian's gay partner. I had no idea of course about their relationship. Needless to say, the proverbial shit hit the fan and I was asked to leave.'

'Can they do that?'

'Probably not, but there's no way I'm going to fight them. They'd make sure that I lost. It's far better that I quit with some semblance of my character intact. Sebastian says he'll write me a reference if I need one but all this is going to look mighty odd on my CV. I mean, no one in their right mind would leave a prestigious firm like that after a few months.'

'You've had a rough time,' Ed tried to be sympathetic but he was still dismayed by her revelation that he had been two-timed. He could also visualise Sebastian, with little pleasure, and was incredulous at Hannah's disclosure. It would never have occurred to him that she would do anything like that. Looking back now, he was unable to make sense of some of her behaviour when he went to visit, her lukewarm welcomes, her departures for work at unprecedented times, her pleas of being too tired to do anything. Despite his thoughts, he did feel sorry for her. She looked quite pathetic sitting opposite him. 'What are your plans?'

'Jasmine has been kind enough to let me stay with her, but that's just as a stop gap. It's far from ideal but I have no income, so I'm not in a position to get a mortgage. The house in Edinburgh is up for sale. I'm applying for jobs around here, but nothing appealing has come up yet. I daresay that I can't afford to be too choosy. There's one job on the horizon which I'm waiting to hear if I've an interview for but I'm not holding out much hope. Sebastian's partner, Ludo, is very well known and if anyone were to ring him direct for an informal chat then I'd be sunk without a trace.'

'Something will turn up, Hannah. Anyone can make a mistake.' The words sounded more confident than the person who spoke them but had the desired result and produced a watery smile from Hannah.

'We'll see. Ever the optimist, still, eh, Ed? That's one of your qualities that I admired so much. I still do, in fact. Along with a lot of other attributes.'

She stopped talking and stared at him.

Ed cleared his throat and averted his eyes, hating the silence that now hung between them, thinking of Zoë, wishing he was there with her, wondering how soon he could decently take his leave.

'Are you sure you don't want a drink? I think I need one after that confession.'

'No thanks,' Ed replied, not wanting anything that might prolong his stay.

She left the room and he was forced to wait, tapping his feet impatiently, getting up to stretch his legs, wanting to be standing when Hannah returned, a non-verbal clue that he was on the point of going. Finally she returned, hands warming around a striped mug which contained an unidentifiable steaming brew, presumably one of her exotic blends. She blew on it and sipped.

'Sit down, Ed. You look uncomfortable.'

'Just for a minute. I can't stay much longer.'

'Sure, I understand. But please hear me out. You rightly commented a moment ago that I'd make a mistake. I'd never have believed I was capable of such idiocy. I suppose part of the blame lies with Sebastian but I thought I was above being deceived by flattery, expensive presents and some words, that I know now to be insincere. It's made me take stock of my life and contemplate what I want out of it. For sure, I want a good job, my career will always be important to me but aiming for such heights, I don't think so. There's more to life than work. I want more time to have hobbies, to relax and one day hopefully get married and have a family.'

'I'm pleased, Hannah. That sounds good. I hope you achieve it. I'm sure you will.' Ed was trying desperately to wind up the conversation.

Hannah held her breath then looked him directly in the eyes.

'I want these things with you, Ed. I've treated you badly and I'm sorry. So sorry. From the bottom of my heart. Can we try again?'

Ed was completely taken aback. He had never seen this coming. He thought Hannah just wanted to use him as a confessional, to exorcise her bad behaviour, to have him accept her apology and give his blessing to her new plans. But to get back together? Unthinkable. How could she ever imagine that he would consider it? Did she honestly think that he had spent the last months moping at home waiting for her to come back to him? Even taking Zoë out of the equation, the fact that Hannah had been having an affair behind his back made him feel belittled and abused.

He placed his head in his hands and wished he was somewhere else.

'Hannah,' he started, searching for the right words. 'You and me – we don't have a future as a couple. What we did have, which was good most of the time, I'll admit, died a long time ago.'

'No, Ed. It might feel like that, but if you give me a chance, I can show you I've changed. We only went wrong because I was selfish enough to move away. Look, for a start, I'd thought we could go climbing tomorrow. Malham or somewhere like that. Then I could come back to yours. I'm sure Jasmine's fed up with having me here. I know we'll have to take it slowly and--'

He interrupted her.

'Stop, Hannah. None of this is going to happen. I've met someone else. We're living together. I love her to bits and won't let anything sabotage what we've got.'

'Ah.'

There was not a lot Hannah could say. One look at Ed was enough to show her that she was not going to change anything.

'She's a doctor,' he added as if this made it all clear.

'Ah.'

He considered telling her more, bizarrely thinking he owed her some sort of explanation but then he felt his phone vibrate within his inner jacket pocket. He fished it out, looked at the caller display. It was Zoë. She had an uncanny sense of when he needed her help.

'Leave it, Ed, while we talk some more.'

'I've got to take this call, Hannah,' he said firmly, getting to his feet and turning his back on her. 'Hi...'

'Ed, it's Clare. I'm about to take her to theatre for an emergency caesarean section. I need you here. Can you come?'

Zoë sounded petrified. Gone was the cool, calm air of a consultant in control, replaced by one who was scared, overly involved emotionally and faced with the terrifying responsibility of two lives to save.

'I'm on my way, darling. I'll be thirty minutes, tops. I love you.'

He turned to see Hannah, who was looking pale.

'I have to go. Take care of yourself. I know you're strong enough to get through this and come out on top.'

She tried to get to the door before him but he was way too quick. He was in the car, engine started when she reached the doorstep and he waved hurriedly and stiffly before swinging round in an erratic three-point turn and roaring off down to the junction.

It was after four. Not the best time of day to get anywhere quickly. The back roads were easy to negotiate but as soon as he hit the main road out of Harrogate, he was forced to slow down to a crawl which lasted for over a mile as temporary traffic lights enjoyed making car travellers' journeys a misery. At last, out of town he could put his foot down, not overly so, for he had always been a careful driver, and know that he was making worthwhile progress. His mind was a-whirl. His heart was thudding. He had no idea what had happened to Clare. There had been no time to ask Zoë who sounded so alarmed and in such a hurry that her clarification might have been indecipherable. At least it was a Saturday so David would be there with her. Heaven only knew what he was going through at the moment.

Zoë was accomplished and professional. By now, he was confident that she would have pulled herself together, re-assumed her capable façade and however much she was shaking inside, would take good care of Clare and the baby.

He thought of how much he loved her, why he loved her, hearing her just now only convinced him of it all the more. A glance at the clock on the dashboard told him that he had already taken twenty minutes and was not nearly half way but there was nothing he could do about it. Trying the cross-country route would add a dozen or more unnecessary miles to his trip all of which would be on meandering single-track lanes, only navigable at gentle speeds. Better to keep on the main roads and just hope they became quieter. He slowed up behind a small squat car that was hogging the middle of the road and apparently incapable of exceeding thirty miles an hour, before overtaking recklessly and thus was able to accelerate again unimpeded. This was better. The road was long and straight. He would make up some time for sure.

More confident, relaxing slightly, he reached forward to restart the music he had been listening to earlier. There was a particular track he wanted to hear, the one Zoë liked best of all. In his hurry, he pressed the wrong button and ended up with the radio instead. Tutting at his stupidity, he took his eyes off the road to rectify the matter and consequently had no awareness of the car, which appeared from nowhere and hurtled towards him on the wrong side of the road until it was far too late to do anything about it.

24

While Ed was visiting Hannah, Clare was trying to do the ironing while sitting down. No easy task and tedious in the extreme but she had to do something. Her whole body was restless and impatient. She'd tried sitting and reading but couldn't concentrate, the crossword had ended up thrown to the other side of the room in frustration and if she had another bath, then there was a distinct chance that she might develop gills and scales.

They'd offered her the option of a water birth when she first booked at the hospital. She'd found the thought beguiling. Patients had been quick to adulate such a means of delivery. The analgesic properties the warm water was supposed to furnish were tempting, a vast improvement on an injection, which she didn't want in case it crossed the placenta and made her baby drowsy. An epidural was a definite possibility, though she thought of it more as a back-up plan to be wheeled in should her labour be very prolonged or her contractions too harsh to bear. Like most women she hoped for a natural birth, following preferably a short labour.

As soon as the complications began to manifest themselves, she had been warned that the option of a water birth was looking less and less likely. It was a territory that only the most straightforward were privileged to have access to. The midwives would want her on a bed, so that they could monitor the foetal heart rate more easily, assess the effectiveness of her contractions, keep an eye on her advancing labour and make sure that if she deviated from what was expected then action could be taken immediately. She'd accepted all this without a murmur, having seen enough when working on the labour ward to know that this was best for her. More than likely she was in for a long, long haul. Pray to God that she went into labour spontaneously which should make things easier than if she had to be induced. Having previously eschewed suggestions of a drive down a bumpy road or the hottest of curries as old wives tales, she was now thinking that she was prepared to give anything a try. That way she could try to stay at home for as long as possible before succumbing to the medicalisation of her supposedly natural event. Yuk, the thought of that was enough to put anyone off. Legs unnaturally wide apart, feet in uncomfortable stirrups which dug into her skin, someone fumbling about down there trying to rupture her membranes. Then drips, hi tech machines that bleeped monotonously and a continuous stream of staff visiting to check up on her. So much for the dimmed lights, soft music in the background, she had had visions of. She shuddered.

David came in from the garden, where he had been fighting a loosing battle sweeping up fallen leaves and raised an amused eyebrow at the sight of his boxer shorts and socks coming into contact with the iron for the first time in their lives.

'Don't laugh,' she ordered him. 'I'm fed up but can't sit still. So it had to be this. I
couldn't think of anything else that I could do sitting down.'

'That's wonderful. They look so nice, I'll probably dispense with my trousers on Monday, just so everyone can see that razor sharp crease in my underpants.'

Clare threw her head back and roared with laughter.

'Careful, they'll be coming to section you, if you do that.'

He leaned over and kissed her.

'How's my baby?'

'He/she is fine and having a nice sleep.'

He placed his hand affectionately on the right side of her belly.

'Fantastic,' was his comment. 'Hey, I felt a tightening. Did you?'

Clare put down the iron to ponder, holding her breath.

'Nope, nothing. Don't get my hopes up like that. It'd just be a

Braxton Hicks.'

'Sorry. I'm going into the study to catch up on some mail, okay? Don't do too much, will you?'

'I promise.'

'And leave the ironing board for me to put away.'

Clare saluted.

'Yes, sir. I've nearly done, as it happens. Then there's a film on TV I thought I'd watch.'

'Good. If you're making a drink, bring me a coffee would you? I need some caffeine or I might end up falling asleep in there.'

Clare stood up, job finished and rubbed the small of her back which ached more than usual that day. She felt exhausted after that simple task, slightly nauseous and for once, not hungry. Good, she thought, I might finally stop putting on weight. Taking care, she adroitly balanced the warm, sweet-smelling clothes in her arms and made for the hall.

Another stab of excruciating intensity left her breathless and on her knees.

Shirts tumbled into rumpled heaps at her feet and rolled-up socks bounced to the four corners of the room.

Taking her time, she gingerly uncurled, hanging on to the arm of the chair for support, ready to brace herself if there was the tiniest twinge. No, careful consideration revealed that the pain had gone, so short lived that perhaps she had imagined it but the debris around her told her otherwise. Just a cramp again, though something this time was more menacing. Fortunately the baby seemed unconcerned. It had been quiet most of the day, presumably sleeping peacefully, more than likely an omen that it was gearing up for a lively night.

Wary of a recurrence, Clare made to pick up her ironing. Calling for David to help would only arouse his suspicions as he would immediately want to know why she had dropped everything. Little damage seemed to have been done either to her or the ironing. Once hung up, the shirts would be fine. More confidently now, Clare crossed the hall. She could see David through the half-open door, intent on what he was reading, probably unaware that she was there. In slow motion, she reached the bedroom and deposited the clothes in their rightful places. Her tummy felt uncomfortable, not really a pain, more restive, a portent of something more. Wind probably. I'm over-analysing things again, she remonstrated with herself. I should eat. I've not had anything since breakfast so my blood sugar must be in my boots.

Satisfied with this interpretation of her condition, Clare tiptoed back down to the kitchen, preparing to make David's drink and raid the biscuit tin. She searched in all the cupboards for David's latest hiding place and finally spotted the chocolate biscuits on the top shelf, cunningly hidden behind a new, unopened box of tea bags. Too high to reach, she had to stand on a chair, a perilous procedure at best, but one far worse when grossly inflated with child. She was successful if breathless as she returned to terra firma and delighted to see that he had chosen her current favourites.

Now that she had them in her grasp, it was queer that, truth be told, she really didn't fancy one at all. Still convinced that she would feel better for one, or two, Clare took a bite and crunched her way morosely through the first mouthful which failed to have its usual satisfying and more-ish effect. Baffled, but secretly rather chuffed, she made David's drink and walked through to the study. He looked up, pleased to see her, proud of her for how she was coping with what had turned out to be such a difficult time for her. He knew her far too well to be fooled by her demeanour, even though Clare thought she was retaining a normal exterior to all who saw her. Knowing better than tackle her repeatedly on how she was feeling, he had opted for the role of constant support, attentive to her needs day and night. The fear was clear in her face, sometimes in the evenings when she was sitting watching television with unseeing eyes, her mind a million miles away. Totally the victim of having too much knowledge, Clare was torturing herself with the very worst visions of what could go wrong. This evening, she had looked more relaxed, he thought, but now her expression was tense again, her smile false, her shoulders hunched negatively.

Taking her hand, he pulled her onto his knee.

'Watch it,' Clare admonished him, 'I'm currently a size that could inflict severe damage to anything or anyone I come into contact with. I really ought to have a health warning attached to me.'

'Don't be daft, come here both of you and have a cuddle.'

She conceded and attempted to get comfy. He massaged her tummy, talking all the while to the baby. Clare hugged him, pulling him to her, needing him as close as she could get him. As she did so something warm trickled down her legs, sufficient to soak through her clothes and onto David's thigh.

'What's that?' they asked, almost in unison, Clare heaving her bulk to her feet.

'I think I must've wet myself.'

A dull ache passed across her lower abdomen, reminiscent of the period pain she knew of old but had not had for months. Suddenly it all made sense. The bad stabs of pain and now this.

'I'm so sorry, David. How humiliating is that? I think I've got another urine infection. I had a bit of pain earlier as well.'

'Why didn't you say something?' David was instantly alert and quizzical.

'It was nothing. Well, actually it was quite bad. We'd better see about getting some antibiotics.'

'Sure,' David agreed, 'shall I ring Zoë?'

'Would you, please? She's on call this weekend, so that couldn't be better. I'll just go and clean myself up and see if I can manage to procure a sample as I expect she'll want one.'

Clare waddled out, like a Dutch doll, keeping her knees together as though this might prevent further leakage, which made for a difficult and ungainly passage up to the bedroom, taking the stairs one at a time, but one she completed without further incident. Discarding her skirt, she peeled down her pants and stared with horror at the sight before her. A gush of liquid came away from her onto the bathroom floor. Specks of blood and sticky discharge accompanied it. Another spoonful dribbled into the toilet when she sat down. There was no way that this was a common or garden urinary infection. For sure this was a sign of something far more significant.

'David!' she shrieked at the top of her voice.

He was with her in an instant, eyes wide, cordless phone to his ear as he waited for Zoë to answer.

'What is it?' he panicked.

'I don't know. It's horrible. I think my waters might have gone. I've got this ache as well, all over my abdomen.'

'What about the baby? Can you feel him?'

Clare was too distraught to quibble about the putative sex of their child.

'No! I haven't felt him since yesterday! David, I need to get to the hospital now! Get an ambulance.'

Zoë was waiting for them when they arrived, Clare too upset to be impressed by the efficiency with which she was transported to the hospital. The journey had been horrendous. Each bump and curve in the road had exacerbated her pain and the constant artificially cheery chatter had made her want to scream. The labour ward was bright but seemed busy. From her horizontal position on the stretcher, she was aware of people rushing this way and that, doors opening and closing. Gosh, they must be busy, she thought, unbeknown that all this frantic activity was for her. Despite her protests that she could quite easily manage to climb on the bed without help, she was tenderly lowered there by two paramedics who wished her good luck before being ushered hastily out of the room. A friendly looking midwife introduced herself as Anna and a younger student midwife as Katy. Between them they kept up a steady patter while working efficiently, taking basic readings of vital signs and adeptly hooking Clare up to a variety of machines with a great number of flashing lights. Not fooled by their attempts at reassurance, Clare was beside herself. The pains were becoming more regular, stronger, gripping her and making her bite her bottom lip as she tried to cope. She couldn't get comfortable. Lying on her back was making her feel as though she would vomit and even when Katy lifted the back rest and propped her up with a veritable mattress of pillows, she felt just as bad. David was on the opposite side of the bed, hanging onto her hand while trying to keep out of the way, oblivious of the way she was crushing his fingers, repeating over and over that she was going to be fine, that they would have their baby very soon. She turned to him wide eyed and ghostly pale, a look that cut through his heart and he wished he could do more to help her. Nobody had told her it was going to be like this. None of those books she had read had prepared her for this. None of her patients had said anything.

Zoë too, had sprung into action, making her own examination while Anna and Katy worked. She noted that Clare's blood pressure was low but her pulse racing. Lifting up Clare's shirt she expertly ran her hands over her abdomen, picking up incoordinate contractions that were flickering through the muscle of her uterus. She looked up momentarily at the monitor, wanting confirmation that the foetal heart was a normal rate but there was nothing. Sharing a worried look with Anna, which Clare caught sight of too and understood the meaning of, Zoë explained to Clare that she needed to perform an internal examination.

'Bend your knees up for me, Clare. This will probably be uncomfortable but I'll be as quick as I can.'

'I don't think I can keep still, I'm so uncomfortable,' Clare apologised.

'Try hard, it's important.'

Clare heard the ripping of paper as Zoë opened an examination pack, then the snap of gloves as they were pulled on. With the help of Anna and Katy, Clare's knees were bent and her hips abducted. Her legs shook uncontrollably. They no longer belonged to her.

Zoë's worst fears were confirmed as she saw the thick, brown liquid draining from Clare's vagina. Fresh meconium. An incontrovertible sign that the baby had opened its bowels and was in dire distress. Clare heard Katy catch her breath. At a nod from Zoë, Anna let go of Clare's knee and ran out of the room. Katy watched her go, unhappy at having been left, however briefly.

All heads turned when a slow, but definite heartbeat sounded on the monitor. Clare gripped David's hand. The baby was still alive.

'It's far too slow,' Katy commented to Zoë, who was nodding.

'Clare,' Zoë swallowed hard and turned to her. 'There's meconium. I'm going to have to take you to theatre now and perform a Caesarean section. We need to deliver your baby as soon as we possibly can.'

Clare, sweating from the pain she was experiencing managed only to croak. Her mouth was devoid of moisture, her tongue stuck to the roof of it.

'Is he going to be all right?'

'I'm going to do everything I possibly can to make sure that you and your baby are fine.'

Giving Clare's hand a final squeeze and nodding at David, Zoë left the room and leant against the corridor wall shaking all over. She had been in this situation many, many times before but never when the patient in question had been a good friend. Somehow she had to pull herself together and perform better than she ever had before.

The well-practised team had Clare prepped and ready for theatre before she had a chance to take in what was happening. Relinquishing any control over her plight, all she could do was stare at the window on the monitor that signalled the baby's heart beat and pray. She knew that sixty beats a minute was pitifully slow but it was something, a glimmer to nurture hope, a sign that her baby was prepared to keep hanging on, waiting for help to come.

Zoë was pacing up and down, ready scrubbed up in the theatre, desperate to get started. Unlike Clare, she was back in control. She knew she could do this. She had to. There was no alternative. Inspired by Ed's voice, the knowledge that he believed in her and that he was on his way, she had reverted to the consummate professional that she was.

'Is everyone ready?' she asked.

Anna was beside her.

'Almost. The paediatric registrar is here and Dr Martin, the consultant is on her way.'

'Good, let's crack on.'

The consultant anaesthetist, Alex Raymond, whose swarthy good looks were completely lost on Clare in her bewilderment, worked smoothly and efficiently, while she submitted to the ministrations of all those around her. As she was wheeled from the anaesthetic room, all she could see were the glaring lights above her and faces half covered with masks. Desperately she looked for someone she knew and mercifully spotted Zoë, her eyes serious but somehow calming. David was at her shoulder, and the last thing she heard before she fell asleep was him whispering in her ear.

The moment Zoë started to work, a hush fell in the theatre. She skilfully made the first incision, too well aware that speed was of the essence to get the baby out as soon as she could. She sliced into the uterine wall and was drenched by a further torrent of heavily stained amniotic fluid, which cascaded down Clare's sides onto the floor. An efficient attending nurse ran to mop it up before someone slipped. With an almighty scoop, the head of the baby was delivered. Its grimacing and wrinkled face was cyanotic. The umbilical cord was wrapped tightly around its neck, twice. Once freed, the limp and lifeless body slithered out into the world easily and Zoë speedily thrust it into the open arms of the waiting paediatrician who ran to the resuscitation area, David in hot pursuit.

'It's a boy,' he announced as proudly as he could, his voice breaking with emotion.

Zoë looked up, able to take her time now.

'Where's Beth?' she yelled, referring to Dr Martin.

'Still on her way. We've rung and rung. She's been held up.'

'Shit. We need her now. How's the baby doing?'

'Not well,' was the agonised reply. 'I'm doing my best. I've suctioned him but I'm going to have to intubate and then we'll take him to Special Care. Oh, thank God...'

The doors banged open and Beth dashed in, not bothering to tie her mask, theatre cap falling off, making a bee line for her registrar and starting to help, their heads bowed over the little form who lay immobile on a blue towel.

'I'm so sorry, Zoë, David. There's been a bad crash just outside town. It took me ages to get past it.'

'No matter, you're here now.'

'We need to get this baby to the unit now. Are you coming with us, David?'

'Yes, of course,' he looked over to Clare, loyalties tugged in opposite directions.

'Go, David,' Zoë encouraged him. 'Clare's fine. I've nearly finished here now; by the look of things, she'd had a placental abruption. She'll be back on the ward before you know it. Your place at this moment is with your son. Go.'

Pulling off her theatre cap, Zoë made a half-hearted attempt to tidy her squashed hair in the rest room. A quick glance in the mirror informed her that she looked shocking. Not that she needed telling, for she felt a million times worse. Kicking off her clogs, she fell back into a chair, put her feet up on a little table and closed her eyes. Over and over she repeated events in her mind, looking for things that could have been done differently and if they had been, would they have made a difference. The conclusion was the same, whichever way she chose to interpret the last few hours. She had done as much as she humanly could. They all had. Her team had more than risen to the occasion, as they always did. All of them, without exception, had reacted slickly, there had been no hold ups at any time, no one had slipped up and now, thanks to them, Clare was safe, sleeping off the anaesthetic, unaware that she had a son.

But Clare was also, thankfully, blissfully unaware of how ill he was. The last bulletin from Special Care had been the same as the one before – that there was no change.

Zoë gratefully accepted a cup of tea from Anna. Her mouth felt parched. Barely warm and stewed to a point way past its best, the tea nevertheless tasted delicious.

'I'll just have this then I'll go up to SCBU and have another word with Beth.'

'Yes, do,' Anna agreed. 'Clare's on her way back to the ward and perfectly stable.'

'Does she know?' Zoë whispered.

'She's been told she's got a son and that he's on special care. She fell asleep again then. There was no point in telling her anything else.'

'Of course not. Let me know when she's properly awake and I'll come and talk to her. I expect Dr Martin will––'

'Zoë,' Alex popped his head round the door. 'Someone wants you on the labour ward.'

'Oh no, not another problem,' she moaned, still inhabiting the mind set where the worse obstetric complications that she had only ever read about occurred.

'They said it was personal...' Alex added.

She changed in an instant.

'Oh great, it must be Ed. Boy, do I need to see him? I'm on my way.'

Pausing only to brush her hair and smooth down her scrubs in a brash attempt to look presentable, she ran through the changing room and back to the labour ward, only to be met by sombre and shocked faces that told her before she heard any words, the very last thing that she wanted to be told. News that was indeed the worst she had ever heard but news that she would never have guessed in a million years.

25

Such a curious place, thought Ed to himself, looking around, wondering where he was. Definitely somewhere he had never been before, there was not one thing about it that he recognised but it was not unpleasant, indeed, quite the contrary, the ambience felt rather peaceful and almost familiar. He seemed to be in a large room, but each way he turned it looked identical, with white walls, devoid of pictures or any decoration whatsoever. No doors, no windows. The ceiling too was white. Looking down, the floor was a thick carpet of the same colour, the pile so dense and long he could barely see his feet. It made him smile, remembering the house call months ago to that converted barn and the child with athlete's foot. Is that where I am now, he wondered. Am I on a visit? If so, where's my bag?

But there was no sign of life, no noise, just warmth, not stifling but enough to make him feel quite inexplicably and irresistibly sleepy. About to lie down on the carpet, suddenly he noticed a chair, huge and soft. That hadn't been there before but how comfortable it looked. Drawn by some invisible thread, he walked towards it, overcome with weariness, his limbs twice their normal weight. I haven't time for this, I mustn't forget that I've promised to see Zoë, were his last waking thoughts as the chair enveloped him like a huge duvet and he fell asleep.

There she was, still working. Or was she? Dressed in her theatre scrubs, she was sitting crying, sobbing uncontrollably, the face he found so gorgeous was messed up by despair. Around her were some midwives, one with her arm around her shoulder, trying to console, placate, another with the inevitable cup of something, doubtless hot sweet tea, urging her to take a drink, a third crouching at her knees, muttering something he couldn't quite catch.

In a flash he remembered what was happening. Clare was in trouble and there was only Zoë who could save her. This didn't look good. Unless she was crying with relief but somehow he knew that she wasn't. He opened his mouth and called her name. For the briefest of moments she looked up, eyes wide, darting from side to side, and then her head turning to look around her, before dissolving into fresh tears.

'I can't believe it,' she wailed.

'Shh, try to calm down,' a midwife suggested, ineffectually.

'I need to see him, where is he?'

She half rose from the chair, only to be coaxed back down into it.

'I'll find out. Give me a moment to ring A&E. He's probably up on the ward by now. They were just about to set off last time I spoke to them.'

'Please, I want to go now.'

A brief conversation on the phone ensued, Zoë trying to work out the gist of the conversation when only able to hear one half.

'He's on ITU. They say you can go and see him when you're ready.'

'I must go now,' Zoë repeated.

'Sure, but I'm coming with you.'

'Thanks, Anna.'

Zoë shakily stood up and Ed put his hand out to steady her. She jumped at his touch and looked towards him but straight through him. He followed the two women as they made their way off the Labour ward and hurried down the straight, empty corridors, their footsteps echoing, to the intensive care unit. The doors opened and they all went in, Zoë instinctively heading for the nearest bed and standing, gazing down in disbelief at the occupant. She collapsed onto a chair and tentatively reached out to hold one hand and Ed felt his own hand tingle as she did so.

A supercilious-looking man came over to talk to her. Unmistakably the consultant in charge but Ed could not hear what they said. Whatever it was, was longwinded and complicated, involving a lot of discussion of figures and charts and pointing to different parts of the patient's body. Ed craned his neck, trying to listen but for all that he could hear the words, they made no sense to him. Instead he had to content himself with watching the emotions on Zoë's face, a melange of angst, anger and sorrow.

What a weird dream, thought Ed. The sooner I get to Zoë, the better. I shouldn't really have taken time out to sleep like this. I can't bear to see her so distraught, it's breaking my heart. I want to hold her and make everything all right. And where's Clare? What's happened to her? Has she had her baby? I must get out of here, nice as it is and get back to the hospital.

With difficulty, he prised himself out of the soft, marshmallow-like chair. The room had changed. Now, he was not alone. There was something over there, a cot, draped with white lace. He wandered over and peered in. A tiny face with beady black eyes smiled back. A shock of dark hair was visible under the edge of the white blanket in which the baby was swaddled.

'Hello,' said the baby.

Not the slightest bit taken aback, Ed smiled too.

'Hello!'

'I'm Tom,' the baby introduced himself. 'What's your name?'

'Ed.'

'Nice to see you. I thought I was here all on my own. I was a bit lonely.'

'Don't worry. I'm here, though I was thinking of leaving soon. How about you?'

'I don't know where to go. Can I come with you?'

'Of course. You're very welcome.'

Ed bent down and picked Tom up. He was a dear little thing.

'You look a lot like a friend of mine, called David,' Ed commented. 'You've the same eyes and nose. I do so hope Zoë and I have a family one day soon.'

'Who's Zoë?' asked Tom.

'My girlfriend. She's amazing. I love her to bits. I'm just off to find her. She's really upset about something and I need to be with her to help.'

Ed looked around. Two doors had appeared side by side in the previously blank walls. Cuddling Tom, he approached and opened the first. He could see nothing but could felt the warmth and tranquillity waiting for them. This must be the way. It felt right. On the point of stepping through, he stopped and opened the other door. Again, nothing was visible but he could hear Zoë talking earnestly, half crying, talking to him, telling him how she loved him and how she always would, reminding him of the good times they had had in their short but passionate relationship, how she needed him more than anything...

'Let's go,' urged Tom. 'Which way is it?'

'I don't know,' Ed replied, torn between the two. 'What do you think?'

'That one,' Tom told him and Ed knew his choice was correct.

26

Frost covered the grass and branches and the air was sharp, just one intake of breath needed to clear the sinuses of the most chronically congested. The country churchyard was a picture, almost white with rime, glistening in the insipid sunshine that transiently crept out from behind the wintry clouds. Holly bushes were studded with bright red berries, warning of a hard winter to come and ivy clung possessively and eccentrically to tree trunks and exposed roots. On either side of the path leading from the road, hefty, venerable gravestones stood tall and proud, lichen splattered, one or two on a lean, each telling a story of the person whom they commemorated. Beyond them were neater rows of newer, lighter-coloured headstones, more frequently visited and recipients of recently left flowers. Further still there was space for those who were yet to join them in their final resting place.

Couples stamped their feet, talking in cloudy breaths and rubbing their hands together as they made their way from the lych-gate to the church door and the slightly friendlier temperature within. Warm clothing was the order of the day and there was a surfeit of woolly hats, long coats and cosy boots.

Ellie, as ever, looked striking in a calf-length coat of lovat green and a matching cloche hat, reminiscent of the nineteen twenties, a perfect match for her auburn hair. Beside her, Ian, pink cheeked from the freezing air was alternately blowing on his hands or wiping his glasses that had steamed up. Exuding elegance, he was in a smart sports jacket of russets and browns, dark brown slacks and a shirt and tie that could only have been chosen by his wife for he would never even have entertained the colour scheme that she had picked out and which actually worked so well. Lydia and Virginia were, despite instructions to the contrary, running around, in and out of the gravestones, pausing every now and then to read the details of who had died and when and how old they had been. Little did any of the congregation realise that the twins had had to be offered serious bribes before they agreed to change out of their jodhpurs and into pretty little dresses and coats.

Waving as she caught sight of John and Faye, Ellie called out to them.

'Over here, John.'

Arm in arm, they walked over to her and Ian.

'It's so cold,' remarked Faye, almost hidden beneath a hat of enormous proportions trimmed with fur, which Ellie hoped sincerely was fake.

'Feels like Christmas,' agreed John, 'even though it's weeks away. Do you know, I think it might snow?'

'Let's go in. It's way too cold to stand out here much longer. I stopped being able to feel my toes some time ago. Virginia, Lydia, come here now, please,' Ellie yelled.

'Shhhh,' Ian remonstrated with her.

'Sorry,' she mouthed. 'Isn't it odd that you feel you have to whisper because you're near a church?'

With no sign of the girls having heard, or more likely that they had heard but were not going to comply with her request, Ian told them to go inside and he would round up his daughters. As usual, the sight of him coming towards him made them squeal with delight and run off in the opposite direction, hoping that he would chase them first. When it became immediately obvious that this was not going to occur and that the look on his face was one that it would be unwise to disobey, they came to him meekly and allowed him to put an arm round each of them and usher them into church.

'Try to remember why we're all here and be good throughout the service,' he begged, straightening their coats and scarves at the last minute.

The church was full. The organ was playing softly, almost drowned by the rustling of clothes, the opening of hymn books and the subdued chatter of the congregation. Ian pushed his girls up the aisle to the front row, where Ellie was waiting, with John and Faye, who were next to Ed's parents, Ailsa, handkerchief in hand, blowing her nose, Alan almost unrecognisable in a smart stiff suit, which smelt of mothballs.

'Is everyone here?' murmured Ian.

Ellie looked around.

'Nearly,' she nodded. 'Apart from two of the most important people of all.'

Ian took her hand and held on to it firmly.

Reverend Aloysius McBretney commenced the service by welcoming each one of them and asking them all to be upstanding for the first hymn. The harmonious swell of voices filled the little church from rafters to stained-glass windows, sending a tingle down Ellie's spine and bringing a tear to her eye. She couldn't join in with them; a lump had appeared from nowhere and was making singing impossible. A quick glance at Ian revealed that he was similarly affected. He winked at her and together, fortified by each other, they performed a passable act of miming for the next five verses.

'This is awful,' Ellie muttered under her breath. 'I can't even look at any of the others.'

'Me neither.'

There was a rumble as the congregation sat down en masse, some seeking out the Prussian blue cassocks to kneel on for prayers. Ellie and Ian bowed their heads reverently, sure that the Lord would not mind the fact that they could not let go of each other to place their hands in the traditional position to pray. A hush fell, save for some throat clearing and nose blowing.

As the service progressed, Ellie tried hard to concentrate, which was nigh on impossible for Lydia and Virginia were becoming restless and needing to be reminded on a very regular basis that they had promised at breakfast to ensure that their behaviour would be exemplary. The reverend's words reverberated magnificently around the building, their meaning was poignant and heart felt.

Simultaneously with his last sentence, the church door banged and a waft of bitter air entered, chilling the necks of the poor souls who were nearest and setting the posters on the notice board a'flutter.

Slowly but surely, two people made their way to the front. Ellie turned and breathed a sigh of relief.

Zoë and Ed.

She'd feared they were going to be too late. Ed was still on crutches, not yet allowed to put his left foot to the ground, his compound fracture one that had tested Gareth Pickering to the full. More surgery was likely in the future and his climbing days were most definitely over; this and the loss of this spleen were but a small price to pay for the fact that he was alive. He could remember nothing about the accident or the following two days, a phenomenon he found on one hand a relief and on the other perplexing.

His first recollection had been the sight of the top of Zoë's head. She had fallen asleep in the chair by his bed, with her head on his shoulder, having kept a virtually constant vigil since the time he had arrived there. He'd reached across with his other hand and stroked her hair and she had sighed, thinking that she must be dreaming. Stirring, she had stretched and looked at him, never for a moment thinking that his eyes would be open and that there would be a half-smile on his face. They'd said nothing, but her reddened eyes had softened as he touched her face as though discovering it for the first time and she had kissed his fingers and hand again and again and again.

That night, he'd been afraid to go to sleep, fearing that he would not wake up, but Zoë had urged him to, impressing on him that he needed the rest, that it was integral to his recovery and that she was going nowhere, that she would be right beside him, touching him. He'd slept deeply and restoratively and felt enormously better the next day. Finally, when it had been decreed that he could be moved to a single room on the orthopaedic ward, he had persuaded Zoë to go home and sleep, where she could rest properly but she refused to go any further than her hospital flat, announcing that she would not go back to his house until they went there together.

As his improvement continued, she had agreed to go back to work, but had found ways to slip out during clinic, walk the long way to the operating theatre so that her route took her past his room and delegate more to her middle grade staff so that she was still his most frequent visitor.

Others came too, amongst them Ellie and Ian, John and Faye, Faith and Rob – to name but a few. Alan and Ailsa had spent almost as much time with their son as Zoë. It had been an unusual way to meet your boyfriend's parents – she could have envisaged far more conventional ways, but maybe this had been easier. Instantly united by grief, they had been bonded together by their common love for Ed and the determination that he should pull through.

The nurses had complained, jokingly he hoped, that his steady streams of visitors were too rowdy and that every time they opened his door, all his dozens of cards fell over. The patients registered with Teviotdale Medical Centre had been generous to a fault. He had been inundated with flowers and fruit, bottles of squash and get well soon wishes. Zoë had fought a losing battle trying to keep track of who had sent what so that they could all be thanked in the fullness of time.

It was Ellie of course who had kept him abreast of news of the practice. As usual, she knew what the receptionists had been gossiping about, the practice nurses had been moaning about and what had been happening to the patients, one in particular. Kathleen Clarke had died four days after Ed had last visited. There had been no word from Tina, nor had the nursing home heard from her when Faith had visited to confirm the death.

The day before he had been due to go home, Ed had three other visitors, allowed to visit with the special dispensation of the Sister on the ward. He had been lying back on his bed, attempting some of the improbably difficult exercises left by a physiotherapist and paying considerably more attention to eating his way through a bag of homemade pecan biscuits that Barbara had sent, when the door had opened.

'Hi, there,' a voice had said. 'Can we come in?'

Ed had looked up to see David and Clare, beaming from ear to ear, Clare clutching a bundle of blankets in her arms.

'Hey,' Ed had been delighted. 'How wonderful to see you. How are you all doing?'

'Wonderfully well. We thought you'd like to meet the latest member of the Jennings family. It's been a bit of a rocky start but we're all fine now, thanks.'

'Congratulations, all of you.'

Clare had sat on the edge of Ed's bed.

'Would you like to see him?' she'd asked.

'I'd love to.'

She had peeled back the blankets from the well-wrapped-up baby to reveal his chubby, healthy, pink face and dark, wispy hair.

'Here, you hold him. He'd like that.'

Ed had looked down and the baby had looked back at him. Weird, he could have sworn that he'd seen him before somewhere, but that was ridiculous. Besides, babies all look very similar, don't they? He had looked closer. This baby definitely had a look of David about him.

'What's his name?' Ed had asked, knowing full well what the answer was going to be.

'Tom. Thomas Gregory Jennings. We'd be delighted if you and Zoë would be two of his god parents.'

'That's a fantastic honour. Thank you so much. I'd be thrilled and I'm sure Zoë would as well.'

'Excellent. Ellie and Ian have agreed to be god parents too. Isn't he lucky?'

'He certainly is.'

So saying, Ed had smiled at the baby and knowing that everyone would have told him that this just did not happen in a three-week-old baby, had been absolutely sure that Tom had smiled back.

This was Tom's christening. At the end of the morning's service, the christening party were invited to the font and Tom, following in the tradition of many a baby, proceeded to complain in a loud and raucous cry at having his head splashed with water. Once the formalities were over, there was a party at Clare and David's with good food and good wine, including champagne to toast long life and happiness to Tom, together with much celebration.

Needing a moment to herself and relieving Ellie of Tom, who was making it clear that he was as hungry as the adults, Clare sat and breast fed him in the relative peace and quiet of David's study. Taking time to reflect, she was aware that her Caesarean scar was still painful, that at times she could barely move from exhaustion and she was still nowhere near getting back into her usual clothes but it only took one glance at Tom, to realise that all these observations were immaterial and of no consequence. This was, without doubt, quite the best thing that she had ever done.

Ed had taken over Clare's place of enforced rest on the sofa. With his leg outstretched and carefully cosseted by cushions to keep it still, there was still room for Zoë to sit with him. She had moved into his house in a charming and unobtrusive way, such that he felt it strange to think he had ever lived there alone. Alan and Ailsa adored her and approved without reservation of her presence in his life. Even Hebe and Toby appeared to approve, often choosing her lap to sit on over his. From time to time he thought about Hannah, able to recall most of their last conversation and setting off from her house before hitting a blank wall of amnesia. She would survive, she was tough and independent enough to rebuild her life and in all probability get her career back on its previous track, as for sure that was where her heart really lay, despite her best attempts to convince him otherwise.

Zoë turned to him and refilled his glass. Their eyes locked and for a moment, everyone else ceased to exist. Their glasses touched and they sipped in unison.

'Thank you for coming back to me, Ed,' she breathed and leant over to kiss him. 'This toast is to you, from me, with love, always.'